Starting Over

Book Four in the Fortune Bay Series

Judith Hudson

The Fortune Bay Series
Lake of Dreams
A prequel Novella
Free to my readers group
At www.JudithHudsonAuthor.com

Summer of Fortune
Book One
Maddie and Jake

The Good Neighbor
Book Two
Frankie and Sean

Home for Christmas
Book Three
Louise and Blue

Family Matters
A Bridge Novella
Everybody!

Starting Over
Book Four
Lily and Marshall

Starlight and Tinsel
A Christmas Novella
Star and Harry

Acknowledgements

I'd like to thank my readers for their ongoing support. While writing the book, I'm usually caught up in the world of the story, but when I finish the book I think, *Now what?*

I know what to do to get it online where people can find it, but like most writers I'm a bit of an introvert and don't like to flog my wares. Your letters and Facebook comments mean so much to me, bringing me out of my seclusion and reminding me that there are people out there who *want* to hear I have a new Fortune Bay book out and can't wait to read it. And your online reviews are icing on the cake.

I also want to thank my beta readers and typo editors on this book, Mara Burnstein, Eve Paterson, Mary Laycock and Jenny Watson. And always, thanks to my story editor, Stephanie Webb, who sometimes knows what I want to say before I write it.

And now, here's ***Starting Over...***

Judy Hudson

Chapter 1

Marshall Mason slammed the motorcycle helmet on his head. *Damn thing won't do up,* he thought. He ripped it off and took it under the light, but the clasp was toast. He threw the helmet aside and pulled his knit cap down over his ears. He just wanted to ride, get out on the road and burn off some of the anger that had been roiling like the hot, acrid smoke of burning tires inside his chest ever since he'd left the courtroom that afternoon.

Damn judge. What right did she have to give custody of his kids to his wife? She may be their mother but for more than a year she'd been his wife in name only. And he'd only hung in that long because of the kids. He scowled as he swung his leg over the seat and kicked off the bike stand. Their time in court had raised doubts in his mind about the years before that, too.

But he didn't even care about her infidelity, now. He just wanted his kids. Or at the very least, equal access. Up until now, he would have called her a good mother, putting her career on hold while he worked on the road, but he couldn't believe that keeping children away from their father was in their best interest. It was spiteful and mean, but like the beautiful ice queen she was, she'd laid him out in court as a disconnected father, living a dangerous lifestyle. A father not interested in his kids.

Who did she think had worked his butt off making the money to keep them in this pretentious lifestyle?

The lifestyle she wanted. The house in the Hollywood Hills. The beach house in Malibu. All her idea. And those fancy private schools the kids went to, which, if he'd had his say, they would never have gone to in the first place. Public school had been good enough for him and it would have been good for them, too. Teach them real life skills they'd need to survive. Better than the artificial values they were learning now.

Straddling his bike, he revved the motor and pushed a button on the handlebars. The garage door rose slowly on an icy scene of sleety rain. Unusual weather, but here in the hills they even got the occasional snowfall in the winter. He'd never liked the house but at least it was out of the city. Above the smog of L.A. where the air was clean.

Easing the bike out of the garage, he drove cautiously down the steep drive, testing the brakes, adjusting for the road conditions. Raw wind stung his cheeks as it rushed by, sucking the anger and hurt out of his lungs.

At the end of the drive he turned uphill, leaning into the bends, first left, then right, soon leaving the rain behind. The sharp night air tasted like winter, with the promise of snow. At the sight of red taillights up ahead, he touched the brake gently, pulling in behind the SUV that was crawling at a snail's pace up the hill. On a straight, starlit stretch, he let her rip, cruising by the SUV as if it was standing still.

Headlights rounded the curve ahead and Marshall boosted his speed, ducking in front of the car he'd just passed. The curve came up fast and with no chance to slow, he touched the brake and held tight to the handgrips. Leaning low, and lower still, he was halfway around the bend when he hit black ice.

The bike skidded along the surface of the road

dragging him with it, the friction shooting sparks into the dark night. The asphalt tore off his glove and his cheek burned as if stabbed by a thousand needles as it scraped the harsh pavement. The faces of his children flashed through his mind. He couldn't die here on this dark icy road. Not without a fight.

The bike crashed into the guard rail and the last thing he remembered was the sting of gravel peppering him like a spray of bullets as the car on his tail drove by. Then everything went dark.

Chapter 2

Six months later.

Lily Brewster took the heavy suitcase out of Dorothy's hands. "Let me help you," she said. If she didn't intervene, Dorothy just might try to carry it down the cabin steps all by herself.

Dorothy held tight to the bag. "Thank you, but I can manage."

Lily lowered her head, letting her hair fall forward to hide her smile. "I know, but I'll take it from here. Why don't you get your purse and then you'll be ready to go?" Lily had grown very fond of the old dear this past month, but now that Dottie and Harold were finally moving out of the cabin, she couldn't wait to have it to herself.

The suitcase was outrageously heavy, so once she'd wrestled it down the stairs, she set it on the ground and tried to pull it along the driveway. The tiny wheels caught on every rut and stone and, stifling a groan, she hoisted the bag off the ground with both hands and stumbled the rest of the way to the car.

Howard, Dorothy's octogenarian beau, stood by the open trunk of the old Lincoln. Thick carpeting covered the floor of the enormous baggage compartment—which was almost as spacious as the apartment Dorothy and Howard were moving into at The Manor, the senior's residence in nearby Majestic.

Together, Lily and Howard muscled Dorothy's suitcase into the trunk, then Lily went back to find

Dorothy standing on the cabin porch, pink purse over her arm, gazing out at the water. Majestic Lake was at its spring-glorious best on this sunny morning, the rim of the far shore beginning to glow white as dogwood blossoms burst into bloom, a bright frill on the hem of the dark cloak of evergreens that climbed the mountainside to the bare rocky peak across the lake.

A spark of excitement shot through Lily at the thought that in a matter of minutes, the cabin and its magnificent view would be all hers. At least for a while. A month ago, when she had arrived in Fortune Bay, her father had exceeded her expectations and welcomed her into his home and for that Lily would forever be grateful. But she and her dad hadn't been close in years and although they were making strides to remedy that, they quickly began to feel cramped in the log house across the road where he currently lived.

Then two weeks ago, her dad's girlfriend Stephanie had offered to rent Lily the cabin on the lake across the road from the log farmhouse. A nice gesture, prompted, Lily suspected, by the older couple's need for more privacy. But when Stephanie had taken Lily and her dad Max across the road to see the supposedly empty cabin, they found Dorothy and Harold had moved in.

As Dotty put it, they were "on the run, like Bonnie and Clyde," running from the threat of being "put in a home" by Stephanie's sister. And obviously enjoying every minute of the adventure. Fortunately, in their minds the senior's residence in Majestic didn't fall into that same category as *the home,* and they were thrilled with the prospect of their new apartment, and the pickle ball court, and the swimming pool, and the availability of meals upon request. Lily had to admit, The Manor sounded more like a resort than an old-folks home.

Stephanie stepped out the front door to join her mother on the porch. "Time to say goodbye."

Dorothy closed her eyes and swayed slightly. Her smile softened and for a moment her aged face took on a youthful glow. Her lips moved and although Lily couldn't hear what she said, she knew Dorothy was talking to her sister, Augusta, whose spirit Dorothy believed still resided in the cabin. Then she opened her eyes. "I'm ready. Let's go."

Stephanie took her mother's arm and helped her navigate the four steps to the ground.

"You and Howard can come by for a visit whenever you want," Lily said.

Stephanie's eyes bulged slightly in warning, but the invitation was out. Lily didn't mind. After years of feeling bereft of all family except her mother, it was nice to have a new grandmother in her life, even if she was a few steps removed.

"It's been nice to reconnect with Augusta," Dorothy said. "I would love to come by for a chat sometime."

Lily wasn't sure if Dorothy meant a chat with her or a chat with the spirit of her sister, Augusta. She cast an appraising glance at the cabin. That was the one kind-of-freaky thing about her new home. The Murphy family all agreed that it was haunted. Everyone who had lived there said so, but they all agreed that Aunt Augusta was benign, even friendly. Dorothy obviously believed it—Lily had witnessed her talking to and apparently receiving messages from Augusta more than once—but Lily wasn't sure she believed the stories.

"Any time, Dotty." She kissed the old lady on the cheek. "You too Howard." She gave the old man a hug and his cheeks flushed with pleasure.

Stephanie gave Lily a quick hug, too. "Thanks for

helping out. You sure you don't need any help moving in?"

"No, thanks. I think I'm all set. I'm travelling light." She was pretty much on the run herself, Lily thought ruefully. Then she straightened her spine. Not running, taking a stand. But her bravado deflated when she remembered her husband Troy's words—*there's someone else.* What stand could she take if he didn't want to be with her? And like every other time lately that thoughts about her crumbling marriage popped up, she pushed them out of her mind.

Stephanie climbed into her yellow hatchback and slowly followed the Lincoln down the bumpy drive—leaving Lily alone in the forest. She wrapped her arms around her ribs. The wind off the lake rustled the branches of the evergreen trees that surrounded the cabin in a protective buffer against the outside world. A city girl all her life, the absence of people sucked at her like a vacuum. But, she reminded herself, coming to Fortune Bay and moving into the cabin was her decision. She wanted a place where she could take some time to figure out what to do next—about Troy and the rest of her life.

The cabin was slightly ramshackle, with the peeling white paint and periwinkle-blue trim, but it was right on the lake and there was no denying that the view of the lake with the backdrop of snowcapped mountains in Olympic National Park was magnificent.

She ascended the steps to the front porch where she'd stashed the two suitcases that held everything she'd brought with her from Seattle. She'd made a quick getaway the night Troy had confronted her, throwing whatever was at hand into her suitcases and heading for the ferry. Now, with one in each hand, she pulled open the screen door with her foot. The solid-wood door stood open and inside, the doormat seemed to *ka'phlump* on the floor. Glancing down in surprise, she read the script on the mat through the glistening dust that sparkled in the air. "Welcome Home."

Although she read the words silently, they seemed to whisper in the air. She froze for a moment, then glanced around the empty room.

"Thank you, Augusta," she murmured under her breath. Then, suppressing a smile, she stepped inside, shaking her head at herself for talking to the "ghost" already.

She'd visited Dorothy and Howard a few times at the cabin, but it seemed different now that it was hers. A yellow Arborite table sat under the sunny window that looked across the porch to the lake. An old refrigerator flanked one end of the kitchen counter on the far-left wall, with a stove bracketing the other end. Not just any stove though, a turquoise stove with a row of push buttons along the back instead of knobs.

A staircase against the back wall led up to a trap door in the ceiling and, next to it, a blowsy flowered curtain covered the doorway to the bedroom. A woodstove stood in the far-right corner, and an overstuffed chair and sofa set, circa nineteen-forties, defined the living room area on the right. Cute. Shabby chic. Her friend Carmen who'd worked with her at the YWCA in Seattle was always looking for pieces like that.

She took her toiletry bag back outside and crossed to an inconspicuous door at the end of the porch. She was sure even Carmen would draw the line though at having to go outside to get to the bathroom.

But it wasn't an outhouse. Far from it. The bathroom was outfitted with fairly-modern fixtures and, most importantly, a shower over the tub. It would do fine.

Stepping back outside onto the porch, she sank onto the faded chintz couch that faced the lake and breathed in the clean damp air. Just what she wanted. Room to breathe. No one to answer to, no one making decisions for her about her life. In fact, if it wasn't for the fact that her dad actually seemed to need her help at the newly opened resort he managed in town, she might feel a little *too* unencumbered, drifting like a rudderless boat on the lake.

She took another breath, shakier than the first. She felt a little rudderless right now. The thought of being on her own scared her a bit after being in a couple for fourteen years. She'd thought when she'd married Troy that the lonely years were over. Yet, here she was, right back at square one. And when she thought back over the past few years, she realized she'd been lonely for a long time. As she and Troy had grown apart she'd filled the void—a void that should have been filled with a loving husband and young family—with her counselling work at the Y and the after-work hours she spent volunteering on the teen crisis phone line. It was rewarding work, but no one could be one hundred percent successful in that line of work, and her one or two tragic failures had left her burnt out and in drastic need of a change.

It was good to have her own place, though, to tide her over until she figured things out. However long that took. She'd taken a six-month leave of absence from work and although she expected to have things worked out with Troy long before then, she was not at all sure she wanted to go back to her old job or her taxing work at the crisis line. And she certainly didn't want their marriage to go back to the wasteland it had been. She wasn't quite ready to give up the fight, though. Not yet. She had too much invested in her marriage to just throw in the towel.

A twig snapped like a crack of a gunshot and she surged to her feet, her fight-or-flight reflexes on high alert. What was she thinking? She knew nothing about living in the forest, alone.

A shadow moved in the trees and a woman stepped into a patch of sunlight on the driveway. Hand to her chest, Lily blew out a breath and laughed. Frankie. Of course. Her neighbor. Lily's father had taken her to a dinner party at Frankie's house a few weeks before where she'd met a whole group of local people who, in some inextricable way, all appeared to be interconnected.

"Hi, neighbor," Frankie said with a smile. "Just thought I'd come over and help you move in." She was casually dressed wearing a woven poncho over tee shirt and jeans, her honey brown hair swinging at her shoulders.

Lily laughed, patting her chest to the beat of her racing heart. "I thought you were a bear."

Frankie laughed and joined her on the porch. "It's not unheard of, but still a little early in the season for the mothers and cubs to come down to the lake. They're probably still hiding out in the forest."

"That makes me feel a *lot* better."

Frankie waved off her concern. "You probably won't see any. I've been here for five years and have yet to see one. So—" she peeked in through the open door. "Need any help?"

"Thanks for the offer but I don't have much stuff to move in. I left Seattle in kind of a hurry and most of my things are still there."

Frankie nodded, then raised her eyebrows. "How

long are you staying?"

"I'm not sure." *About anything.* The open look in Frankie's soft, caramel-brown eyes was encouraging and Lily was surprised to hear herself continue. "My husband and I are separated—not necessarily forever. I'm not sure yet." She stopped herself just in time, before she blurted out the whole ugly story.

Frankie nodded sympathetically. "I hope you work it out. Good to have your own place, though."

"No kidding. I was beginning to feel like a bit of a third wheel over at the farm. Would you like something to drink?" Lily walked into the cabin. "I don't know if Dorothy left anything, but we can see."

She put the kettle on the stove and punched in a button, hoping it still worked. In the cupboard, a tin of Constant Comment tea sat in the middle of the almost-empty shelf. As the kettle began to hiss, she pried up the lid of the tea, releasing the aroma of oranges and cloves.

"I really appreciated Dad taking me in like that. We hadn't seen each other in almost a decade, he was always on the road, working. But after a couple of weeks of togetherness in the farmhouse, I think we'd both had enough. I need room to think, and he and Stephanie need some privacy."

Frankie took a seat at the table. "Max is a great guy. My boyfriend Sean works for him at the resort."

"I know Sean. I'm working at the resort myself. Just helping out. At first, I thought maybe Dad just asked me to help because he didn't know what else to do— he's always been all business—but I really do feel like I'm being helpful. He was kind of a troubleshooter for a hotel chain, moving around a lot, wherever he was needed. For the first few years of my life, until I started school, my mom and I travelled with him across the country, from one hotel or resort to another."

"That must have been fun," Frankie said as Lily put the mug of fragrant tea in front of her.

"I remembered those days in a kind of golden glow. It was the last time we spent any time together as a family. When I started school, my mother and I settled in Seattle and Dad continued on the road." Lily frowned, remembering how, a few times a year, he'd stopped in for a week, and how as the years went by, the visits became increasingly awkward and the gifts for her increasingly inappropriate and juvenile as they lost touch. "So I'm glad to be able to help out. It gives us some common ground."

"What are you doing at the resort?"

"Anything I can. I straightened out the bookkeeping. He'd been doing it himself during the building and hiring phases." She laughed. "He really needed help with that."

They took their tea back out to the porch and sat on the couch. The sweet smell of cloves drifted up from Lily's mug and as a soft breeze played across her cheek, she felt the strain of the past months slip away. The sun streamed onto the porch bringing with it a hint of spring. Waves sparkled on the bay and the snowy peaks of the Olympic Mountains rose startlingly white behind the hills across the lake.

"The water's still really high," Frankie commented. "There was a lot of snow last winter. It'll take a while to melt. I always feel a nip in the air as long as I can see snow."

Sounds of construction and the faint strains of country music radio drifted through the trees from Frankie's house next door. Putting down her empty cup, Frankie sighed dramatically, but smiled. "I guess I'd better get back to work."

"How's the reno coming?" Lily asked. When she'd been there for the dinner a few weeks ago, she'd heard Frankie and Sean's plans to enlarge Frankie's bungalow to suit their newly formed family, which included Sean's teenage daughter Amber.

"Sean hired part of the crew who were working on the resort to frame up the addition, so it's gone up pretty quickly. Now, on the weekends, a bunch of the guys come over and they do what they can." She grinned. "I'm just the gopher, but they keep me busy. When you get settled, you'll have to come over and see."

"I will," Lily said. "Thanks for dropping by." She lifted her hand to wave goodbye as Frankie disappeared on the path through the trees.

While Lily loved the wilderness, she had never lived all on her own before, and certainly not in a cabin in the forest, so the knowledge that people lived just beyond the fringe of trees was reassuring. Fortune Bay was a tight community. Frankie's boyfriend Sean was one of Stephanie Murphy's children, and Lily's dad seemed to have found his niche with the sprawling Murphy family.

As an only child, Lily found big family gatherings a bit overwhelming. Everyone she had met here seemed very nice, though, and Fortune Bay seemed like as good a place as any to settle while she got her head, and her life, together.

She went back into the cabin and stopped at the foot of the attic stairs to study a black and white photograph on the wall of a young woman waving out the window of an old car with a split front windscreen. Somehow, she knew the woman was Augusta. Maybe she should call her *Aunt* Augusta, to be polite. Everyone except Dottie did.

A breeze whispered by her cheek carrying a sweet aroma like fresh baking.

Wait a minute. She reined in her thoughts. She wouldn't be calling the so-called *ghost* anything!

But back to work. Opening the suitcases on the bed, she looked around, suddenly realizing there wasn't a closet in the bedroom, just a rod, like an old broomstick, with hangers on it secured to the wall in the corner. She'd make do.

As she hung up her clothes, an electronic disco melody sounded on her cell phone in the next room. It wasn't her husband. Troy's ring was a foreboding, descending, *Duh, duh, duh.*

She located her phone and saw her friend Carmen's name displayed on the screen. Carmen was the only person in Seattle that Lily had been in contact with since she'd walked out of her apartment that cold, rainy night. All her other so-called friends seemed to have decamped to Team Troy.

Refusing to play the forlorn refugee game, Lily put as much pep as she could into her voice. "Hi there."

"So how did the move go?" Glasses clinked in the background. Carmen must be at a restaurant. Probably Sunday brunch with friends. Lily tried to push down the envy as she looked around the small bedroom—from the rod hanging from the ceiling to the time-speckled, full-length oval mirror on the wall—and plunked herself down on a steamer trunk at the foot of the bed. "Everything went smoothly. I don't have very much to move at this point."

"How's the cabin?"

Lily hesitated a moment as she looked around the bedroom, searching for the right word. "Charming." Standing up, she went out onto the porch and looked out at the lake. "Picturesque." She glanced at the bathroom door. "And quirky."

"Fun!"

Lily smiled. Carmen saw the fun side of everything. "It will be fun, since I'm only here for a while."

"Have you spoken to Troy?"

Lily grimaced. "Not since the first week. I have to admit, I've been ducking his calls since the first one when he wouldn't agree to go for counselling." She sighed. "I guess I'll have to speak to him sooner or later. I'd just like to wait until I don't feel like..." *such a loser.* "Until I have some kind of plan."

Carmen's voice softened. "Go easy on yourself. Give it time. You had the rug pulled out from under you. You'll figure something out."

"I know. I just hope it's soon."

Chapter 3

The next morning, there was a chill in the air. Lily had found a cozy patchwork quilt in the chest and in her sleep, had pulled it tight up under her chin. The sharp, clean scent of closet-cedar wafted into her nostrils as she pulled the soft edge of the faded blanket to her cheek. Staying with her dad had been a godsend, but she realized now that she'd been on edge, on her best behavior the whole time. She and her dad had a long way go to make up for the years he'd been away working. Even as an adult, she'd only seen him once since her wedding fourteen years ago and had relied on her mother for news of his life. Last year, when her parents divorced, she'd worried she might never see her father again unless one of them took action, so she'd been happy when he'd reached out with the phone call last fall. After that first awkward conversation, Lily had vowed to reciprocate, not to drop the thread, but she hadn't done anything about it until Troy's declaration. *I'm seeing someone.*

She and her father had been distant for so long that she hadn't felt comfortable telling him much about what had gone down with Troy. And he hadn't asked. Not that she wanted him to pry but a simple question would have opened the door. They obviously still had a long way to go, but by helping out at the resort, his baby, she was showing him she cared.

Throwing back the covers, she stepped onto the chilly linoleum floor. The May air was cooler here in the mountains than it had been in Seattle, but the on-again off-again pattern of spring rain and warm sunshine was the same.

As she made her way across the porch to the bathroom, a smile formed on her lips at the thought of how different her life was here, with this view of the lake and snowcapped mountains greeting her each time she stepped out the door. Other than some of her clothes—and not even all of them—her electric piano and her books, there was very little in the apartment that she would miss. And very little she could call her own. Pretty sad after fourteen years of marriage.

She'd been aware of issues in her marriage for years but had told herself she was in it for the long haul, that she and Troy would make it work. At first, she'd thought that having a child would bring them together, but when he didn't get on board, kept putting her off, she had tried to convince herself that they were happy just the way they were, that she didn't need children to be fulfilled. The constant dull ache in her chest told her otherwise, though. Growing up as a lonely only-child, she'd always dreamed of being part of a big family. If he really didn't want the same, he should have let her know from the start.

Strong talk, but it didn't stop the ache in her chest. What hope did she have of having her dream family without him? At thirty-eight, it was almost too late to start over.

She might not have any other choice, though, if Troy was serious about moving on. And it certainly looked like he was. She wasn't exactly sure what *I've met someone* meant. That he'd *met* someone interesting? That he was ready to date her? Already dating? That they were sleeping together? Hopefully it hadn't gone that far. Hopefully, her leaving had brought him to his senses, but she was less sure of that each day. It had been three weeks and he hadn't come crawling back. In fact, after the first contentious conversation, she hadn't answered his next two calls and he hadn't called again.

She searched the kitchen cupboards and found an old percolator and—thank you Dorothy—a bag of ground coffee. After a piece of toast and a cup of coffee, she washed out her cup and made her bed ... then she didn't know what to do next. It had been so long since she'd been truly on her own that she had no idea what her own version of *moving on* would look like.

Her dad had suggested she take the weekend off from work to move. Well, she'd moved, and now the day spread out long and empty before her. Troy had always made their weekend plans. It hadn't started that way, but gradually over the years she had decided it was easier just to go along with whatever he wanted to do, rather than try to get him to go along with her ideas. Pathetic, now that she thought about it, but he could be such a pain in the ass if she talked him into something he didn't want to do that, eventually, she had given up trying.

Maybe being alone to think wasn't the best idea. Not yet, anyway. She didn't have to figure out her whole future the first day. The faint banging of hammers and whine of an electric saw drifted over from Frankie's house next door, but Lily didn't feel comfortable dropping in on the work party there so, in the end, she pulled a pair of dress pants off a hanger and dressed for work. The resort had opened two weeks before and the hustle and bustle of the reception area was a comforting distraction. There was always something to do. Even if she was just helping out at the main desk, answering phones or taking reservations, it felt good to be with people.

And she was surprised at how easily she'd slipped into the routine. Her dad was the general manager and part owner, but Lily didn't want anyone to think she was taking advantage of her position, so she'd made a point of trying to learn every job in the organization. The turning of the wheels within wheels was fascinating.

Choosing a pink silk blouse with a soft droopy bow at the neck, and a pair of black pumps, she was ready to go. As she got out of the car in the resort parking lot, the sky opened, and rain poured down. She ducked onto the long deck with the square fieldstone pillars holding up the roof that ran alongside the dining room, and made her way to the oversized glass front doors of the main entrance.

The doors swung open effortlessly and, brushing the rain off her shoulders, she hurried into the spacious, hexagonal lobby. From the first time Lily had walked through those front doors, she'd felt right at home. Her father had carefully designed all aspects of the Fortune Bay Resort to make the best use of the forest and lake-front setting. Bringing the outside in with giant windows and judicious use of local materials, he had managed to make it both classy and welcoming at the same time.

Warm-colored cedar paneling clad the walls and in the center of the room stood an eye-catching one-of-a-kind table made by local carver and furniture-maker Blue: a glass top over an organic wooden base that looked like the roots or branches of a tree.

On her immediate left, an arch decorated with swimming salmon—also courtesy of Blue—led to the dining room and next to it a massive fieldstone fireplace soared the full two stories to a beamed wooden ceiling. The fireplace took up most of the wall between the dining room arch and the entrance to The Cedars Bar. Directly opposite the front doors, a corridor ran off the lobby with elevators to the rooms above. On her right was the front desk and behind it, the administration offices.

Sean was working the front desk this morning and smiled up at her as she walked in. As marketing manager, his clean cut, blonde, blue-eyed good looks, easy charm and perpetual smile made him the perfect face of the resort.

"How are you settling in at the cabin?" he asked.

"It's great. I love my dad and appreciate him taking me in unannounced, but I really needed to get out of his house."

Sean laughed. "I hear you. My daughter and I are living with my mom right now. You know Stephanie, don't you? It's kind of a zoo. I can hardly wait for the addition at Frankie's to be finished so Amber and I can move in." He leaned toward her, forearms on the counter and a grin on his face. "How are you getting along with Augusta?"

"I haven't heard too much from her," Lily said cautiously. "Sometimes I think I feel a kind of ... I don't know—a presence? A breeze, or a smell. Dorothy seemed to hear her pretty consistently, though. You lived there, didn't you? Did Augusta ever speak to you?"

"Not directly. She just moved things around and sort of left me notes. But Grandma hears her talking and Louise, the pastry chef here, lived in the cabin last winter and saw and even spoke to Augusta."

Lily's eyes widened. "Seriously?"

Sean nodded. "So she says. I kind of believe her,

but it might have been wishful thinking. She was going through a lot at the time."

"I don't want to *see* the ghost," Lily said with a nervous laugh.

Sean shook his head and waved a hand vaguely. "Don't worry. She's harmless." He focused back on the computer screen before him. "Now, what do you know about this column marked, "Extraneous Expenses"?

Half an hour later, Lily finally went into her office. They were in the process of hiring more staff, but at the moment, she pretty much *was* the accounting department.

Three weeks ago, shortly after she'd arrived in Fortune Bay and a week before the official opening, she'd quietly started working in the resort office. She'd heard about the splashy soft opening just before the previous Christmas with a few invited guests, mostly the press, that coincided with a Christmas Artisan's Show they'd held in the dining room. Because of that, Max hadn't planned anything dramatic for the real opening. Just as well. To the public it looked like business as usual—but behind the scenes they were scrambling to make it all work. Everyone in the place was new and in training, from the wait staff in the restaurant, to the room cleaners, to the chefs and the front desk clerks. Some were local, some from away. Lily had jumped right in, partly for the distraction, taking the training sessions right along with the new staff, and she had quickly become fascinated by all aspects of running a resort of this size. She wanted to prove her worth, not be just a figurehead, the boss's daughter.

She'd tweaked the computer systems that handled the bookings and payroll, billing and accounts payables, a job she'd worked at summers while completing her social work degree, before moving into counselling at the Y. Luckily, her dad had given her free rein, because she could see he was in over his head when it came to computers. He was a big picture guy; people loved him and bent over backwards to please him. She'd seen it before and knew that was why he'd done so well as a trouble-shooter. He could read and analyze a spreadsheet, but that was about as far as his recordkeeping expertise went. They would be opening more rooms as the season progressed, but this weekend all of the rooms they had opened so far were fully booked. She was sure she could find a way to help. They'd gone from one mini-crisis to the next since the opening but somehow, with her dad at the helm, they always made it through.

She found Max on the phone in his office, rubbing his forehead with his free hand.

When he hung up the phone, she asked, "What now?"

"One of the cleaning staff has a sick child and can't make it in until after noon. We do the rooms in the morning so they're ready for the afternoon turnover."

Lily nodded. "I know. I took the orientation with the cleaning staff my first week. Hilda will be pissed. She runs a tight ship."

Max looked at the schedule on the desk in front of him, a frown creasing his forehead. "I need someone to do three of the cottages on the point. Frankie's dad Philip and Ellen are in Cottage One, long term. Ellen insists she only needs a cleaner once a week, but the other three need the full run-through." He ran his finger down the staff list. "I hate to call Hilda in again today. It's her first day off in two weeks."

"I can do it," Lily said.

Her dad looked skeptically at her outfit. "You're not exactly dressed for cleaning. And taking the orientation is not the same as doing the job."

"I've cleaned toilets before, Dad. It will only take me a minute to go home and change. Or, isn't there an extra uniform here I could wear?"

She was pleased to see the worry lines in her father's brow ease. "It's really only the three cottages. We can cover the rest. It shouldn't take more than an hour or two."

"No problem. Are they turning over today?"

Max checked the schedule. "Two are, but Cottage Four, the last one, kind of back in the trees, it's another long term." He looked at her strangely, as if deciding how much to say. "The renter, Mr. Morris...likes his privacy. He'll be there, so try not to disturb him."

Lily nodded. "Morris. Cottage Four. Got it."

An hour later, having finished cleaning Cottages Two and Three and having developed a new respect for the cleaning crew, Lily stood on the veranda of Cottage Four and tapped on the door. The reception building, that everyone referred to as the Lodge, and first building of suites looked out on the other side of the point at the quiet vista of Fortune Bay. This side of the point, however, had a spectacular view across the lake to the Olympic Mountains, their snowy peaks blindingly white in the afternoon sun.

Lily had pulled her almost-shoulder length honey colored hair into a short ponytail to keep it out of her face while she worked, and now she tugged at the front of the steamy uniform tee shirt she'd changed into before starting the first cottage. The pants were a good idea, but she'd have to speak to her father about the synthetic blend of the tee's. If she was hot and sticky on a cool day like today, the workers would melt in the hot summer sun.

No one seemed to be home in Cottage Four. The curtains were drawn even though it was almost noon. She rapped again and considered opening the door with her pass key, but her father had said Mr. Morris would probably be there, so she gave it another minute. Soon, she heard sounds of movement inside and the turning of the lock.

"Cleaning staff," she called in a cheerful voice.

The door opened a few inches and warm stale air brushed by her. Inside, the cottage was dark. She hesitated. "I could come back later, if you want."

There was a slight pause, then the door opened a few more inches and she got her first glimpse of Mr. Morris. Probably six feet tall if he'd been standing up straight, long straggly hair hung over most of the left side of his face. He'd pulled the other side back behind his ear, revealing a face ravaged by some kind of misery only he could see, so obviously painful that she took a step back, then quickly hoped he hadn't noticed.

His lips pressed together into a tight line. He had noticed. He had one hand tucked into the pocket of a dressing gown he wore over baggy sweat pants and a faded rock concert tee shirt. Not one of the crisp white gowns the resort provided for guests, but a droopy, striped terry that had obviously seen him through—a lot. A lot of what she wasn't sure, but something harsh. She was somewhat surprised her father was letting him stay. And surprised Mr. Morris could afford a long-term stay in a cottage.

"It's alright," he said. His voice sounded hoarse, as if her hadn't spoken in a while. "Might as well be now. Just give me a minute." He closed the door, leaving her standing on the porch.

Dragging her hands over her hot face, Lily pulled back the stray hair that had escaped from her ponytail. The first two cottages she'd cleaned had been empty. They'd probably had families in them, though, and she suspected there'd been a dog in one. They'd been sticky and sandy but nothing she couldn't handle. She had hoped this last one would be quick, but now she waited with trepidation for Mr. Morris to open the door, half expecting to see the remains of a bender—bottles and pizza boxes and god-only-knew what else. She pulled the service wagon closer and checked her supply of plastic gloves.

The door swung open but in the dimness, all she saw was Mr. Morris's back as he walked away.

"I'll be in the bedroom until you finish the rest," he said, and the bedroom door closed silently behind him.

Cautiously, Lily turned on the lights. The living room was surprisingly neat and clean, as if he never used it at all. She threw open the curtains, illuminating warm wood walls, a stone fireplace and a new, nubby-textured couch and chair set, like in the other cottages. No sign of the debauchery she'd expected. The only personal item in the living room was a beautiful electric piano. Lifting the cloth dustcover to peek at the keys, she flexed her fingers. She'd left her own piano in Seattle—although it was nothing like this. Not nearly as grand.

She looked around. Other than the piano, the cottage could have been unoccupied.

There wasn't a crumb on the kitchen counter and other than a take-out box from the Fortune Bay Cafe in the garbage, the place looked barely lived in. The second bedroom hadn't been touched.

She wiped her way through the rooms anyway, as

per the training; checked the dishwasher for dirty dishes but only found a few forks which she washed and put away. She emptied the recycling container, which was full of empty water bottles, washed the still-clean kitchen floor and, plugging the vacuum hose into the built-in unit, gave the spotless carpets in the living room and spare bedroom a once-over.

Everything shone in the main bathroom, but orders were to sanitize it all anyway. It only took a few minutes to scrub the shower and sink, clean the toilet, replace the unused towels with fresh—folded like Hilda had demonstrated—and wipe the already shining mirror.

The whole time she worked, the bedroom door stayed closed. When she finished the main rooms, she hesitated in front of the door. Mr. Morris had looked pretty rough. She didn't want to bother him, but her instructions were to service the whole cottage. She had to at least offer to clean the bedroom and ensuite bath.

Taking a deep breath, she knocked on the bedroom door. No answer. She raised her hand again and was trying to decide whether to knock a second time when the door silently swung open. Surprised, she stepped back to let him pass. Mr. Morris looked down and away, and asked in his rough voice as he shifted past her, "What happened to Hilda?"

Lily didn't know what to say. She hadn't known Hilda actually cleaned any of the rooms herself. "It's her day off. I'm Lily."

The eye she could see glanced at her and away. "You can call me Morris."

Something about him looked familiar; sharp cheekbones, dark sculpted brows, piercing blue eyes. Eye, really, because he kept his face strangely averted, hair hanging over the hidden side.

"I'll wait out here," he said. "Just the bedding, and

the garbage. Please, Lily."

Certain her smile looked as fake as it felt, she said, "I'll just be a few moments. It's a lovely day. Enjoy your beautiful view." She wondered if he'd even noticed it, or if he kept the shades drawn all the time. She picked up the clean linen and walked into the bedroom.

The shades were drawn here too, and the air was stuffy, like a sick room. Suddenly she wondered if Mr. Morris—Morris—was sick. Maybe she'd been too quick to judge. Maybe she should ask if he needed help.

This was obviously where he'd been living. The air conditioning was off—it wasn't warm enough to warrant it—but she opened the blinds and wound open the windows to air out the room while she worked. She would respect his wishes and just do the bed, the small bathroom and give the room a quick vacuum. As she cleared six beer bottles off the dresser, she noticed a couple of photos of two children, one picture framed, under glass, and the other, a smaller one, stuck into the frame, covering whoever else might have been in the framed print. The children looked about four and six years old, with the boy being the older. They were both very sweet, with straight black hair and high cheekbones. The little girl's eyes had a slight, possibly Asian tilt, but the boy's eyes were very much like Morris's. What she could see of them. His kids? None of her business.

She found more empty water bottles in the trash and carried the linen laundry and refuse into the living room on her way to the service cart. Morris had closed the drapes and in the dim light she saw his silhouette on the couch, head resting back on the cushions. His eyes seemed to be closed.

She stopped with her hand on the front door. "I'm finished."

He didn't move. "Thank you."

It wasn't her job to interfere, but she hated to think of him here, ill and alone. "Is there anything I can help you with?"

He hitched himself up on the couch, but continued to stare straight ahead, not at her, his hair covering much of his face. "No, thank you."

"If you're not well, I could get a doctor..." How presumptuous, but she couldn't help feeling that something was wrong.

"I'm fine."

She shifted uneasily. "Okay then, I'll get out of your way." She opened the door and maneuvered the cart out onto the porch. Morris stood and followed her to the door.

Unaccountably nervous, as she busied herself organizing the cart for the trip back to the Lodge, she glanced back to where he stood, hand on the doorknob. She must have caught him by surprise, because this time he was facing her, and she sucked in a breath when she caught a glimpse of the cheek he'd kept hidden. An angry scar formed a ring of fire from the corner of his mouth to the top of his cheek bone, the colorless skin inside the ring looking unnaturally smooth.

Her eyes flashed to his and for a split second, held his gaze. Then he shut the cottage door.

Chapter 4

Lily pushed the cleaning cart down the path to the service entrance of the Lodge, her heart racing as she considered the implications of what she had seen, the glimpse of ravaged flesh on Morris's cheek. What could have caused his injury? Possibly a fire. Her dad probably knew. She didn't want to pry, Morris deserved his privacy, but the poor man. She hated to think of him alone in the cottage, although he must want to be alone, to have come to this isolated area from wherever he was from, to heal. Or to hide. It didn't look good, staying alone in the cottage with the curtains drawn. That wasn't curative, or restorative. That was depression.

She recognized the symptoms. Her mother had often sunk into depression for weeks at a time and all through Lily's teenage years, her mother had been in denial, hiding from the world, taking it all into herself, not dealing with the problem, leaving Lily to deal with her teenage life as best she could. Over the years, particularly at college where Lily had majored in social work with a minor in psychology, she had done extensive research and learned that many depressives don't know they're depressed. Some think it's their fault they can't cope, are ashamed and don't seek treatment. She had an uneasy sense that Morris had yet to look that demon in the eye.

Lily let herself into the large service area in the rear of the Lodge. Although the guests never saw this area, it was the heart of the resort operation. Laundry and storage, the back entrance to the kitchen for deliveries, staff changing rooms and lunchroom, it was all there through the inconspicuous doorway just past the lobby elevators marked *STAFF ONLY.*

Her dad came in just as she was putting the soiled linen in the industrial washing machine. His eyes twinkled. "How did you make out?"

She smiled wanly and rubbed her lower back. "I have a new respect for the cleaning crew. You probably don't pay them enough. And seriously, you have to do something about these synthetic tee-shirts. It's like being wrapped in plastic."

He nodded. "I'll take that under advisement. Thank you. That was a big help."

His appreciation made her heartbeat faster, but she just smiled. "Wait until you get my bill."

"How about I take you to dinner?"

She squinted one eye and tipped her head suspiciously. "Here?"

He had the grace to look chagrinned. "I hear the poached Steelhead is fabulous."

Lily smiled. "It's a date."

As she changed back into her own clothes, she wished she could take a shower. She hadn't worked that physically hard in years. Bending over, she let her fingers hang toward her toes, trying to release the kinks in her lower back, cringing when her fingers didn't actually touch her toes. Long hours at the computer had left her in terrible shape. She had to get more exercise. But right now, she'd settle for some air and lunch.

The landscape designers had left a grove of mature fir trees lining the resort driveway and Lily always enjoyed the short walk down the drive and across the road to the Fortune Bay General Store. The brisk breeze off the lake made her think about Morris and how restorative the lake and this breeze could be if he'd just get out and enjoy it. But she didn't know him well enough to suggest it and, as his chamber maid, her dad would probably say it wasn't her job to interfere.

The Fortune Bay Café was housed in the General Store, a one-story blue frame building directly across the main road from the resort driveway. The store's large windows faced the road and were plastered with posters proclaiming local events. Center stage was Sean's large, colorful poster for a kid's fishing derby, sponsored by the resort. There had been great debate in the office over the date. Some wanted the derby to kick off summer on the Fourth of July, but eventually they decided to put it on the quieter, first weekend in August, maybe adding an outdoor dance at night, thinking it would lend excitement to the mid-summer weekend.

Inside the General Store, Lily waved to the woman behind the counter. Fiona was a gruff old bird, but Lily had detected a kind heart under her rough exterior. Right now, she was at the checkout counter talking to an elderly woman wearing a tweed suit and a felt hat bedecked with flowers.

"You're kidding," Fiona said.

"We needed something to replace the Gazette," the woman argued. "It's been three years since it closed."

Lily stopped at the counter. She had quickly learned that the checkout counter at the General Store was gossip central. And that anyone was welcome to join in.

Fiona looked at her over the reading glasses sitting on the end of her nose. The frames were bright fuchsia, a new purchase she'd proudly displayed the week before, and the sight of them on the otherwise dowdy shopkeeper always made Lily smile. Fiona had said that time was running out and she had to start checking things off her bucket list. Apparently 'fuchsia glasses' was at the top of the list.

"Lily, do you know Ms. Bowden? She used to be the teacher at the school here in town. She's starting an online newspaper. On Facebook." Fiona spat out the word with suspicion.

"It may turn out to be more of a bulletin board," Ms. Bowden said modestly. "Anyone can post, although I'll moderate and make sure no one posts anything too racy or nasty. Local services can post specials, too, or people who are looking for something," Ms. Bowden added, her barely contained excitement making the flowers on her hat bob. "A ride to Seattle or something like that."

"I think it's a great idea," Lily said. "I'll be sure to join."

She headed to the café through the arched entrance beside the counter before she could become embroiled in the latest local scandal. It was already hard to keep a secret in Fortune Bay, and this new Facebook page was bound to make it even harder. She was glad she was still flying under the radar. Not that she really had anything to hide.

The small café was a throwback to earlier times, with six red vinyl-topped stools lined up at the counter and a couple of scarred wooden tables by the windows that looked out at the forest. The room buzzed with the chatter of people waiting by the till for their take-out lunch.

Lily snagged the one empty stool at the counter. She ordered a fried egg sandwich and the soup of the day—chicken vegetable—and Star, the elfin, short-order cook, while seeming to do ten things at once, still managed to fill a stainless-steel teapot with boiling water and a tea bag and place it on the counter in front of Lily, along with a heavy white mug.

Lily had discovered that Star was relatively new in town too and seemed eager to be friends. As Lily ate, the take-out crowd left with their orders and the lunch rush slowed. Star poured herself a cup of coffee and came over to lean against the stainless prep counter to chat.

"Someone is starting a community Facebook page," Lily said.

"I know. Ms. Bowden came in all excited a while ago and told me. Up until now, the store and café have been the first place to hear most of the news, but I guess people will still come in to talk it over. I don't think the Facebook page will replace the need for face to face gossip."

Lily laughed. "Probably not. I always look forward to coming into the store and getting the news from Fiona—and you."

Star grinned. "I do hear things."

Lily nodded. "Who ran off the road on a rainy night, whose dog had puppies, who is having a baby."

"And the speculation over whose baby it is." Star sighed. "I'll be sorry if that changes." Then she brightened up. "Some new courses are starting at the Hall this week. Colleen is teaching line dancing. I've signed up. You should come too. It'll be a blast."

"Seriously? Line dancing?"

"Come on. It'll be fun. When was the last time you had any real fun?"

Was it that obvious? Lily couldn't remember the last time she had let down her guard enough to have fun. Most of what she considered fun, Troy had considered frivolous. She had told herself that moving to Fortune Bay signified a new start, but so far, she had been at a loss as to what that really meant. Maybe she had to actually try something new to find out what her new life could look like. And line dancing was certainly new to her. "Okay. I'll come."

"Great! You don't need cowboy boots, although they are pretty fun." Star came out from behind the counter and in her tight jeans and turquoise cowboy boots, demonstrated a grinding hip swivel and a turn-and-stamp, then giggled her girlish laugh.

Lily blanched—*what have I gotten myself into?*—but she found herself laughing, too.

With plans in place to meet Star at the Hall on Thursday evening, Lily headed back up the winding tree-lined drive to the resort. Stopping in front of the Lodge, she watched a family walk down the path to the dock. The girl and boy, probably six and eight, skipped excitedly ahead of their parents. Both of the children wore shiny yellow boots and colorful waterproof jackets, and each carried their own fishing pole.

Lily took a deep breath and blew it out. Seeing happy families together always caused a twinge of longing—but she'd better get used to it because after Memorial Day, when the season really got rolling, lots of families were booked into the units. In Seattle, none of their friends had had children, but even though her specialty was counselling at-risk adults, Lily enjoyed working the kid's classes at the Y. She firmed her lips. Families were good business and while she was part of the Fortune Bay Resort team, she'd have to get over herself and embrace it.

And it wasn't such a hardship, she thought as the parents joined the kids on the dock, because the little ones were so darned cute. It would have been nice, wonderful in fact, to have children of her own, but Troy had always put it off until now, at thirty-eight, she had to accept that it might not happen at all. She'd have to learn to be content being everyone's favorite aunt—although, as an only child, that was problematic too. There seemed to be a baby boom here in Fortune Bay. Maybe she could become an honorary aunt to some of those kids. If she stayed.

Her dad stepped through the French doors from the dining room onto the long porch. He leaned his forearms on the heavy wood railing and looked at the crisp whitecaps out on the lake.

Lily climbed the steps and joined him at the rail. "Surveying your domain?"

He smiled sheepishly. "Just taking a break. It is darn nice, though."

"It's great, Dad. You've really pulled it off." She looked back to the parking lot. "Where's your car?"

Max puffed out his chest. "I walked."

"Wow. I'm impressed. What is it, a mile?"

"And a half."

"I might start walking too, once the weather gets a bit more reliable."

"You could take one of the resort bicycles. Or even a rowboat."

She laughed and shook her head. "I'd be rowing in circles. I don't row well enough."

"Take out a boat sometime and see how you like it." Max looked back at the lake and took a deep breath. "You know, I don't miss the city at all."

"Strangely, neither do I."

"It's something your mom never understood, but I guess I couldn't understand what kept her in the city, either. Well," he said, straightening up. "I'd better get back to work. It's been ten minutes. Surely there's another crisis by now. See you at dinner?"

She smiled. "You bet."

Chapter 5

Lily worked in her office until it was time to meet her father in the restaurant. The spacious room was only a third full, having been designed for the crowds Max anticipated when the resort was complete, with the other wing of rooms and two more condo pods he planned to build for next season.

Her father was waiting. He had secured a table by the corner windows where they would both have a view. A bottle of Washington State merlot sat open on the white tablecloth and someone had poured her a glass.

She sank gratefully into her seat and took a sip. "Busy day."

"Thanks again for helping out with the cleaning service. That was above and beyond, especially on your day off. It saved my neck, though. One crisis I didn't have to handle."

She waved it off. "No problem. I like knowing how things really work around here."

Her dad grinned. "Next time there's a clogged toilet, I'll give you a call."

After the server took their order, they talked about the problems Sergio the chef was having with his deliveries, but regardless of the minor crisis in the kitchen that day—or maybe because she was dining with the boss—their food arrived quickly.

As she ate the delicious Steelhead poached in wine, with early asparagus and fresh green salad, the sky above the fir trees on the point took on an orange glow as the sun set behind the mountain across the lake. The Olympic Mountains were visible from Seattle, but here they were immense, immediate, towering over the lake and swooping down from the snowy peaks of the peninsula interior to the far shoreline.

As twilight settled, lights came on in the first two cottages. Lily sought out Cottage Four, but it was dark, almost hidden by the trees and the gathering dusk. Frowning at the thought of Morris, Mr. Morris, sitting alone in the dark, she hoped he was watching TV. Lots of people turned off the lights when they watched TV. Her frowned deepened as she remembered how miserable he looked and how he'd drawn the blinds during the day, and suddenly she wasn't hungry anymore.

Pushing the food around on her plate, she said, "Mr. Morris seems to be kind of a special guest. He said Hilda had been doing his cleaning." She tried to sound nonchalant even though she was dying to know the story behind the mystery man in Cottage Four.

Her dad looked up briefly from cutting the meat on his plate. He put the forkful into his mouth and chewed thoughtfully. Then he swallowed and took an exasperatingly slow sip of wine. Finally, he said, "He was in a bad motorcycle accident. Sliced up one side of his face and burned his left hand."

She inhaled sharply in surprise. "I didn't see his hand."

Her dad nodded. "It's pretty bad. He was in the hospital for a long time, has had a couple of surgeries already and will probably have at least one more, as I understand it. Now he just wants to be left alone to recover."

Lily went back to her meal as she mulled over this

new information. "I can't pretend to understand what he's going through, but I don't think it's healthy to be holed up there all alone in the dark, day and night."

"Now Lily, don't interfere. He's not one of your strays."

She *tsked* her tongue indignantly. "I don't have strays."

"You always brought home strays. Stray cats, wounded animals, kids who you thought needed help one way or another. Your mother was not amused."

Lily chuckled. "She particularly hated the birds."

"I repeat—Mr. Morris is not one of your strays. He came here looking for peace and quiet and...anonymity. I mean to give him that. His...friend comes by once a week to check on him."

Lily *humphed* at that bit of information. He needed more human contact than one visit a week. Left on his own, he could shrink even further into his shell.

"I'm really glad to have you here, sweet pea," Max said.

Tears sprang to her eyes at the childhood term of endearment. Their connection was still so new and tender. "I'm glad to be here. I—I missed you." She took a drink of water to cover her emotion.

"I missed you, too." Max cleared his throat. "I want to apologize for leaving, for being on the road so much. The problem was between your mother and me, but at the time I didn't consider what it must have been like for you, living alone with your mom."

Lily thought over her response before she spoke. "It wasn't *horrible*, she didn't abuse me, but...she had problems. I never really felt like she *loved* me."

"She did," Max said firmly.

"Really?" Lily raised one eyebrow skeptically. "She didn't show it."

"You should have heard how she talked about you when we spoke on the phone. She was *so* proud of you. Your music, your art. Your mother isn't cold, just so finely tuned and, I'm afraid I have to say, selfish. She likes it to be all about Marion, and when you have a child you can't do that. It has to be all about them. She knew that, but I'm afraid she resented you a tiny bit."

Lily remembered the long, lonely weekends when her mom was shut in her room. "It wasn't just that. She...she had problems." Her dad had been away so much, she wasn't sure if he knew to what degree. Her mom always hid it when he was around, had always seemed overly bright and cheery when he was home. Lily thought her mother had suffered from depression, but maybe she just really missed him when he was away. Lily had been a child at the time, so it had been hard to tell what was really going on.

"Just remember, she does love you—a lot. And so do I. I relied on her to keep us connected. A weak connection at best and I admit, I was lazy. And busy." He looked her in the eye. "But that is no excuse and I'm sorry. I loved it when you and your mom were on the road with me. Do you remember?"

"I remember the swimming pools, and the meals arriving under silver domes. I felt like a princess."

Max laughed. "Room service. Probably stainless-steel covers, but I guess that is how a child would remember it." He shook his head and when he spoke again, his voice was gruff with emotion. "It was no kind of life for a kid, though, and when you reached school age, rather than send you to boarding school—which I admit we considered—your mother decided to get an apartment in Seattle and stay put. She was tired of travelling. There wasn't much for her to do at the hotels."

He was silent for a moment. "I always missed you, but eventually the work took over and the lonely life on the road became the norm. I'm sorry I wasn't there for you more. You deserved better."

"Well, you were there when I needed you this time." She sighed deeply. "I don't know what is going to happen with Troy. I have fourteen years invested in that relationship. We've had some problems lately. We just have to try to work things out." Tears pricked her eyes. "Otherwise, I don't know what I'll do."

"Stay here with me, in Fortune Bay?" Max asked hopefully.

"That would be great," Lily said dryly. "Living with daddy at forty."

"I don't mean living together."

"No," she said, giving him a teasing smile. "I think I rather cramped your style with Stephanie."

"No," he blustered, his cheeks turning a cute shade of red.

She became serious again. "Regardless what happens with Troy, I don't want to go back to my old job. I didn't realize how burnt out I was until I started working here."

"There's always room for you here, honey. You're doing a great job helping us get organized. And just in time. I'd hate to think how we would have gotten through this last couple of weeks with the reservation system I had set up."

"I'm happy to help out, but I don't really think I'll be staying long."

"You are looking better. When you arrived, you looked like you'd been run over by a truck."

Lily nodded. "That's how I felt. I'd had a couple of terrible experiences. A client at the crisis line died. He was just a kid. Then Troy announced he thought we should separate, and I snapped. I guess it had been coming for a while. I just hadn't seen it."

Max put a hand on her arm. "I'm proud of how you've pulled yourself together."

Lily thought for a moment then nodded. "I feel much better—quite good in fact. It isn't over with Troy, I'm still hoping we can get back together, but some things will have to change if we do." She shook off those worries. "But I feel stronger, now. Ready to face him again."

"That would be good, I guess. Although I hate to see you go back. I could use you here, at the resort. And I feel like we are just getting to know each other again," he added shyly.

Lily reached across the table and touched his arm. "I feel the same way Dad." Then she picked up her knife and fork. "But if Troy wants to try again, I have to go back."

"Do you love him?"

She raised her eyebrows. When had her dad become such a softie? "I think so. I do," she said more firmly. Then she sighed and her shoulders dropped. "I think so. We have a lot invested in this. I want to have a family. Children. I'd hate to throw it all up and have wasted the fourteen years we had together."

"I'd love to have grandchildren, too," Max said gruffly. "But if you aren't happy—and you certainly didn't look happy when you arrived on my doorstep— then I want you to know there's a place for you here."

Lily blinked away her tears. "Thanks, Dad."

"And in the meantime," Max said, obviously trying to hide his emotion. "Just try to have some fun."

Lily grinned. "That's number one on my bucket list. Learn to have fun. Star wants me to take line dancing classes with her."

Max let out a whoop of laughter. "Line dancing. Whatever turns your crank."

Lily smiled wryly. "Time will tell. I won't know if it's for me until I try."

* * *

Once darkness fell, Marshall opened the living room blinds in the cottage. From his seat on the couch, he could see the moon, almost full, hanging over the lake, its silvery light streaming in through the window, falling on the shrouded piano. Why had Harry insisted on bringing that useless thing to Fortune Bay when he'd moved Marshall in? Managers could be such a pain, especially one like Harry Santino who'd been a bossy son of a bitch ever since they were kids.

Marshall rubbed his good hand over the taught, dry skin of his badly scarred left hand. He'd never play again. They all knew it. Sometimes he wished he'd died in that crash instead of surviving. Music was his life and it had been ripped away in those few minutes of fire and pain. What the fuck was he going to do now? Be an *invalid* for the rest of his life?

They said with more surgery they could restore some use to his left hand, but he'd still never play the guitar again. Or the piano. His voice would come back, slowly. It might not be the same mellow baritone that had sold millions of records, but he would probably be able to carry a tune.

He looked away from the piano to the mountains across the lake, their snowy peaks glowing in the moonlight. He was too old to start over. Until the accident, he'd managed to hang onto his heart-throb persona into his forties, probably because he'd gone easy on the drinking and drugs that plagued so many of his buddies in the business. He'd tried them early on in his career, but they'd never delivered as much of a kick as the music itself.

That was all he'd ever wanted to do—make music. And he'd planned to play forever, counting on his talent and reputation to get him gigs even when his looks had gone. But now he wouldn't be able to play well enough to get a job as a back-up studio musician, and even that would have been a difficult step down from being a name that pulled crowds into the stadiums.

The stage and spotlight weren't kind to a face like his was now. He saw the way people looked at him. The pity. Harry was used to it, he'd been by his side since the accident, but others couldn't hide their reaction. Like his ex-wife, who'd been horrified. And like that maid today. He'd seen the look—well, to be fair, it had only been a widening of her honey colored eyes when she registered the shock of the taut skin and warped features on the left side of his face.

Admit it, man. His vanity was the greatest victim of that life-changing accident. He'd better get used to it because he had to live with the consequences of that one stupid decision for the rest of his life.

Chapter 6

The next morning, Lily searched out Hilda in her office. As Head Housekeeper and Facilities Coordinator, Hilda was responsible for assigning the cleaning staff rotations.

"Thank you for pitching in on the weekend," Hilda said. She wasn't one to show much emotion. If anything, she was more like an army drill sergeant, so her thanks came as a bit of a surprise.

"My pleasure. I met the man in Cottage Four. I'm surprised you are cleaning that cottage yourself."

"That one is a special case." Hilda shook her head. "I don't really have time for it, but your father insisted. Said the guest can't be bothered by the regular staff. Can't risk news of his being here getting out. I take it he is a bit of a celebrity, although I don't know what for and I don't care. All guests should be treated the same, in my opinion."

Lily nodded seriously, trying to hide her eagerness. "I understand the need for confidentiality. You know," she said, as if the idea had just come to her. "I could help you out with that one cottage."

"You! What do you know about cleaning—"

"I took the orientation last week. Anyway, it's no problem. Mr. Morris doesn't seem to make much mess."

"That is true." Hilda squinted at her. "And we do need someone discreet."

And, Lily couldn't help thinking, *someone more*

cheerful than you. Morris certainly wasn't one of her strays, but Lily did have experience dealing with depression.

Relief settled on Hilda's normally stern features. "Thank you. That would be wonderful. I don't have time to traipse through the forest every other day with the service cart to take of care of an invalid. This is not a sanatorium."

"I'm happy to help."

* * *

Thursday evening at seven, Lily pulled into the parking lot at the Fortune Bay Hall, a multi-purpose building built in the nineteen-sixties by the forest company who at that time owned the town and the now long-gone sawmill. Star was waiting on the steps, the rays of evening sun sparking her cinnamon curls as it dipped toward the mountain tops across the lake.

Lily stepped out of the car to the sound of driving country music blasting out through the open doors of the hall. She'd never considered line dancing before, but she was determined to get out there tonight and *have some fun.* As she walked across the parking lot toward Star, her friend did a welcoming slide, first to one side then to the other. Her elfin grin always made Lily feel like her new friend had some mischievous master plan.

"Great. You made it. I wasn't sure you'd show up," Star said, leading the way inside.

The bingo tables had been pushed to one side of the cavernous room. Like everything else in Fortune Bay, the building was made entirely of wood, with wood paneling covering the walls and exposed beams holding up the high wood ceiling. A large stage dominated one end of the room and a doorway led to an industrial kitchen at the other. A dozen people milled around on the open hardwood floor. There were two men present, but the rest of the group was comprised of women. Two pregnant women stood by the sound system looking through cd's. One was tall with short, cropped, white-blonde hair, and Lily recognized her as Louise, the pastry chef at the resort. The other woman had long, bouncy black hair and she looked vaguely familiar, too. By now, though, most of the people of Fortune Bay fell into that 'vaguely familiar' category.

Star greeted a few people Lily didn't recognize. "Do you know all these people?" she whispered to Star.

"You get to know everyone when you work in the café."

Lily soon realized that she did know a few people in the class, too. Ms. Bowden, who she'd met at the store, resplendent in a lavender track suit, chatted with a group of younger women who, to her surprise, included Chloe, a receptionist at the resort. She gave Chloe a wave, but just then the dark-haired pregnant woman, wearing a cowboy hat, boots and jeans under a long form fitting tee-shirt that highlighted her tummy bump, clapped her hands at the front of the room.

"Welcome to the first class of the season. I'm Colleen Porter, and I'll be teaching the class with my lovely assistant, Louise. And no, this is not a pre-natal class." She grinned as a snicker went around the room. "But line dancing is great exercise at any age or stage. And lots of fun, as well."

She went on to demonstrate the grapevine, stepping to the side, one foot behind, then in front, then behind, explaining that it was a basic step. As the class tried it, it quickly became obvious who the experienced students were, like Star, and who, like Lily, were the awkward beginners.

In the fifteen years they'd been together, Lily had never danced with Troy. As her legs tangled together almost throwing her to the floor, she began to think that had probably been a good thing. She was just beginning to wonder why she'd come when Colleen said, "Hit it, Louise."

Shania Twain's voice rang out, "Let's go, girls." And they were off.

They shuffled and vined and coastered for an hour. Lily laughed when her feet twined around each other— "So *that's* why they call it the grapevine!"—and at the sight of the two pregnant mommas, bellies bobbing, hips swiveling, at the front of the class. In fact, she couldn't remember when she'd laughed as much. When the class finally poured out into the evening dusk, she felt charged, exhilarated, not ready to head home.

"Thank you for talking me into this," she said to Star. "I'm going to have to get some boots. You can't really stomp in runners."

"And it's so satisfying." Star demonstrated with a stamp of her size five turquoise cowboy boots. "Want to go for a drink?"

The Cedars Bar, just off the foyer at the resort, was the only watering hole in the village. Long and narrow with a bank of tall windows at the end, it had more glitz than the rest of the resort, despite its name. Lily had been there once before with her dad and Stephanie on the opening Saturday night when Max had brought in a lounge band from Seattle. Weeknights at this time of year were pretty quiet. Just a few locals and resort guests.

Nick, the cute bartender, approached with a wink

and a smile. "What can I get you girls?"

"What do you recommend?" Lily asked. Was he flirting? Her singles radar was rusty. A little bit, perhaps, and she returned his smile. There might be life in the old girl yet.

He chatted while he made the drinks, then left to go to the far end of the bar to talk to Sergio, the resort chef.

"I wonder if he's single?" Lily asked.

"Sort of single," Star replied, then took a sip of her cocktail. "But I think he's got something going with Sergio."

Nope, her singles radar was completely dead.

"How long have you been line dancing?" she asked Star.

"All my born days," Star said with a grin. "My Momma used to take me to the local where we lived in Colorado when she didn't have a sitter, so I learned really young."

"No wonder you're so good. It did kind of feel like a prenatal exercise class, though, but Colleen and Louise seemed to do just fine."

Star nodded. "Louise is having twins."

"I know. I remember Colleen, too, now that I think about it. I met them both at a party at Frankie's shortly after I arrived."

Star's eyebrows shot up. "*That* party? The one where Louise and Sean *both* announced they were getting married?"

Lily laughed and nodded. "But not to each other. Yes. Quite the introduction to the Murphy family. Do you know them well?"

"I know them, but not that well. I'm still pretty new here. I live in the apartment at Louise's fiancé Blue's shop, so I know him pretty well, and of course Louise is in and out. They are not really part of the Murphy family, but they've been friends forever."

"Sean and I work pretty closely together," Lily said. "And Dad is seeing his mom, Stephanie...so yeah, I've probably met them all, too."

Star laughed. "A tight family. Hard to keep up with."

Lily shook her head and smiled. "You're not kidding." She struggled to keep the smile relaxed. "And soon there'll be a bunch of babies."

Star nodded and took a sip of her drink.

"You ever want kids?" Lily asked.

Star tilted her head in thought. "Not really. Not yet. It's never really been the right time, you know?"

Lily nodded. "I know. But time flies by. You're how old?"

"Thirty-three."

Lily winced. "I'm thirty-eight. I don't have much time left and I really want to have children."

Star's eyes softened. "How long were you married?"

"Fourteen years." Angry tears sprang to Lily's eyes, and she blinked them away. "My husband always said it wasn't the right time, but now time is running out. I don't know what to do."

"Aren't you separated?"

"Taking a time out. I'm hoping he'll come around and agree to counselling. I think we still have something, although we've drifted apart in the last couple of years." She sat up straighter. "But I'm willing to work on it. I'm not willing to throw it all away. I want to have a family. While there's still time."

Star held up her glass. "Here's to happy endings."

* * *

A few mornings later, Marshall sat in the dim living room of the cottage, listening to Lily as she cleaned the bedroom. An uncomfortable buzz of energy hummed down his arm, electrifying the nerves in his otherwise-dead left hand. The doctors had told him the nerves might come back to life and the feeling might return, but so far it was just an often-painful buzz he'd be better without.

Lily had been coming every second day for over a week to do the cleaning Harry had arranged when he'd checked Marshall into the resort. Last time, she'd told him that she'd be his regular cleaner for a while. He was glad to hear it. Hilda meant well in a hearty, head nurse kind of way, but she wasn't easy to have around. Lily was easy, soothing. She didn't push. Too bad she wasn't permanent.

But he wouldn't be staying forever either, although he couldn't think of anywhere he'd rather be. His breath tightened, and he pressed his hand to his chest. He'd broken a couple of ribs last year, but they'd healed months ago so he didn't know why he sometimes still had trouble breathing.

His energy had never come back after the accident. Just getting out of the bedroom took everything he had. He used to play music for twelve hours a night, often going from a gig to a party and straight to the next job, his mind buzzing with ideas for the next song he wanted to write. He remembered feeling that way, but like a hazy dream he couldn't really remember the physical feeling of having so much energy.

Now everything was too much trouble. Even eating and watching TV. Harry had arranged for food to be delivered from the café across the road every day, but half the time Marshall didn't eat it. It tasted okay, but he wasn't hungry, so what was the point?

He couldn't see the point of anything anymore. If he even started to think, his thoughts plummeted to the question, the only real question: *What am I going to do now?* Without his hands and his face, he had nothing. He didn't want to see his family—even for the limited time the court had allowed. Couldn't stand the horror he imagined seeing in his children's eyes when they saw his face. His future was a black hole, a terrifying vortex that pulled him in until he craved oblivion. For the first time in his life, he preferred a drug induced daze to the pain of reality. A reality that had no future.

How many times had he dragged himself out of bed and stared at the bottle of pills in the bathroom cabinet, wanting to take more? Wanting to take them all. Something always stopped him, but it was a thin, fragile cord and it was beginning to fray. One of these days the last thread would snap, and he'd pour the whole bottle into his hand, instead of just one.

Lily bustled out of the bedroom. Although it was only late May, the last few days had been hot. She was wearing shorts and a tee shirt, and had pulled her hair into a short, bouncy ponytail. She looked so bright and fresh, it hurt just to look at her.

"I guess I'm done. Anything else I can get for you?"

She said that every time. It made him hot and cold and ache all over, like he was getting the flu.

"No. Thank you." He looked straight ahead, making sure she could only see his good side. He couldn't bear to see rejection in her eyes. Although the desire to talk was like an ache in his jaw, he felt like a thick pane of glass stood between him and the rest of the world.

She hesitated. "Well, I guess I'll be off then."

And she left, quietly shutting the door behind her.

A moment later, the loneliness reached for him again, grabbed him by the lungs and squeezed.

Chapter 7

That evening, the weather changed. Wind raced down the length of the lake and over the course of a few hours a storm rose up, puffing like a dragon, blowing hard rain across the peninsula from the Pacific. The mountains formed a wind tunnel that increased the velocity to gale force, and Lily, trapped inside the cabin as darkness fell, listening to the howling and the rattling of the windows, realized for the first time the limitations of her new home. No TV. No internet. She laughed at her sorry self. *Can't you spend one evening alone without screens?*

The night had turned cold, so she closed the door and all the windows, trying to trap inside whatever heat might remain from the afternoon sun. The weather report said it might rain all week. As she waited for the kettle to boil, she eyed the black, cast iron stove in the corner of the living room. If this storm kept up, she might have to light a fire. For tonight though, she'd just grab a blanket off the bed and curl up on the couch with a good book and a nice cup of tea. But she dug the emergency candles and matches out of the drawer. Just in case.

A knock sounded on the door. A reprieve. *Thank god!* Smiling to herself at her relief, she hurried to open the door.

Frankie stood on the porch, water dripping off her yellow raincoat. "We're having an impromptu girl's night next door. We thought you might want to come but nobody had your phone number."

"Let me get my raincoat."

Outside, the wind churned angry black waves on the lake and moaned through the long branches of the fir trees. Rain pelted their faces as they dashed for the slight cover of the trees between the cabin and Frankie's house, splashing through puddles on the path, then racing across Frankie's slippery lawn to the front door.

Shaking the rain off their jackets like dogs, they stumbled into the light. The living room was warm with the laughter of a dozen women, sitting on the couch and chairs and standing around the food covered island that separated the state-of-the-art kitchen from the dining area.

She recognized a few people: Louise and Colleen, Stephanie and Fiona, and Star, bobbing to the music playing in the background, beckoning her with a glass of wine, and her shoulders relaxed. It was all just fun, and wasn't that her new motto? *Have more fun.* Lily didn't have a group of friends like this in the city, just the women from work, and their couple friends had turned out to be mostly Troy's.

Louise had taken charge of the stereo and was playing easy-listening country tunes. Lily wasn't a big country music fan, but she recognized this as a Carry Underwood song that had crossed over to the pop charts the year before.

Lily took a seat in the dining room, and Louise came over and plunked her sizable bulk down on a dining room chair next to her. "Glad you could come. We decided to do this late this afternoon and then realized we didn't have your number. How are you enjoying working at the resort?"

Lily smiled. "It's only temporary, but I love it.

There is always something going on."

"I was thinking of having my wedding there next month." Louise called over her shoulder, "Frankie, get over here."

Frankie came over with a fancy-drink glass in her hand. "We're making Bellini's," she said in a loud aside to Lily. "Help yourself but keep Momma here away from the blender."

"I'm being good," Louise said, waving her bottle of sparkling, non-alcoholic cider. "We were talking about the wedding," she said to Frankie. Then her head swiveled back to Lily. "Frankie's organizing it for me. I don't have an extra ounce of energy after putting in my mornings at the resort. And I want to get this out of the way before these babies are born."

"Out of the way?" Frankie said in exasperation. "This will be the party of the year!"

Louise patted Frankie's leg, which was all she could reach from where she sat. "I know. You'll do a great job. I just thought we should get Lily into the loop. Maybe you can coordinate the event with her."

Frankie turned to Lily. "Is that part of your job?"

Lily laughed. "Right now, my job is anything and everything that needs doing, from accountant to chamber maid. I know Sean is busy. He'd probably be glad if I took it on. And anyway," she turned to Frankie. "Isn't he your...?"

Frankie nodded. "Fiancé. Might be better if we don't plan the wedding together."

Louise grinned. "I'm trying to talk them into making it a double with Blue and I."

Frankie started shaking her head, *no,* and didn't stop as Louise outlined her plan. "Two separate ceremonies, one right after the other, could be in different locations around town, then one giant hoopla after, at the resort."

Frankie was adamant. "No."

Louise tilted her head, showing she wasn't convinced. "There's still time to change your mind."

Frankie turned to Lily, deliberately shutting Louise out. "Sean and I are planning to get married sometime soon, but building the addition is enough of a challenge for now. I'd love to work with you as the go-to person at the resort for Louise and Blue, though. We're thinking the middle of June."

"That should work," Lily said, mentally running over the resort calendar. "Get it in before the Fourth of July."

"I'm due the middle of July," Louise put in.

Frankie walked over to the calendar on the kitchen wall. "So, let's make it—soon."

"Mid-June gives us less than a month," Lily said. "I don't know if I'll be here then—it's still kind of up in the air—but I'd be happy to work with you until I leave."

Frankie held up her empty glass. "I'll drink to that. Come into the kitchen and I'll get you fixed up."

Lily followed her into the kitchen where Star was mixing more Bellini's. "I used to work as a bartender in Austin," she explained as she poured frozen peaches into the blender.

Lily took a stool across the marble counter and, a minute later, Star handed her a drink.

Follow Me, a country crossover that had been a mega-hit, started playing in the background. "Turn that one up," Colleen said, and Louise reached over and cranked up the volume.

Lily smiled. You didn't have to be much of a country music fan to recognize Marshall Mason. His honeyed voice had caressed both the country and pop charts with this tune non-stop, a few summers ago.

Some of the women sang along. "*Follow me when you stumble.*" Lily knew most of the words too and, when the chorus rolled around, she joined in with everyone else.

The singer's face flashed into her mind. Darkly handsome, killer cheekbones, dark stubbled jawline, hawkish eyebrows and—

Her jaw dropped and just—hung there.

She looked up and saw Star grinning at her. "What?"

Lily closed her mouth and shook her head. She recognized that profile. She'd seen it just yesterday—in Cottage Four.

It couldn't be. Must be the combination of the Bellini blur and *Follow Me* blaring from the speakers. Lily stood up and grabbed the CD cover off the pile, and there was Morris—no, Marshall Mason, the mystery man in Cottage Four—smiling his hot, sexy smile on the cover.

"What is it?" Star asked again.

Lily smiled, but her face felt like cardboard as she replaced the CD cover to the pile. "Just trying to remember who sang this."

"Marshall Mason."

Lily nodded. "Has he done anything new lately?"

"He put out one new song this year, but they must have had it ready to go because, remember? He was in that horrible motorcycle accident last year. Apparently, he almost died."

The woman on the other side of Star leaned across and shook her head sadly. "They say he'll never sing again."

Another woman nodded. "He's gone into retirement. It was in the tabloids."

"I saw him once in Seattle," Star said. "He was amazing."

Louise nodded seriously. "He's a god."

The song ended, and silence hung in the room for a few moments, then one of the singers said, "What a loss."

A hard lump formed in Lily's stomach and she put down her glass. That was the misery she'd seen in his face, the something that went beyond the physical trauma. His career was over.

Glancing up, she caught Stephanie's eye across the room. Steph shook her head ever so slightly. She knew. Of course she did. If Lily's father knew, Stephanie was bound to know, too. And she was right. They couldn't tell anyone. They couldn't expose Marshall when he'd come to them for shelter. That was why Hilda had been cleaning his cottage. And now they were counting on Lily to be discreet.

She stayed at the party for a while after that but was no longer in the mood. What she wanted was to go home and think. By the time she finished her drink, people had begun drifting away. She thanked Frankie for inviting her, gave her both her work and cell numbers, and agreed to meet later in the week to talk about wedding plans.

Pulling on her raincoat, she put her head down and battled the wind and the rain back to the cabin. As she broke through the trees she could see a light in the cabin. She didn't remember leaving it on, it had hardly been dark when Frankie had come to get her, but it nice to see it now, welcoming her home.

She shook most of the rain off her jacket on the porch and was hanging it up on the hooks behind the door when her cell phone rang. *Duh, duh, duh.* Troy's ring. She looked at the phone on the kitchen table and her stomach rolled over as it rang again. She inhaled a shaky breath and blew it out. Sooner or later they had to talk. She had to find out if he was willing to work on their marriage. He'd been dead set against counselling when she'd mentioned it before, but now that she had been gone for a while, now that he saw she was serious, maybe he had changed his mind.

"Hello."

There was a pause at the other end. "Uh, hi. I didn't think you'd pick up."

"Yeah, well, we have to talk."

"Yes. We do."

Her shoulders unhinged from their position up around her ears. She collapsed into a kitchen chair. Maybe he'd come to his senses. Maybe he wanted her back.

"I'm moving out."

That hurt. So nothing had changed. "I don't think we should give up so easily. Maybe counselling would help."

"I'm moving in with Melissa."

Melissa. Lily was stunned into silence. His assistant.

"She's pregnant."

Lily jumped to her feet, swept up by a tornado of swirling emotions. Anger won out. "I asked you— begged you, over and over—to start a family. You said you didn't want to have children."

He cleared his throat. "Yeah, well, it just never seemed like the right time."

She pulled herself in like a crouching tiger, her voice becoming dangerously soft. "And now does?"

"Well, yeah."

He sounded uncomfortable. Well good. "You can keep the damn apartment, I'm staying here. I'll come back for my things."

He cleared his throat. "We'll have to talk about how to divide the furniture."

"I don't want it," she spat.

"Any of it?"

She looked around the cozy cabin and thought of the glass and chrome furniture in the apartment. It had never been her choice. "None of the furniture. Just the things that were mine to begin with. You can write me a check for my share of the rest." She named a sum off the top of her head.

When she heard the breath of relief on his end, she knew she'd let him off easy. He'd been expecting to pay more, or to have to move out completely. She didn't care, she just wanted out. Out from under his fussy, dominating ways. Out of the marriage completely. She was sorry she had to go back at all. "I'll come for the rest of my things one day this week."

"That would be great," he said quickly. "I've been packing up your stuff. Melissa is moving in."

Moving in. Of course. That had been his plan all along.

Melissa was pregnant. Lily's eyes filled with tears. "I'll come during the day." She didn't want to see him.

"That will be fine." His tone was somber, but she'd just bet he was cheering inside. She wiped the back of her hand across her eyes.

"I'm sorry, Lily, but I think we've both known for a while it was over."

She hadn't known, but obviously she'd been the only one who thought they still had a chance.

There was nothing else to say, so they both hung up. She collapsed onto a kitchen chair, leaning her elbows on the table and staring at the phone in her hand. Numbness set in, pushing out the anger and pain. She raked through the emotional shrapnel left from Troy's announcement and realized that although it hurt, he was right, she had known it was over for a while. A new wave of shame crashed over her. She'd known—or at least suspected—that something was going on, but she'd shielded her eyes and her heart from the truth, unwilling to let go of her dream of a family, clinging to what was known, what was safe.

She huffed out a hoarse laugh. *Safe.* There was nothing safe about a loveless marriage. And that was what theirs had become in the last few years. Two people living together, but not working on a life together.

Had they ever?

She thought back to the first years of their marriage, when she was so thrilled to have someone to love her that she hadn't focused on anything else. She'd been happy to cater to him, to go along with his plans. And they had seemed very reasonable at the beginning. Get better jobs, save some money, maybe for a down payment on a house. That had been her dream, but she wondered now if it had ever been his. Had he ever said it out loud, or had she just imagined—hoped—that they had the same dreams?

When had she put her dreams on hold? Had she ever known what his dreams had been? Had she ever really known him at all?

Now the life she had wanted was swirling away, her dreams of a family had been flushed down the tubes along with it.

Chapter 8

Lily wasn't sure she got any sleep that night, but she must have dozed off toward dawn because she awoke the next morning feeling weak and fragile, as if she'd been dragged through the mud. She groaned when she saw her reflection in the bathroom mirror, the black circles her fair complexion left her prone to, darkening her eyes. She bathed her red-rimmed eyes with a cold washcloth because yes, there had been tears, too. Anger, tears and self-recrimination in an endless, draining cycle.

Dragging herself into the kitchen, she glanced at the clock on the turquoise stove and wasn't surprised to see she was already late for work. But she couldn't go in—not yet. She had to pull herself together first. Her dad wouldn't mind if she was late. So far, she had set her own pace, worked her own hours. It always added up to more than forty a week because she enjoyed the work, found the atmosphere at the resort exciting and enjoyed solving the inevitable problems that emerged as the fledgling business took flight.

But there had been another reason for the long hours—she hadn't liked being at home alone. Didn't want so much time to think.

Troy's announcement had pitched her into a pit of quicksand and the ground continued to shift beneath her feet. What would she do? Where would she go? She couldn't stay in Fortune Bay. The panic rose in her belly like a swirling flock of pigeons, spiraling into her chest.

She put her hands on her hot cheeks and her thumbs felt the rapid pulse beneath her jaw. She had to get control. She took a drink of her cold coffee. She needed a plan, *baby steps,* something to make her feel like she still had a say in her life.

First, she had to get her things out of the apartment. The flutter of wings began to subside with the suggestion of a concrete plan. As long as she had this connection with Troy holding her back, she wouldn't be able to move on to her new life—whatever *that* would look like.

Cold and alone.

The anxious wings fluttered again, and she forced herself not to look too far ahead, just to concentrate on what she could control. *One step at a time.*

She'd go into work, play it cool, see if she could borrow a van tomorrow. The move wouldn't take long. Just into Seattle and back. Get her things and get out.

When she arrived at the resort an hour later, she searched out her father.

He didn't comment on her late arrival, just asked, "Everything okay?"

She nodded. "I'm getting my things from the apartment."

His eyes widened. "That's pretty sudden."

She shrugged. "It's time."

"Need any help?"

"No thanks. I can manage. Just the van."

He nodded briskly. "Sure honey, anything you need."

She was glad he didn't ask any more questions. She didn't feel strong enough to fashion a reply. In her office, she tried to concentrate on the spreadsheets open before her but couldn't make any sense of the numbers. She didn't want to go home to the cabin, though, so she went to the café for an early lunch.

Star was alone. She took one look at Lily and said, "Coffee, hon?"

Lily nodded gratefully and sank into the seat. "I'm going to Seattle tomorrow and getting my things. Moving up here. For now."

Star's brow wrinkled prettily. She was small and fairy-like, her manner gentle but surprisingly direct. "Things not going well with the hubby?"

Lily had never told Star why she'd come to Fortune Bay, but suddenly she desperately wanted to talk to someone. Staring into her cup, she told her the story, how she had wanted children for so many years, but Troy had not.

"And now," she said, biting her lip to hide a hitch in her breath that was close to a sob, taking a moment to compose herself. "He's having a baby with someone else."

Star drew in a horrified breath. "Oh my god! The scum!"

Lily nodded morosely. "He's scum, all right. She's ten years younger than him. Than me." She lifted one shoulder in resignation. "It's pretty well too late for me to start a family now. By the time I meet someone, assuming I ever do, and..."

"It's not the only way," Star said brightly. "Women are having babies well into their forties these days. Look at Colleen. She's no spring chick."

Lily shook her head. "I don't see myself marrying again. Not anytime soon, anyway. And I don't know if I'm up to having a child alone. That's such a huge responsibility." She shook her head. "I'm just starting over. I don't know what I'm doing or where I'll be in a year."

Star tipped her head to the side, considering. "I guess it depends on how badly you want to have children."

More than anything.

* * *

At noon the next day, Lily unlocked the door to the apartment she had shared with Troy for the last four years. As the door swung open, she tensed, expecting a jolt of pain. Instead she was met by a blank wall of silence. After a month away, it didn't feel like home anymore.

She dragged the nested pile of boxes she'd brought with her into the stark white foyer. At first everything looked the same as it had when she'd left, but when she opened the hall closet to grab her things and found Melissa's unfamiliar coats hanging there instead, the reality hit home. Melissa had wasted no time moving in. Lily winced at the jab of pain in her heart. She was out, and another woman had taken her place. Snap, just like that, their fourteen-year marriage erased.

Lily walked through to the kitchen, taking mental inventory of what she wanted to take with her. Not much. It wasn't that these things, the things they'd shared, held painful memories, just that they were meaningless. She felt no connection to the pure white Wedgewood dishes that had been Troy's choice. *Wasn't the china supposed to be the bride's decision?* Or the cut-glass nut bowls they'd received as a wedding gift from his aunt. But the matching orange *Le Creuset* skillet and big round casserole—those she wanted. Even though they did weigh a ton.

She pulled a few things out of the cupboard and set them on the kitchen island. She'd take the pots, and some of the paintings on the walls, but just her paintings, the ones she'd bought while she was in college of the river and the mountains around Portland. The rest, the minimal abstracts, had been Troy's choice. She thumbed through the cd's on the living room shelf. Also mostly Troy's. That's what they listened to when they were at home. She kept her own music on her phone.

No, she thought as she walked into the bedroom, it wasn't really Troy or the life they had here that she mourned. It was the life she'd *hoped* they would have. Children. A family. As an only child of a disjointed family, from a young age she'd dreamed of having a family of her own. How she'd bake for them, give them crayons and paper, let them play outside. Not over-book their every-moment like her childhood had been. Probably less bother for her mother that way and, to be fair, she had been a single parent struggling with depression. But, even so.

For years she'd clung to the hope that somehow, she and Troy would pull it together. That she would miraculously become pregnant and then everything would be back on track. That, she admitted now, had been her secret plan.

But it would have been miraculous indeed because, looking at the king-size bed, she realized they had probably not had sex for months. Not since Christmas. In some ways she had been fine with that, even feigning sleep the odd time in the hopes that he wouldn't reach for her when he came in late—and she had been relieved when he hadn't, because the intimacy had become forced and unpleasant. That's right—she turned and faced herself in the mirror, lips pressed firmly together—she might as well call a spade a spade. Sex with her husband had become unpleasant because they weren't in love anymore.

Catching sight of the bed behind her in the mirror, the bed he now shared with Melissa, she sadly realized that he obviously felt the same way.

So, if they hadn't had a loving marriage, what was this pain in her chest about? It wasn't really about Troy, although the deception stung, but the loss of her future family really hurt. Had she been using him to get the family she'd always wanted? Putting up with a less than stellar relationship in the hope that a baby would pull them together? If so, how sad was that?

Not as sad as losing that hope altogether.

Best thing now was to get her things and get out. She opened her closet doors. Her coats were stuffed in with the rest of her clothes. And a box of her books. Her eyes slanted to Troy's closet. It was none of her business what was inside, but it was still her apartment and he was still her husband—in the eyes of the law at least. She stalked across the room and opened the doors. Melissa's clothes were crammed into one end. She slammed the doors shut. No wonder Troy sounded relieved when she said she was coming to clear out her things. It gave her some satisfaction to know it must be killing him to have his shirts scrunched up on the rod like that.

Tears of hurt and anger rolled down her cheeks. She was hurt that their life together meant so little to him, and angry that he could dismiss her—*replace her*—so quickly. *He's sorry, my eyeball!*

She ripped her clothes off the hangers and threw them onto the bed. She was doing fine with the clothes she'd taken to Fortune Bay. The corporate suits didn't really suit her life anymore, but she'd take it all with her and go through it later. The last thing she wanted was for tiny Melissa to go through her clothes and keep any of it as maternity wear.

An hour later, Lily was back in the hall, fighting the elevator door that kept closing as she loaded her boxes. She'd taken everything of hers from the apartment and was suddenly desperate to get out of the building. The van she'd borrowed from her dad was parked in her space in the underground garage. After loading up these last few boxes, she'd go through the storage locker and be on her way.

She opened the wire storage cage with her key and stepped inside. Her bicycle leaned against the wall— along with Troy's and one she didn't recognize. She grabbed her bike and huffed a few short breaths. The hurt she'd felt earlier had burned itself out. What she felt now was anger, growing like a fire taking hold. She forced herself to concentrate as she lifted her electric piano into the van. She had stopped playing when they moved into this apartment. The keyboard had never even made it out of the storage locker. Troy thought it didn't match the decor. Her temperature gauge continued to rise.

She'd take her tennis racquet, even though she'd never really learned to play. Troy loved to play, but Lily hadn't been able to improve fast enough to please him. What did he expect? He'd been playing since he was a kid. Melissa could get her own damn tennis racquet.

Come to think of it, what did she and Troy have in common anymore? Nothing that she could think of.

The photo album was definitely hers. Flipping through it from back to front, all there was were a few photos they'd taken at a resort in Mexico years ago, and their wedding photos. They'd pulled out all the stops for the wedding and Lily remembered being blissfully happy. It had seemed so right, her and Troy.

She'd never have believed it then if you'd told her it wouldn't last.

She put the last few things into the van and slammed the door. They'd decided they'd live in an apartment for a while, while they both worked on their careers and saved up a down payment for a house. She took that to mean a house *and then kids*, but that was obviously not what he had meant.

"In good time," Troy always said, but there had never seemed to be a good time. It was always the *wrong* time and now it was too late.

She stepped on the gas and the van leapt out of the parking space. She could have had a teenager or two by now. Sure, she'd have been a single mom when she and Troy split up—because she could see now that it had been inevitable—but she would have had her kids and wouldn't have been alone.

At the exit of the garage, she sat for a moment. If she wanted a new life she'd have to take charge. She needed to do something concrete. Right now. Something she would never have done with Troy.

Like buy cowboy boots. She pulled the address Star had given her for the western wear store out of her purse, put the van in gear and roared out of the parking lot.

Chapter 9

The following morning Lily woke early. She'd come back to the cabin, unloaded the van and, in a blaze of energy, had unpacked most of her things. When the clothing rod in the corner of the bedroom sagged and the dresser drawers would barely close, she left the clothes she didn't need here in Fortune Bay in boxes in the corner. Going through them and deciding what to discard could wait, but for now the sheer volume was reassuring, made her feel like she'd got everything that was important from the apartment. That she was done.

She wiped off the dust on her electric piano, plugged it in and played a few chords. She didn't need a TV—she could practice in the evenings. She discovered an empty shelf in the bookcase that she had never noticed before and unpacked her books. There weren't very many. Troy always discouraged her accumulating *things.* Well, she liked *things,* and was planning on accumulating a lot more. Her hoarding nature had been stunted during her marriage and she looked forward to a lot of shopping. Maybe even second-hand shopping. Troy hated that. He liked sleek and modern furnishings while she favored antiques and kitschy collectables. Like in furniture in the cabin. Now she could finally indulge herself.

But this morning, the work she'd done the night before just generated sadness, tinged with a slightly metallic residue of anger.

The silver was wearing off the edges of the antique

mirror in the corner of the bedroom, but her image was clear enough to see why Troy had chosen Melissa over her. At some point, without her even really noticing, she'd become drab and dowdy. Extra weight had crept on around her waist and her hair hung limply around her face. No wonder he preferred cute, perky Melissa.

Last night, when she'd been riding a high of adrenalin and emotion, she'd thought she could cope. Now she wondered how.

Take one step after another.

She stopped and looked at the front door expecting to see someone there, speaking to her through the screen. But the front door was shut. No one was there.

She'd heard the voice so clearly, though. And it wasn't the first time. Sometimes she heard a voice in her head, and thought she was going insane. That was all she needed.

Shaking her head, she headed for the porch where she stopped to take a deep breath. As always, the smell of lake water mixed with the wet musk of the forest calmed her. The fir branches that hugged the cabin swayed in the breeze and the sight of the first white trilliums, twinkling in the forest shade, made her smile.

Come on. Admit it. You've landed in paradise.

There it was again. That voice. Not her voice and possibly not audible, either. She was starting to think there really was a ghost and that it was talking inside her head.

Regardless of the source of the words, as usual, the sentiment was right. This *was* paradise. And she no longer felt she had nowhere to go. Her future started here. She could stay in Fortune Bay, working at the resort, until she figured out what she really wanted to do. Where she really wanted to be.

"You're right, Augusta," she murmured, heading into the little bathroom off the porch. "This is perfect. For now."

After showering and dressing, Lily headed for the resort. As she pulled the van into a parking spot behind the Lodge, she swooned as the aroma of cinnamon buns hit her olfactory buds. Louise's breakfasts and coffee were infinitely better than her own. It was one of the perks of working here—like having her own breakfast chef.

Her dad was at the front desk and she dropped the van keys into his open palm. "Thanks for the loan." Unexpected tears flooded her eyes and her throat swelled and suddenly she wanted to tell him everything. "He's moved another woman into the apartment."

Her dad frowned, his shoulders rolling restlessly.

"She's pregnant."

Now he actually growled, and the show of support made Lily feel infinitely better. Smiling blearily through her tears, she put a hand on his arm. "It's okay, Dad. Let it go. At this point, I just want out."

"He shouldn't get away with that." Her father's hand clenched around the van keys and for one disconcerting moment Lily thought he might jump in the van and go and deal with Troy himself. Instead he just looked at her, lips pursed. "I'm sorry, honey. But I'm glad you're going to stay." He looked suddenly worried. "You are going to stay, aren't you?"

She dashed the tears from her eyes and smiled. "For a while, anyway. And thank you. You are making this a lot easier. I'd like to keep the job I've been doing, make it official. At least for the summer. If you'll have me."

His face broke into a smile. "Of course I will.

Having you work here is a dream come true."

A couple emerged from the elevator pulling their suitcases behind them and made for the front desk. Lilly gave her dad one last smile and headed for the dining room. "I have things to do, I'll let you get to work."

It being mid-week and early in the season, the dining room was only half full. As Lily helped herself to coffee from the urn at the coffee station outside the kitchen door, she noticed again how seamlessly the elements of the Lodge reflected the wilderness outside. Even the coffee station was a work of art, a thick slab of heartwood with the wavy bark edge of the tree intact.

She looked longingly at the tray of pastries next to the coffee. Louise's baking was delicious, but Lily wasn't a guest here. This was her life and she couldn't eat pastries every day or soon she wouldn't fit into any of the clothes she'd brought back from Seattle. Virtuously, she reached for a yogurt cup and spooned Louise's homemade granola into a bowl. A fresh start, that's what she needed, in every way. Starting with a healthy breakfast. Eat better, exercise more, and have more fun—and maybe shed a few pounds in the process.

As she scraped up the last spoonful of yogurt, the door to the kitchen swung open and Frankie came into the restaurant, her laptop under her arm. Her face lit up when she saw Lily. "There you are. I've been looking for you."

She made a detour to pour herself a cup of coffee and then sat down across the table from Lily, settled her computer and cup, then raised her eyes. When they focused on Lily, Frankie's warm brown eyes softened. "Everything alright?"

Lily cringed, realizing the remnants of her anger

and tears must still show. She purposefully put on a cheerful smile. "More than fine. My plans have changed, and it turns out I will be here for the summer, so I'll be able to help you plan the wedding."

"That's great. I know Louise is downplaying it, but she deserves a first-class affair. I want to do this up right."

"It will be good practice for the resort too. I know Sean wants to host more weddings in the future."

"I don't know how good this one will be for publicity. Louise will be pretty large by then..."

Lily laughed. "She already is. I just hope she makes it to the wedding date without having the twins. We can still get some shots of the facilities with the decorations in place, though."

Frankie opened her laptop and turned it toward Lily. "I have gathered some ideas online. Want to see?"

They oow-ed and ahh-ed over flower arrangements and gorgeous outdoor settings for the next hour. Frankie had some ideas of her own. "I hope that by the middle of June we'll be able to hold most of the events outside. I thought we'd hold it on a weekday so it won't be too busy here and, if necessary, we can move the dinner inside. We can include any of the resort guests who want to participate. Sean and Louise are cool with that."

"Fun idea."

"Sean said we could keep The Cedars quiet and let the resort guests who don't want to join in, eat in there."

"So, you *are* talking to Sean about this."

"Hard to avoid." Frankie's eyes sparkled. "He and Amber come over every evening to work on the addition and it just comes up."

"How is the reno coming?" At the impromptu

women's party at Frankie's a few nights before, the entrance to the new addition hadn't been cut through the hall wall yet, to try to stop construction dust from seeping into the rest of the house.

"Great. You'll have to come over tomorrow for a tour. A bunch of people are coming for a work-bee. You'll probably hear the noise from the cabin. Why don't you come and join in?"

"I'd love to help," Lily said. She glanced at her watch. Marshall would be waiting. "Gee, it's time for... I have to be... somewhere."

Frankie closed her laptop and stood. "Sure. Let's get together next week and try to settle a few things about the wedding. I'll try to get a handle on the food. Louise wants to make the cake herself and that might be okay, actually might be the easiest way since she knows exactly what she wants and won't be satisfied with anything else. But she can't cater the reception."

Lily shook her head, eyes wide, as she walked with Frankie to the lobby. "The woman doesn't know how to pace herself."

"So true. See you tomorrow."

Lily smiled to herself as she ducked through the *Staff Only* door to the utility area, pleased to have something to look forward to this weekend. A work party with neighbors and friends was a new experience and sounded like fun. She wasn't very good with a hammer and saw, but hopefully she'd find some way to help.

* * *

Marshall sat on the couch in the dim living room, waiting for Lily to finish cleaning the bedroom. He usually found her presence in the cottage soothing, but today a crackling current—the high side of his mood swings—rushed through his body. He felt edgy, but at least he felt something.

Lily came into the living room, bundling the laundry into a bag. "I'm done." She wiped a hand across her damp brow.

The current buzzed under his skin. A part of him wanted to hide in bed between the cool, clean sheets, but another part, the part that was crawling out of his dark lonely cave, craved companionship.

Before he could stop them, the words tumbled out. "Hot day. Want a drink?" He plucked a bottle of water from the table in front of him and held it out to her, turning his good side slightly toward her.

She hesitated and his high plummeted. What was he thinking? With the scar disfiguring half his face, he looked like the phantom of the opera. No wonder she didn't want to spend any more time with him than was absolutely necessary. The hand holding the bottle started to shake. He was seconds from pulling it away when she smiled, stepped toward him and took the bottle out of his hand.

"Thanks. I could use it." She cranked open the top and took a swig. "It is hot today. Sign of things to come, I guess."

"Can you sit for a minute?" God, he sounded pathetic. He'd never had to beg a woman to sit with him before. Not since he was a thirteen-year-old acne-faced punk.

She took another sip and glanced at the open door to the porch. He braced for whatever excuse she would use to get away.

"Nice breeze outside," she said. "You ever sit on the porch?"

"I haven't, yet."

She smiled, a friendly, girl-next-door smile, and his heart clenched. "Let's, then," she said, and walked out the door.

The desire to sit with her, even for a few moments, washed over him like the ache of a lost love. A lost life. All he had to do was follow her out the door.

Shakily, he got to his feet, grabbed his sunglasses and hat from the shelf by the door, and stumbled outside.

He hadn't been outside in the three weeks he'd been here—had hardly been outside for half a year—and even with the tinted glasses on, the blast of sun hit him like a gamma ray right between the eyes. He clutched the door frame with his scarred claw of a hand. For a moment he thought he might pass out.

She was waiting by the cushioned patio chairs. He pushed himself away from the door and, looking down and away, walked past her and sank into the furthest chair, in the darkest corner, leaving her the chair on his good side.

Good side. That was a joke. He remembered the photoshoots in the past and how aware he'd been of having his good side to the camera. Now his good side was his bad side. She'd seen the scars, was aware of the damage, but he didn't want to inflict it on her unnecessarily. Sitting like this, his new bad side was screened by the trees that shielded the end of the porch.

He let out a deep breath and relaxed, leaning back in the chair. "Sorry. I haven't been outdoors much in recent months. I...I had a stretch in the hospital."

She pressed her lips together and nodded, motioning with her bottle to the lake view before them. "This is a wonderful place to recover. I've always felt that, when I'm injured, all my energy focuses on the part of the body that needs to heal, and that can really sap your strength. Maybe the air and the water will help you recover."

He hadn't thought of that. When he'd asked Harry to find him a place to stay, away from L.A., he had just wanted to hide. Harry had made the arrangements for him to move into Cottage Four a week before the resort officially opened, when the place was quiet. It was still quiet, no loud parties, but it hardly mattered since he hadn't stepped foot out of the cottage since he'd arrived. Until now.

He glanced at her, just moving his eyes, but Lily seemed content to sit in silence and look at the lake. Marshall relaxed back in the chair and soaked up the soothing warmth of her company.

When she'd finished her water, she flashed him a smile. "I don't do this enough. Just sit and relax. Thanks for the drink." Setting the empty bottle on the table between them, she said, "See you Sunday." Then she stood up and left, pushing the cart up the path to the Lodge, her short ponytail bobbing and her hips moving under her shorts.

Christ. Don't go there.

When she disappeared into the screen of spring leaves that separated the cottage from the Lodge, Marshall let out a long shaky breath. He put his hands on his thighs, preparing to hoist himself up to go inside, but remembering what his therapist had said, he stopped and took a tentative body scan. Some of the uncomfortable buzz, the electric current that had run through him since his surgery, had subsided. But that short encounter, the act of reaching out, had left him exhausted.

Leaning his head back on the chair, he closed his eyes and listened to the waves slapping rhythmically against the dock. The breeze, like gentle fingers, massaged his forehead and a moment later, he slipped into a doze.

When he awoke, he had no idea how much time had passed and, for a moment, where he was. But warm air caressed his face and he felt more relaxed than he had in many months. His lips softened into a smile. The lake and the forest were nice, but the woman with the friendly smile was becoming his restorative balm.

"Hi neighbor," a voice called out.

Marshall's head instinctively snapped to the side so that only his good side was exposed, but other than that, he was paralyzed in his chair. Trapped. This was why he did not come outside.

A man was walking along the communal lakeside path that ran between the cottages and the shore. He had a slight build and although older, from his spritely walk he was obviously quite fit, and made Marshall feel like a frail old man by comparison. Would he ever feel that light and energetic again?

"Hello," he replied, without inflection, keeping his face turned away, not to encourage the stranger. *Just keep walking.*

"Lovely day," the man countered, but did not break his stride, and soon was swallowed up by the trees along the shore. Marshall let out a long-held breath. Glancing furtively to both sides, he stood up and hurried into the cottage.

Lily pushed her cart down the path with a purposeful stride. Getting Marshall outside was a positive step, but only step one. The road to recovery from depression was long and could be slow, with many potholes along the way. This was another good reason for her to stay in Fortune Bay. For as long as Marshall needed her.

Chapter 10

The following morning, Lily awoke to the high-pitched whine of a straining electric motor in the distance. She glanced at the clock. Seven o'clock. The work crew started early.

She stretched and groaned, her muscles reminding her she had biked home from work the previous day. But the aching muscles were proof that she was following through on her vow to get in shape.

She was nervous and excited about Frankie's work-bee. Quaint idea, but probably very efficient. And a good way to get to know her new neighbors.

When she got to Frankie's, Sean and Louise were in the kitchen. Louise was pulling something that smelled amazing out of the oven.

Sean poured Lily a cup of coffee from the carafe on the counter. "I see you're taking the pre-natal line dancing class," he said, a grin on his face. Louise guffawed.

Lily smiled. "How did you know?"

Sean flipped open a laptop that sat on the counter. "Facebook."

Lily's jaw dropped when she saw the photo of Louise and Colleen in profile, baby-bellies prominent, and a row of dancers facing them. All except Lily who, front and center, faced in the opposite direction.

Her cheeks burned. "It was my first class."

Sean laughed and patted her shoulder. "You'll get the hang of it."

Lily couldn't help smiling. It was hard to take offense with Sean. He always had a twinkle in his eye. But still, she couldn't help feeling like a bit of a fool—up on the page for the whole town to see.

Sean excused himself and went out the sliding glass door to the back deck, leaving Lily in the kitchen with Louise. Wearing a pair of droopy denim overalls that did nothing to hide her maternity bulge, she kneaded a mound of bread dough at the kitchen counter.

Lily grabbed a warm muffin—Apple Crunch, one of her favorites. "Who's doing breakfast at the resort?"

Louise plopped the dough in a bowl and propped herself on a high stool. "I started it at my regular time—"

"Which is?"

"Four."

Lily groaned.

Louise shrugged. "I can't sleep for too long at a stretch these days anyway. I'll probably head home for a nap soon. I got most of the prep work done by six when Amber came in to take over."

"Have I met Amber?" Lily asked. She thought she knew most of the kitchen crew.

"Sean's daughter? Long blonde hair? You probably met her at a family gathering."

Lily remembered a young girl with long blonde hair and heavy black eye makeup at the first dinner party she'd been invited to shortly after she'd arrived in Fortune Bay. But that night had been her introduction to the Murphy clan, and she hadn't gotten everyone straight. "Is she experienced enough to leave in charge?"

Louise nodded. "I've been training her since before Christmas. She's going to take over for me with breakfasts for the summer when the babies come so I thought she might as well start by taking the weekends alone now. Or almost alone. My sister Brandy is helping her today and the regular kitchen crew are on at six, too. On the weekend, now, I only do pastries, but we serve a lot of those in the morning."

"Sean's daughter." Lily said, still processing.

Louise nodded. "They reunited last fall and now they are moving in here with Frankie. As soon as the addition is finished."

"Frankie mentioned that."

"Sean had the crew who have been working on the resort take two weeks and frame up the addition and do the plumbing and wiring. Everyone's working on insulation and drywall today, and once they are finished, these guys, Sean, his brother Jake and my Blue, can do the rest. Between them, they are quite experienced with construction. Especially the finishing work."

Lily nodded, wiping the crumbs from the counter into her hand. "My dad told me about the work Blue did at the resort."

Frankie hurried into the kitchen and came to an abrupt stop. "Time for a break. I've been going steady since six." Pouring herself a cup of coffee, she settled on another of the stools and took a sip. "Mm-mm-m. Why does my coffee taste better when you make it?"

Louise laughed. "Anything tastes better when I make it."

Frankie sat taller. "Hey. I'm learning."

"You certainly are," Louise said, obviously trying not to sound patronizing but not quite succeeding. "Lucky you have Sean as a teacher."

Frankie stuck out her tongue at Louise. Then she slapped her hands on her thighs and stood up. She looked at Lily. "Ready for the tour?"

Lily popped the last of her muffin into her mouth and mumbled around it. "Ready."

"We have to go outside," Frankie said, leading the way out to the back deck. "We haven't knocked out the new doorway yet. Figured we might as well keep the dust contained for as long as we can."

Frankie's lakeside deck had the same breathtaking view that Lily had from the cabin porch, the spring-green blush of new leaves across the lake climbing the hills to the exposed rocky cliffs above, but Frankie's deck was furnished with a matched set of padded lounges and chairs.

They walked to the far end of the deck where the structure was obviously new, built to match the original but the wood still unfinished, and stepped through a large opening in a plywood wall into the addition.

"There'll be sliding glass doors here," Frankie said. "This will be the family and music room." The room was full of unidentifiable people in coveralls and masks stuffing pink insulation between the open studs of the walls.

"Music?" Lily asked.

"The guys, Sean, Jake and Blue, have had a band called Busted Muffler ever since they were teenagers. They're pretty popular around here."

"I saw the electric piano in your living room," Lily said. "Do you play too?"

"No. That's Sean's. He plays a lot of instruments, all kinds of music, and composes, too. The band plays mostly classic rock and country covers, though. They're hosting an open mic at the resort on Thursday night. You should come."

Frankie led the way up an open staircase to the second floor. "Up here, we'll have a couple of bedrooms. The master, with a little Juliette balcony over the lake, a bathroom, and another smaller bedroom in the front." Frankie blushed.

Lily smiled. "For?"

"We'd like to have a child of our own, sometime." Frankie held up both hands, palms out. "But not now. There's too much going on with the addition and getting the three of us settled in the house." She frowned as she looked at the second bedroom.

"Is there a problem?" Lily asked.

'Not really." Her brows pinched more, then she said in a burst. "Sean thinks we should get married. Soon. He doesn't want to live together, with Amber, without being married. He wants to be a good role model. She... Amber hasn't had very many good role models."

Lily nodded. "Makes sense. Before or after you move in?"

Frankie forced a smile. "That's the question." She shook her head. "We'll work it out."

Sean's voice echoed up the stairway. "You two going to yack all day or are you going to get to work?"

Frankie yelled back, "Okay, okay." She grinned at Lily. "We'd better go down."

"I don't know how much help I'll be," Lily said as they carefully navigated the open, plywood staircase. "I've never worked construction before."

Frankie rolled her eyes. "Insulating is not construction. It's the second level of hell. Come on. We'd better suit-up."

Soon Lily, attired in an attractive yellow plastic jumpsuit, gloves, goggles and mask, *and* a with scarf covering her head, was teamed up with Colleen's husband Alex. She began to see the organization in the seemingly random mass of people working in the music room. Husky Blue carried in a giant bag of pink fiberglass insulation. When he cut it open with a utility knife, pink insulation batts mushroomed out. Lily and Alex worked their way around the big room, stuffing the insulation into the stud walls.

Someone—probably Louise—put on Carrey Underwood's *Storyteller.* The men all groaned good naturedly, but the work seemed to go faster with music. Sean, working with Frankie's dad Philip, followed the insulation with a big role of plastic, stapling it to the studs, imprisoning the pink bats. Two guys Louise hadn't met before, followed them, nailing sheets of drywall from a stack in the middle of the floor into place.

Time flew by and the temperature rose as the sun streamed in through the windows. Just as Lily began to feel like she was being baked alive in her plastic jumpsuit, they reached the last bit of wall, finishing at the opening facing the lake. Stepping out on the deck, she stripped off her protective gear and held her arms wide, letting the breeze off the water cool her overheated skin.

Stephanie stepped out of the dining room on the far end of the porch and smiled when she saw her. "Hello, dear. Would you tell everyone lunch is ready?"

Lily stuck her head into the big room and, over the noise, yelled, "*Lunch.*"

Suddenly she was surrounded on the porch by a lot of men, stripping off their yellow suits, feeling their muscles and acting like, well, men. This was a new experience for her. Something about doing physical work had spiked their testosterone levels and Lily could almost smell it the air. They all grabbed a beer and a bowl of the chili Stephanie had dished out, and a slab of Louise's fresh sourdough with butter, and hunkered down on the deck chairs to eat. They talked about fishing and power tools and the bass guitar Jake was thinking of buying. Alex was teasing Colleen, Blue stole a kiss from Louise, and then Jake's pregnant wife Maddie arrived with their daughter Sarah, and Lily suddenly felt like the only woman in the house who wasn't pregnant.

Her throat swelled, and she escaped to the cool, quiet kitchen and ran water at the sink, patting some on her forehead and filling a glass to drink.

"Everything okay?"

She turned to find Stephanie had followed her in, a concerned smile on her face.

"Yes. No." Lily laughed self-consciously. "I'd just kind of hoped I'd be in that position someday myself. Married to a man who wanted to have a family." Then, struck by the irony, she closed her eyes and absorbed the painful jab. She *was* married to a man who was excited about having a family—just not with her. She took an involuntary, shaky breath.

Stephanie rounded the counter and gave her a quick hug. "It's a hard time. Regardless of what your husband did, and how mad you are at him, it's still hard."

Lily nodded, tears in her eyes.

"Your dad is very glad to have you here. And believe it or not, you're still young. You have lots of time to find your place in life."

Lily shook her head. "I wasted so much time on that marriage. I should have known it was going nowhere."

Stephanie laughed. "Hindsight is twenty-twenty. But," she said, obviously changing the subject, for which Lily was grateful, "Max tells me you're taking care of our 'mystery guest'."

Lily nodded, her thoughts going to Marshall who on this lovely day, was probably sitting in a dark, silent room instead of with a group of friends on a bright, airy deck. "It's sad, really. He's hiding away in the cottage at the resort, not seeing anyone."

"It must be hard to go from a man who everyone envied, who women swooned over and men wanted to be like, to having your career and your future in jeopardy. To have it all stripped away in an instant. Does he talk about it?"

"I've just gotten him to talk, period. He's just beginning to come out of his shell. He actually sat outside for a while yesterday."

Frankie's father Philip came in through the patio door. "I saw him. Sorry for eavesdropping but I couldn't help overhearing. Cottage Four? I'm in Cottage One. Max told me a bit about him. It's a shame."

"It can't be healthy to be all alone like that, but that seems to be what he wants," Lily said.

"Maybe that's what he needs," Stephanie said thoughtfully. "Maybe he's processing. Men process things differently than women. Where we might call our friends and have a sympathy session or a pity party, they tend to retreat into the cave and mull it over. Alone. It's good you are watching out for him, though."

Lily nodded, hoping she could think of a way to help Marshall emerge from his shell.

After lunch they went back to work, Lily and Frankie drawing the job of unrolling the eight-foot roll of plastic vapor barrier and stapling it up behind the insulation team as they worked their way around the second-floor rooms.

When they finished, there was much back slapping and mutual congratulations on a job well done. Then everyone congregated on the deck for barbequed steak, salad and baked potatoes. They spilled into the dining room and kitchen as their numbers increased with spouses and children, including Amber, Brandy and Max, arriving to join the party.

Lily indulged in her annual beer, enjoying the way it cut the dust in her throat, and the easy comradery of being part of a group who'd accomplished a major job. In the course of one day, the addition had gone from a stud and plywood shell to recognizable rooms and a staircase. After dinner, Lily wandered the upstairs rooms alone, looking out through the opening in the bedroom where the full-length glass doors would embrace the view of the lake.

The first tentative guitar chords drift up from the deck below, muffled by the sound of overlapping conversations. Someone started playing quiet chords on the electric piano, a different song than the guitar, and she listened, intrigued by the casual jumble of noise. She'd taken piano and voice lessons all through school, sang in a city choir and once performed a duet with a friend at the high school talent show—a medley from the Lion King—but she'd never been to a jam before. How did they all know the same songs? She was adrift without sheet music. Sure, she could figure out the chords, if she had enough time, but just playing from the heart—that was magic.

Another guitar joined in and she ran down the stairs and out onto the porch to watch. One of the men she didn't know—someone called Guy—was strumming a mandolin, the pick in his hand moving as fast as a hummingbird's wings, producing a plaintive melody that bordered on melancholy. Then all playing stopped and someone suggested a tune she didn't know, strummed a few bars and they were off. Sean sang the lead in a clear tenor with Jake coming in on harmonies. More people joined in on the chorus, leaning from side to side as they sang. Not everyone got the words right all the time, but nobody seemed to care.

When the song ended, the mandolin player kept right on going, segueing into *Ripple*, by the Grateful Dead. Lily'd had a job one summer in high school where her boss had played the Grateful Dead and other seventies bands all day long. When the chorus came around the second time, she joined in with the rest of the room. Sean was sitting beside her, and his face brightened in surprise. He nodded encouragingly along to the beat. When the song was over and everyone took a break, he turned to her and said, "You've got a great voice. You must have sung before."

Lily felt her cheeks turn pink. "A bit, years ago."

He strummed a few chords. "Would you like to sing something?"

Her hand flew to her chest. "I couldn't. Not alone."

He smiled as Frankie held out a glass of wine to Lily. She took it automatically, her eyes still on Sean. His chords drifted into another song, Jake picked up on it and the moment passed.

An hour later, Lily was deeply relaxed, from wine and food and a day of hard work, and lounged in a chair on Frankie's deck, wrapped in a blanket to ward off the evening chill. Although it was after nine o'clock, the sun had just sunk behind the mountain and the sky was still that beautiful turquoise-fading-to-peach it turns just before nightfall.

Someone had filled her wine glass again and when the band started playing *Wild Willow,* one of Marshall Mason's songs, Lily joined in from the start.

After the first chorus, Sean said, "Take it, Lily," and she did, her voice rising clear and brilliant, gaining strength as she wandered the paths of the melody, until the rest of the group joined in on the chorus. She stopped singing, invigorated by a flush of energy to have sung like that, with a *band* for goodness sake.

She joined in again on the final chorus and when the last chord faded away, Sean reached for his drink and said, "You should come to the open mic on Thursday. We'll back you up. The crowd likes it when we have a woman singer."

Blue's voice rumbled, "Like we ever get a crowd."

All the better, Lily thought. Less pressure on her. "That was fun. Maybe I will."

* * *

Marshall stood in the doorway of Cottage Four, breathing the night air through the screen. Slowly the sky darkened, dipping from turquoise to indigo, then to slate. The stars slowly flickered to life in his patch of sky, a narrow horizontal band cut off by the porch roof. He pushed open the screen door and the next thing he knew, he was outside. He took a sharp breath and glanced around. Surely in the dark he was safe from prying eyes.

Moonlight silvered the weathered boards of the dock. He slipped down the stairs, the flagstones chill on his bare feet as he walked to the water's edge. The dock was about twenty feet long, only five feet wide, meant to service the two last cottages on the shore. The lapping waves drew him out to the square platform at the end where he squatted, arms wrapped around his knees. Music drifted across the water, reminding him of his cottage summers as a teen when there was always a party somewhere on the lake on a Saturday night.

The sky stretched overhead to the void across the lake where the mountains blocked the stars. The snowy peaks traced a ragged moonlit line between the firmament above and the darkness below. Hidden by the night, he lay flat on his back, breathing in time to the rhythmic lap of the waves. The stars pulled him up and sparkled around him, away from the trouble, away from the pain.

He'd lost the people who he loved more than life. He'd never been a model father, always on the road too much, but he loved his children, looked forward to seeing them at the end of a tour, spoiling them whenever he could. He couldn't blame his wife for getting fed up, and he'd been dense not to see it coming. But he'd never expected to lose them like this. Even after the divorce, he'd been committed to fight for his right to his kids. He'd thought—he'd hoped—his children loved him. How could he face them now, though, looking the way he did? They were kids, for Christ sake. He didn't want to scare them with his monster face.

Then his song, *Wild Willow*, drifted up to meet him in the sky, claiming him and bringing him to his knees on wooden dock. Back to the reality of his life.

Chapter 11

It was a beautiful morning, bright sun, brisk breeze, and Lily had no excuse not to bike to work. Her muscles protested with every stroke of the pedal, but the lakeshore road was flat, and it was easy to convince herself that the burn felt good. She was still fired up by the jam at Frankie's the previous night and wondered if she could ever learn to play the piano well enough to join in. It wasn't a case of learning to play 'better', it was more a case of learning to play with a different part of her brain. Or maybe of turning her brain off altogether and learning to play from the heart.

At midmorning, like clockwork, the aroma of the last batch of Louise's morning baking drifted temptingly into Lily's office. Louise made the last batch of the day's special pastries for the guest brunch, but from the stream of staff passing through the staff kitchen door, Lily wondered how many pastries made it out to the dining room.

Her stomach growled in anticipation and she pushed back from her desk and went to the kitchen. Today was cherry brioche, her favorite, and although it was too early to clean for Marshall—or Morris, she wasn't sure what to call him now that she knew who he really was—she suddenly wondered if he ever got any breakfast. She licked a drip of gooey cherry custard off her wrist. Probably not. There was never anything other than leftover take-out in his refrigerator.

She might just have to do something about that.

She grabbed another pastry.

"Hey," Louise said. "One each for the staff. Orders from the top."

"This isn't for me. It's for a guest in one of the cottages."

"Well then, he should come in and get it himself," Louise said peevishly.

"He's kind of incapacitated. I'm sort of looking out for him."

"Does—" Louise started.

"Dad knows," Lily said quickly. She grabbed a tray from the clean stack by the dishwasher and put the brioche on a napkin on the tray.

"If you're going to do it, then do it right," Louise grumbled, snatching away the tray and putting the pastry on a plate with a napkin on the side, as well as a small pot of coffee and a mug. "There."

She sat heavily on a stool and rested her elbows on the stainless-steel island in the center of the kitchen. "Sorry I'm so snappy. This is harder than I thought it would be, working and having a baby. Granted, I didn't plan on having two. And to think, at one point I was planning to do it alone."

It was common knowledge around town that Louise's fiancé Blue wasn't the babies' biological father—although he certainly acted like the proud papa and everyone agreed that was all that mattered.

Lily hadn't realized Louise was originally planning to go it alone. "It would have been hard alone, with twins."

"Even with one. I'm so thankful Blue and I figured ourselves out. This is what we should have done in the first place instead of donkeying around for all those years." She stood up and put a hand on her lower back. "I couldn't have done it alone. I don't have any savings.

I would have ended up living back with my dad, his wife Belinda, and Brandy. And, while I'm lucky to have them around—they're very supportive and Belinda and Brandy are going to make a great babysitting team this summer when I go back to work— I would have gone crazy back living with them."

Lily nodded. She didn't have much in the way of savings either and didn't want to live with her dad. If she had a baby on her own, she might have to. Although that wouldn't really be *on her own—*

"Better get that tray out to the client before it's stone cold," Louise said, snapping Lily out of her rumination.

"Right."

She added cream and sugar to the tray along with a second empty cup, then hurried out the back door of the kitchen, through the laundry room door and along the trail to Cottage Four. It was her morning to clean for Marshall, but she didn't usually start before eleven—he wasn't an early riser. She'd come back for the service cart after she delivered the tray.

When she rounded the last bend in the path, she was surprised to see him sitting on the porch. When he heard her, his head spun in her direction, but like he was on a short leash, it stopped before facing her full-on. The standoff-ish mask he wore most of the time softened when he saw her, and he turned a few more degrees in her direction. "You're early."

She walked up the service ramp onto the porch, and his eyes lit up when he saw the tray of pastries.

"I try to schedule my break for when Louise is pulling these babies out of the oven," Lily said.

"I can see why." He shifted the coffee table toward her.

"Half the staff does it. The pastries are actually for

the guests, of course, and it occurred to me that you're a guest but you may never have had one. Do you have the meal plan?" She set the tray on the table and sank into the other chair.

"I don't know. I guess not," he said. "I didn't make the arrangements." He reached for the pastry and Lily busied herself pouring two cups of coffee.

"Cream?" she asked.

He nodded and took a big bite. Then he looked abashed and offered the pastry to her.

She laughed. "No thanks. I've already had one. So much for my healthy eating plan. But I thought I'd have a coffee before I start on the cottage."

They sat in companionable silence while Marshall devoured the brioche. Then he reached for the cup.

"What do you do for breakfast?" she asked.

"When I first moved in, it wasn't an issue. I wasn't up in the morning, and anyway, I didn't have much of an appetite. The resort kitchen wasn't open then, so we arranged to have meals delivered once a day from the café."

Lily was aghast. "That's terrible. You shouldn't be starving out here."

"I'm not usually so...helpless." He laughed, in a sweetly self-conscious way. "Well, maybe I am. Harry usually takes care of my living arrangements when I'm on the road." He hunched his shoulders. "It's kind of embarrassing."

"Well," Lily said briskly. "You are looking a better than when we met but I think you're still a bit thin. I'll see what I can do about having regular meals sent out to you here, if you don't want to come into the dining room."

"Thank you," he said. "That would be great. The food from the café is okay, but the menu is limited. It keeps coming, but I don't really want to eat it anymore. Too many French fries."

"Why don't you call the café and cancel the order. I guarantee the meals from our kitchen will be better than what you're getting from the café. Star, the cook there, is a good friend of mine, but she's not on the same level as Sergio, the resort chef."

Marshall settled back in the chair and watched a rowboat stroke by. Lily recognized the resort colors, white with blue stripes on the sides.

"You seem to know everyone," he said. "Have you lived here long?"

"Just over a month. But it's a small town and I had kind of an in, working here..." For some reason, she didn't want to tell Marshall that she was the boss's daughter.

He sighed. "I come from a small town. Couldn't wait to get out. But right at this moment, it seems kind of perfect."

"I've never lived in a small town before. It takes some getting used to, but I think I like it. Of course, I'm just here temporarily, I think. Until I figure out what I'm going to do next."

Marshall shot her a look with his good eye, and she quickly changed the subject. "Fortune Bay is like one huge family. Kind of nosy, and everyone seems to be related, or at least connected. Married to someone's sister or cousin, or childhood friends at the very least. I don't have much family so it's kind of new to me."

He nodded, looking at the lake. "No brothers or sisters?"

She pressed her lips together and shook her head. "No. Just me."

"Parents?"

She gave a half laugh. "Those I have. But they've

always been kind of—distant. Actually, I moved here to be closer to my dad." She was surprised to hear herself telling him that.

His good eye glanced over. "How's that going?"

She nodded. "Surprisingly well."

He nodded. "Good." Then he said softly, almost to himself, "It's good to have family."

Lily finished her coffee and stood up. "Lovely as playing at being a guest is, I have work to do."

"Must be tiring, cleaning all day."

She wondered how much to say. She didn't think he'd appreciate being the poor guest in Cottage Four. Didn't think he'd appreciate her knowing his story. "I don't clean all day. I have various duties."

He grinned. "Like bringing breakfast to shut-in guests?"

She smiled. "That's a one-off. We'll organize something so you're not starving out here."

The drop dead gorgeous side of his face he customarily showed her suddenly became serious. "Thank you. I mean it."

"No problem," she said, her cheeks suddenly on fire. *For no logical reason*, she thought as she hurried back to the Lodge for the cleaning cart. Breakfast was a simple courtesy, like she'd offer any guest.

Marshall needed taking care of, and she would see to that.

Chapter 12

Two mornings later, Marshall woke before eight. Lily was coming today. She had become part of his routine—actually, his only routine. The other days he could easily stay in bed until late afternoon, but the mornings Lily was coming, he was up and ready by ten.

She had become his lifeline to the real world, and he wasn't sure if that was safe. She was easy to talk to, and cool about his scars. Not that he didn't hide them when he could, but he knew she'd seen them, and she'd handled it well. So far, anyway.

But something wasn't quite right with her. He couldn't put his finger on what, exactly, but she didn't strike him as your typical maid. And he should know having spent half his adult life in hotels. After the first time she came, she had never worn the official uniform again and he'd felt something was just...off.

But she was coming this morning and the least he could do was get out of the sweats. She was only coming to clean, but still, last time he'd been kind of embarrassed by the sweatpants and robe. And he figured he may as well shower, too. Just so she could change the towels.

After his shower, he polished the steam off the mirror, opened the drawer and pulled out his electric razor. He used to sport a carefully cultivated two-day stubble. Kind of a bad boy-cowboy look. It was his signature look and the ladies loved it, but now it just highlighted the fact that there was next to no beard on the scarred side of his face. On that side, the growth stopped at the edge of his lips where the worst of the injury had removed most of the skin from his cheek, except for a few spots that still grew in spurts which for some reason kind of freaked him out.

He had let his hair grow to chin length, partly because he hadn't wanted to go to a barber and partly because this way it fell forward and hid his cheek. He studied his good side in the mirror. It looked strangely the same, as if nothing had happened. Then he turned his head and looked at the other side where a stranger stared back. Both eyebrows were intact, and he hadn't lost the eye. He knew he should be thankful for that, but still, after a minute, he looked away.

He pulled on some jeans, although he'd lost so much weight he needed a belt to hold them up, and with only one functioning hand, it took him five minutes to get them on and to do up the zipper and buckle.

He'd barely finished when Lily's brisk knock sounded on the door. Sweat popped out on his upper lip and forehead and his pulse went wild. Glancing at the clock, he opened the medicine cabinet and took out the pill bottle. Although prescribed for pain, they also seemed to calm the jittery feeling that sometimes ran through his veins. He thought just one wouldn't hurt. And he still did have some pain. Soon he'd stop altogether.

He downed the pill with a shot of water, then went to answer the door.

"Hi," she said. He liked to think that Lily's sunny smile was just for him, and even though he suspected that she greeted all the guests with that same smile, he basked for a moment in its warmth.

As he stared at her through the screen, so fresh and

pretty in her jeans and yellow resort tee-shirt, she reminded him of the girls he'd known back home, years ago. She always wore her hair pulled back in a ponytail, maybe because she was working, but he'd love to see it loose on her shoulders. He could imagine it, silky and golden brown. He'd caught glimpses of red and blonde strands in the sunlight.

He blinked. "Hi. Come in. I'm ready." Opening the door, he stood to the side so she could pass on his good side. "I think I'll wait outside today."

She looked pleased. "Great. You're paying for that view—you might as well enjoy it."

Once outside, though, he couldn't relax, not with her inside and able to walk out any time. She didn't, though. And really, why would she? It was kind of her to sit with him for a few minutes at the end of her visit.

Half an hour later, she came out, laughing and shaking her head. "You are the neatest guy I've ever met."

Embarrassed, he mumbled, "I don't do much that makes a mess." He held out the water bottle he'd brought out for her. "Care for a drink?"

It was only water, but she smiled and took it and flopped down on the other chair. She closed one eye and twisted her face into a smirk. "Don't let the boss catch me."

"If you think it's a problem..."

She brushed it off. "No. I can take a break."

They drank in silence for a moment. The last couple times she'd been by, he'd berated himself later that he hadn't spoken more so, heart pounding, he asked, "Have you worked in other resorts?"

She shook her head. "No. I was lucky there was a job here for me. I was..." She glanced at him. "Sort of between lives."

He blew out a breath. "I know what you mean."

She pressed her lips together and nodded. "I guess you do. That a recent injury?"

A ball lodged in his throat and he had to swallow to clear it. "Six months ago. I've been in and out of the hospital ever since. Mostly in. Thought I'd come here for a break. And...to think."

She bobbed her head several times, but kept her eyes fixed on the lake. "I know what you mean."

His shoulders were tense, and he held the bottle in a white knuckled grip on the arm of the patio chair, waiting for her to follow up on that, but instead, she asked, "Have you spent much time on lakes?"

His shoulders relaxed, and his eyes caressed the sparkling water as he went back in his mind. "We had a cottage on a lake in Minnesota when I was a kid. In the summer, my brothers and I would spend the whole day in the water, building rafts and goofing around."

"You the oldest?"

He grinned, the feeling stiff and unfamiliar, stretching muscles long unused. "How did you know?"

She shrugged and smiled. "I don't know. Just the way you mentioned them, kind of protective but bossy at the same time. Did you have boats?"

He nodded slowly at the memory. "We did. An old, flat bottom, wooden rowboat and a waterski boat. It didn't have a very strong motor. When we got to be teenagers, it could barely pull us up out of the water. But still, we had a blast."

She turned to look at him. "Is the cottage still there?"

He shook his head sadly. "They sold it a few years ago. I hadn't been up there for years, but somehow just knowing I could go again was important. I always planned to take my kids." He was quiet, contemplative for a moment. "But as they say, you can never go home again." He looked back at the water, lost in the memories.

"They have rowboats and canoes here for the guests to use," she said. "If you want to go out sometime, Johnny will fix you up."

He stiffened. Not if he had to go down to the dock. "I'll keep that in mind."

"Time for me to get back to work," she said, standing up and tossing her empty water bottle into the cart.

He hoped he hadn't come across as ungrateful. "Thank you for arranging for the meals. They are much better than the ones from the café."

She grinned. "I won't tell Star you said that. See you in a couple of days."

She left then, but Marshall stayed on the porch, watching the waves break on the gravel shore. He'd thought he'd lost the ability to smile the day he woke up in the hospital bed. But, damn! She'd made him smile.

* * *

Marshall's childhood cottage seemed to hold a special place in his memory, Lily thought as she pushed the service cart up the path to the Lodge. Maybe getting out on the water would help in his recovery. He obviously wasn't going to go down to the docks and talk to Johnny on his own, though. Not yet. If there was one thing Lily had figured out about Marshall, it was that he was a modern-day Dracula—he didn't leave the cottage in the daylight.

As she approached the Lodge, a glimmer of an idea formed in her mind. There was nothing to stop *her* from taking out a boat and rowing by his cottage. Maybe sometime at dusk when, possibly, she could lure him out onto the dock.

After disposing of the service cart, Lily went into the restaurant for coffee. Frankie and Louise were hunkered down at a table in the corner with Frankie's laptop open in front of them, all barely visible behind a mound of ribbons and lace, colored cups and fancy napkins.

Lily grinned as she walked over to join them. "How are the plans coming?"

Frankie pressed her lips tightly together, then said, "We can't seem to agree."

Louise struggled to turn a chair around in front of her and lifted her legs onto it one at a time. "I don't see what there is to agree on. I want a black, white and red theme, the guys in tuxes and the bridesmaids in red."

Frankie rolled her eyes up to the ceiling. "It sounds more like a bachelor party than a wedding."

"They won't be jumping out of the cake," Louise said in exasperation.

"I don't think they wear tuxes to a bachelor party," Lily added.

"It's in two weeks, for heaven's sake," Frankie said. "I thought we were keeping it low key. I thought you could wear that lovely black maternity dress you have. It would go with the black and white theme," she added hopefully.

Louise looked appalled. "Black? It's a wedding, not a funeral."

"When did you get so traditional?" Frankie asked.

"It's going to be my only wedding; I want *the dress*."

Frankie and Lily's eyes met—and held. Louise was just so *big*.

"Well, okay then," Frankie said, throwing up her

hands. "We get the dress."

Lily grinned at Louise, and Frankie closed her eyes and dropped her forehead to her fist. "But where are we going to get a white bridal gown in your size at this late date?"

Louise shrugged. "Surely I'm not the only bride who's getting married when she's eight and a half months pregnant. There has to be something out there."

Frankie pulled her computer directly in front of her and frantically started to search. "This might mean a trip to Seattle. It would have to be this weekend." Then she mumbled under her breath, "As if we haven't enough to do."

Tears sparkled in Louise's eyes. "I just want it to be perfect." She wiped the corner of her eye with the hem of her oversized chef's jacket. Then she sniffed and hauled herself to her feet. "I have to get back to work."

Frankie heaved a reluctant sigh and did her best to smile. "I'll do my best."

When the doors to the kitchen swung shut, Frankie moaned. "I'm not sure we can get tuxes for all the guys by the fifteenth." She pulled out a notebook and made a note in red. "They'll have to get into Bremerton for fittings right away. And then there's the pickup and drop off..." Her brow furrowed.

"I can help," Lily said. "Anything you need. There might be other things to pick up right before the wedding, too."

"Even keeping it simple, there's bound to be a list of things. She wants it mid-afternoon with dinner and dancing after. She wants Busted Muffler to play. It's kind of crazy with her being so close to her due date and all the groomsmen being in the band." Frankie's voice had a shrill edge. "I had so much fun planning

Maddie and Jake's wedding last year that I was considering becoming a wedding planner. But this is making me rethink the whole idea."

"Hey, we can pull it off. As long as Louise doesn't have the babies right in the middle of the ceremony—"

"Don't even think it! Or Maddie, or Colleen."

Lily frowned. "It's pretty early for Colleen, but Maddie's a distinct possibility."

Frankie groaned again. "I'm counting on Maddie for the photographs."

Lily held up the black crepe paper streamers and looked at them skeptically. "Let's take this one problem at a time and concentrate on the dress."

Chapter 13

Saturday, Lily was determined to take the day off. She got up at her regular time and drove into Majestic to do a big shopping, stocking up on fruits and vegetables, things that were in short supply at the Fortune Bay store. When she got back to the cabin, she made herself a melted cheese on tomato sandwich. The smell of melting cheese made her mouth water, and the tomatoes were starting to have better color and flavor this time of year. They should be delicious paired with the Asiago cheese she'd picked up at the store.

The sun was high and warm, so she took the sandwich out to the porch, setting it on the end table. When the kettle started to sing, she went inside and made a cup of the Constant Comment tea that had become her favorite. Taking the steaming cup back to the porch, she sat down, took a sip and reached for her plate. It was empty.

For a minute that didn't compute. Had she eaten the sandwich? No, there was no delicious taste in her mouth and, come on, she wasn't that absent minded. She sniffed. The smell of Asiago still hung in the air, so she hadn't imagined making it. Had Augusta eaten the sandwich? No, that was too silly. Much too corporal for a ghost.

She heard a rustle of leaves and her chest clenched. Something was making its way through the forest. Probably the big, lumbering bear she'd been dreading ever since Frankie mentioned they were hiding in the forest. She glanced around but all was quiet. Too quiet?

She heard the rustle again, too stealthy for a bear, and it seemed to be coming from under the porch steps. Taking a step forward to the top of the steps, she glanced down and saw a slim black tail sticking out from under the steps. It was hard to tell what kind of animal it belonged to, it being so matted with burdocks and god knows what else. Too big for a squirrel? Raccoon? Did raccoons have tails?

It scraped, back and forth along the ground. Whatever it was, it could be injured, and an injured animal could be dangerous. She'd nursed more than one injured squirrel back to health in her childhood. The tail moved again, raising a small cloud of dust. Then the animal whimpered. A dog!

She was down on her knees on the ground in a second, peering under the steps and trying to lure it out. The dog—because she could see now that it was a dog—glanced over its shoulder at her, then wolfed down the remains of her sandwich—leaving the slices of tomato behind in the dirt.

It was hard to tell in the dark what kind of dog it was, but it was smaller than a Beagle. Its fur was so dusty she couldn't tell what color it really was, either.

"Come on Sweetie. You can trust me." The tail wagged quickly back and forth, raising a cloud of dust that drifted into her nostrils. Lily sneezed, sat back on her heels and thought. Then she said, "Are you hungry?"

The dog scooched around and stuck its longish nose out through the opening. A tiny pink tongue licked its black lips. Lily stood up and started up the stairs, smiling to herself when the head peek out and cocked to follow her progress as she walked away. She'd never brought home a dog—wouldn't have dared, her mother had been clear they were not getting a dog—but she had brought home every other animal that crossed her path.

She rooted around in the refrigerator and found half a hamburger, a few days old, wrapped in tin foil. *Perfect.* Taking it outside, she sat on the top step. There was no sign of the dog, so she broke off a piece of the burger and dropped it over the side of the steps. It landed outside the opening where she'd last seen the furry muzzle. The sleek head popped out, snatched the nugget and disappeared again.

"Come on, Sweetie," she crooned, dropping another piece a foot from the opening, nearer the first step.

The pup did a belly crawl out of its hiding place to the burger and gobbled it up. This time it stayed there, lying low on the ground, chin resting between its paws. She moved down one step and the dog did a one-two wag, but otherwise didn't move.

Now they were only a yard apart. Breaking the last little piece in half, she placed it on the bottom step. The dog jumped to its feet and, tail wagging, took the piece off the step, swallowed it in one gulp, and let out a yip.

Lily laughed. "More, please? Aren't you polite?"

She held out the last piece of the hamburger. The dog put its front paws up on the first step and she got the first view of its long shape. It took the piece of burger delicately out of her hand. The meat disappeared into its mouth, then the pink tongue darted out and licked her fingers.

"You say, 'thank you', too?" she said, although she was pretty sure it was the taste of the burger the pup was after. Still, the contact was nice. She reached out and patted its dusty forehead. As a teenager, Lily had gotten books on dogs out of the library and studied all the breeds, even though she could never have one herself. She was pretty sure this was a Dachshund. But very small.

The dog stepped back onto the ground and when she reached toward it, it rolled over onto its back and showed her its stomach. Her stomach. Lily was pretty sure it was a girl. She patted her chest and was rewarded with a lick and this time she thought it really was for her. The dog rolled to its feet and stood watching her, tongue hanging out, tail waving, obviously over its fear and wondering what treats might be coming next.

Lily went into the bathroom and found a wide toothed comb, and when she came back, the dog was watching for her, matted ears perked. She sat on the bottom step for a moment and the dog sidled over. She gave it a pat and it came closer, pressing its ribs against Lily's leg.

"This is nice, Sweetie pie."

Starting at the top of the head, Lily skimmed off the burrs, pleased to see the relief in Sweetie's eyes at the attention. She sat back and looked at her work. "But you stink, Sweetie pie. What have you been rolling in? Dead fish?"

Lily picked her up and carried her carefully into the laundry room between the porch and the bathroom, where a deep, square, concrete laundry tub sat in the corner. Grabbing her organic, all-natural shampoo from the bathroom, she set Sweetie in the washtub. The dog didn't fight, just started shaking when the water hit her, even though Lily was careful to make sure it was warm. Once she was soaking wet, Lily could see how thin she was, with an angry red scratch on one shoulder.

"You look like you've been through the war. Crawling under barbed wire to escape the enemy."

Looking like a shivering rat, Sweetie just looked up at her with trusting, big, brown eyes.

Lily toweled her dry and put antibiotic cream on the scratch. "Now you look like a beautiful dog," she said, sitting back on her heels. Sweetie, clean and dry, sat in front of her, long soft ears perked, watching her every move.

"I have nothing else to feed you. We'll have to go back to the store."

Sweetie loved the ride in the car and wagged happily when Lily carried her into the Fortune Bay store.

"What have you there?" Fiona said, reaching out to pat Sweetie's head. "Isn't she cute. Where did you get her?"

"She's a stray. Just turned up at my door," Lily said. But then she had a terrible thought. Maybe Sweetie had a loving owner who was missing her. Maybe some sweet little old lady who doted on the dog. "You don't know who she belongs to, do you?"

To her immense relief, Fiona shook her head.

"She was in pretty bad shape when I found her," Lily said, hearing the hopeful note in her voice.

"You should put her description on Facebook," Fiona suggested. "You could give it to Ms. B. right now. She's in the café."

"Good idea," Lily said without enthusiasm, and with Sweetie still tucked under her arm, went into the café.

Ms. Bowden was there all right, talking to Star, who came around the counter to make clucking noises in Sweetie's face. The pup lapped it up, her tail beating against Lily's side in a steady rhythm.

"Either of you recognize this dog?" Lily asked.

Neither woman knew her, which raised Lily's hopes again, but she tamped them down. Finding Sweetie's real owner was the right thing to do. "She's a stray. Fiona suggested I put her description on the town Facebook page."

"Don't you want to keep her?" Star asked in surprise.

"I do," Lily said. Then thought for a minute. She really did. She wanted a dog and there was nothing—and no one—to stop her now. "I really do. But we should see if there's a family or someone looking for her."

Ms. Bowden pulled out her cell phone. "Let me take a little picture." She snapped a few quick ones. "I'll put up a notice today."

"Thanks," Lily said, and squeezed Sweetie a little tighter.

* * *

The next day, Lily stopped on the porch of Marshall's cottage. Low-pitched, monotonous voices leaked through the door. *Baseball.* She knocked and heard a muffled response. "Come in."

Marshall sat on the couch, watching the game. She was pleased to see him dressed again today and looked like any other resort guest on a warm summer day in a tee shirt, a ball cap and shorts.

"Hi." He glanced over at her, then his eyes went back to the screen.

She smiled. "Baseball?"

"I'm a fan," he said, not looking away from the screen, as if he was embarrassed to be caught actually doing something, even something as passive as watching baseball.

She felt a surprising surge of pleasure to see him show an interest in anything. That was progress.

"I hope you don't mind but I brought my dog. I just found her, and I don't want to leave her alone at home, yet," she said. "I'll just leave her tied up outside."

Marshall got up from the couch and came to the door. "Let's see the mutt. We always had a dog when I was a kid."

He knelt down and Sweetie was all over him, licking his face and neck like he was he long lost love. "A wiener dog. What's her name?"

"Sweetie."

Marshall laughed. "Really?" She rolled over on her back and offered him her tummy to rub and he obliged, saying, "Well, I guess you are pretty sweet, aren't you?"

Lily left them getting to know each other and went into the bedroom, smiling to herself as she threw open the curtains. When she saw the window was already open, her smile broadened. *Baby steps.* She went through the now familiar motions of cleaning and sanitizing the rest of the cottage before finally going back into the living room. Sweetie was up on the couch with her head on Marshall's knee. His hand unconsciously rubbed the dog's ear. Sweetie eyed Lily warily as if waiting be shooed away. Not today.

Lily plugged in the vacuum. "Lift your feet."

Marshall obliged, his eyes leaving the screen to watch as she bent to vacuum under the couch.

When she put the hose away, she perched on the other end of the couch and watched in silence for a few minutes.

"You like baseball?" he asked.

"I do." She grinned and punched the air gently. "Go

Seahawks. But I don't have a television."

"They're playing my team, the Twins."

She settled back on the cushions. "They don't have a chance."

They watched in companionable silence spiced by competitive baseball trash-talk. After half an hour, he asked, "Don't you have to go back to work?"

Lily blushed. "It's my day off."

He turned to her in surprise, for once forgetting to hide his scar. "You're cleaning on your day off?"

She sighed. "It's not like that."

He tipped his head. "What is it like?"

She caught her upper lip between her teeth. "I'm not really...a cleaner."

He looked non-plussed. "You're not."

"No. I'm not."

He continued to look at her, but she didn't go on, so finally he asked, "Then what the heck are you?"

"I'm...well, I don't really have a title, as such. I help out in the office and wherever I'm needed, so when I found out Hilda was cleaning this room herself, I said I'd do it."

"Because Hilda is...?"

"Head of housekeeping."

He took a moment to register that. "So, also not a cleaner."

She nodded. His eyes narrowed as he thought that over, then turned back to the TV screen.

"There's something else I think I should tell you."

His look became suddenly guarded.

Her voice dropped. "I know who you are."

He jerked around to look at her, forgetting to hide. She looked into his eyes, both deep, dark eyes, as he looked out from the long curtain of hair. Her voice was a whisper. "Marshall."

"Who else knows?" His voice was hoarse and his eyes wide, like an animal pursued.

"No one!" she said quickly. "Just my dad—"

"Who's your dad?"

"Max Finster. The director of the resort. Your friend had to talk to someone when he registered you here. And his girlfriend, Stephanie. But neither of them will tell anyone. That's why he asked me to do your cottage."

Marshall ran a hand through his hair, pulling it back off his forehead and inadvertently giving Lily her first full view of his battered face. But that wasn't the important thing right now. Calming his panic took precedence.

"Do you know what will happen if the press finds out I'm here? Photographers and reporters will descend on Fortune Bay. They'll hide in the forest, rent boats and moor them in front of the cottage, hoping I'll step outside. That's why I don't go outside. No one can know I'm here."

"How long can you keep that up?"

"I don't know. It's something that nags me night and day. I don't see how this will end." He turned his head and let the curtain of hair fall over his face. "Until they forget who I am."

She shrugged in exasperation. "We are trying to keep you...quiet."

He sobered and leaned toward her, putting his hand over hers on the couch. "Thank you. But you don't have to come and clean on your day off."

She blushed again. "I wanted to." She shrugged. "And besides, I didn't have anything else to do. I'm new here too, you know." She frowned and turned her eyes back to the game. "Now be quiet and let me watch the game."

She could feel his eyes on her for another minute, then he squeezed her hand where it burned under his and took his hand away. She wished she could scooch over and sit beside him, but she stayed where she was on her own end of the couch.

It was hard to get back into the game after that and her mind churned over ways to get him out of the cottage safely. Surely she could think of something.

Chapter 14

Nothing on Lily's closet rod looked vaguely suitable to wear to an open mic. The cocktail dress she'd bought for Troy's office Christmas party? Too fancy for Fortune Bay. But it was at the resort, and she might be onstage, but just for one song and there might not be anyone in the audience anyway from what Blue had said. What if she arrived in a little black dress and everyone else was in jeans? The guys in Busted Muffler certainly would be. Jeans would probably be the safest thing for her, too.

And on top? A button-down shirt? A glittery tank? Tomorrow was the first of June and the evenings were still quite chilly. Nothing she had looked remotely suitable until a silky sweater fell off its hanger and landed in a soft heap on the floor.

Try this.

The aroma of cinnamon and cloves drifted by.

She picked up the sweater, pulled it on over her head and looked in the speckled mirror. The neckline was wide, almost off her shoulders, the three-quarter sleeves hitting just the right note. The room seemed to take on a golden glow. She felt like a spotlight had fallen on her, picking up the threads of silver that ran through the top. *Perfect.*

Maybe Marshall will come to the open mic tonight. That would make it truly perfect.

She closed her eyes and shook her head. "Don't go putting thoughts in my head," she murmured. Marshall didn't go anywhere and certainly wouldn't be showing up at the bar tonight. She feared she was getting a fan-girl crush, just knowing who he was behind the mask. Or maybe the celebrity persona was the mask, and *this* was who he really was. Who knows what the truth really is when the media is on the hunt for a story?

Why was she even thinking about this? Nothing was going to happen tonight.

She pulled the elastic off her ponytail and bent at the waist to shake out her hair. When she stood upright, it settled like a starlet's soft curls on her shoulders, not like her hair at all.

She rolled her eyes and murmured, "Just stop that Augusta."

Then, grabbing her jacket, she headed for the door.

* * *

Marshall heard the music, distant and thin, but it pulled him to the cottage door.

He'd heard it last Thursday evening too, coming from the main building of the resort. There had been music on the weekends, but that was different. This was his kind of music, a band playing country covers and classic rock. He'd found his feet tapping to the rhythm last week and had ventured out onto the porch to listen.

Since then, he'd been going out at night, sometimes to the dock, sometimes to roam the empty, foot-lit paths of the resort, out of range of the parking lot lights. His body responded to the exercise and cried out for more. More exercise, more oxygen, even more sunlight. But he wasn't willing to brave the light, so he walked in the dark.

This evening, tugged by the music, he took the trail,

Lily's trail, back to the main building. He approached from the rear where a phalanx of tall, narrow windows covered the end wall of the wing that stuck back into the forest. Standing in the shelter of the trees, he watched as the band finished up an Eagles cover, a skinny guy in a ball cap singing the lead at the mic. The band was pretty good, but if that was their lead singer, they needed a new one. Then the singer took his seat and a busty redhead took the stage. He grinned. An open mic. He leaned against a tree and settled in to enjoy the show. This singer was better than the last guy and more fun to watch. The guys in the band seemed to know her, know her moves. She must be a regular.

Then the band called a chick singer up onto the stage and— *Christ Almighty. Was that Lily?*

She looked good, her hair loose and falling over her bare shoulders. And she sounded amazing, sharing the vocals with the lead guitar player, doing Carey Underwood's part in *The Fighter.*

No, not just a room cleaner. That was the magic of small towns. You could be a room cleaner by day and a rock star by night.

When they finished the number, she turned, radiant, smiled at the guy playing lead guitar—and Marshall's heart broke. He'd give anything to be that guy, to have her look at him like that. But the odds were she never would. She turned her head and her eyes seemed to meet his over the distance through the glass. It couldn't be. She shouldn't be able to see him, not blinded by the stage lights and him here in the darkness. She squinted, then shook her head, smiled and made a comment to the guy that should be him.

She disappeared off the stage and an older woman took her place. He didn't register the singer or the song—his mind fixated on the beautiful Lily.

Gravel crunched on the path and he sunk back into the shadows. What was he thinking coming out here so early? Hypnotized by the music, he'd put himself in jeopardy.

"Marshall?" Lily called softly from the darkness. He should hide, retreat, but instead he shifted forward into the light.

She'd thrown a jacket over her shoulders, but her hair caught the golden light falling from the windows. Her face lit up when she saw him. "I thought I saw you."

"I didn't think anyone could. It's so bright in there..."

"And dark outside," she finished. "I wasn't sure, but look at you, out for a walk."

In spite of himself one corner of his mouth turned up. "Yeah. I've been out a few times at night."

"I love walking at night. It's one of the things I love about being here in Fortune Bay. No city lights to interfere with the stars."

Come watch them on the dock with me. The moment stretched out, but he couldn't form the words.

"Well," she said. "Do you want to come in, or..."

He straightened from where he leaned against a tree. "No, I think I'll head back." *Walk with me.* Again, he couldn't say it out loud, but as if she could hear his thoughts, she started walking to the cottages.

"You were wonderful," he said. "I didn't know you could sing."

She laughed with pure delight. "I haven't sung in *years*. In fact, I'm embarrassed you had to hear that, my maiden performance." She giggled again. "But it was so much fun. Sean told me what song to learn, but we never even had a chance to practice."

"Well, you were great." Their arms brushed as they

walked the narrow path and lightning sparked, in his head and his heart, and like Frankenstein, he felt himself come alive. But just for a moment because, of course, she would never sing like that with him.

Still, they were here now and that alone was more than he'd thought could happen. When they got to the cottage, she looked out at the sky over the lake. He glanced at the cottage, dreaded going in alone. Then they were staring into each other's eyes and he was falling.

"Want a drink?"

She smiled. "Water?"

"I have other things too. Wine, beer. Bourbon." He felt like he was telling her his secrets.

She chewed her bottom lip for a moment, then said, "Sure. A glass of wine would be great. Let's sit outside. It's such a beautiful night." She walked up to the porch and put a hand on a chair. "Need any help?"

"No. I can handle it." He hurried inside, opened the cupboard and pulled out a bottle of red Bordeaux and two wine glasses. He poured the wine, then flexed his left hand. The movement was limited. The skin was smooth with a ropelike scar across his palm. The plastic surgery had left the hand shaped like a claw, but he could hold a glass, at least long enough to carry it out onto the porch.

Kicking open the screen door with his foot, he stepped outside—and froze. Lily had taken his seat at the far end of the porch, the chair that protected the scarred side of his face from her sight.

He cleared his throat. "Wouldn't you be more comfortable in this chair. The view of the stars is better."

She looked at him and smiled. "I'm fine here." Then she leaned forward and held out a hand for the glass. She seemed totally unaware of the discomfort she caused him—and of the discomfort awaiting her when she had to look at his disfigured face. She reached out, her eyes on the glasses in his hand. Looking at his claw. He countered, thrusting out his right hand so quickly that the wine sloshed over the rim of both glasses.

She laughed gently and taking a tissue out of her pocket, wiped the base of her glass and took it from him. Then to his horror, she reached up and wiped the drops that had fallen on his scarred hand.

She settled back in her seat. "This is nice. I don't really have any friends here yet," she said shyly.

Friends. He could go with that. Cautiously, he took the other seat, careful to make sure his hair covered most of the left side of his face. He kept the hair on his right side hooked behind his ear so he could see, but he couldn't see her, so he angled his chair slightly in her direction.

She was staring into her drink, lips pursed. He had upset her. Well, they'd make this quick. He took a slug of his wine.

"You have children," she said suddenly, catching him off guard.

His head jerked toward her, but she was staring into the darkness over the water. "I do."

"Where are they now?"

Seriously? She didn't know? It had been splashed all over the tabloids last year, and he was egotistical enough to think the whole world knew. That the whole world cared. Then he felt laughter on his lips. She didn't know. She didn't read the rags. If she'd known, she would say so.

"They are with their mother. My ex-wife."

She pressed her lips together and nodded. "You

must miss them."

Sitting there in the darkness with this straightforward woman, he found himself answering honestly. "I do. I miss them a lot."

She was silent for a moment, then she said, "I have no children." She blew out a breath. "When I got married, I thought I would have some by now." A laugh that almost sounded like a sob bubbled out. "My husband didn't want any, but now he's having a baby with someone else." She sucked in a breath and her shoulders straightened. "I'm thinking of doing it on my own.

"It's kind of scary, though," she continued. "I mean, could I really do it alone?"

He knew that feeling. The fear of facing life's turning points alone. "It's a big commitment. I wouldn't have wanted to tackle it alone." He was silent for a moment as the last view of his children's faces through the rear window of the limousine fixed in his mind. "I've hardly seen them since the divorce. I guess now when I see them, I will be seeing them alone."

"Is that scary?"

He gave a self-deprecating grin. "Terrifying."

"You'll do fine," she said.

He looked in her eyes and a warm glow spread through him when he saw that she meant it.

* * *

Why had she told him about her longing for children? Lily wondered as she walked back along the dark path toward the lights of the parking lot. She was still feeling the pinch of seeing all of her new Fortune Bay friends with their young families at Frankie's the other night. *Just two lonely people confiding in each other, I guess.*

She might be lonely, but at least she was out there, meeting new people, not hiding out, like Marshall. That didn't sound like a workable solution to his problems.

Yes, he'd been in a bad accident and his injuries had been serious, but other people got through similar problems, with the help of their family and friends. Why was he hiding away like this? Although, who was she to judge? She had no idea what his life had been like or, for that matter, what he felt like now. Maybe he didn't feel like he had any family and friends to confide in. She could certainly relate to that.

She went into the Lodge, where the open mic was still rolling and stood in the lobby watching the crowd in The Cedars. They looked like they were having fun. She'd missed so much over the years by going along with whatever Troy wanted. But she didn't feel like going back into the noisy bar. She'd had enough excitement for one night. She wished she had someone she could talk to about Marshall, but silence was part of the deal. She could talk to her dad and Stephanie, but it was too late to stop in and see either of them tonight.

Instead of joining the crowd in the bar, she slipped into her office. She only knew Marshall in his new persona, as his alias, 'Morris', not as the man he had been before the accident. She knew he'd been a star, a big star, straddling country and popular music, winning major awards in both arenas, but she didn't read the tabloids or watch entertainment news on TV, had never bought his music or been to his concerts—Troy would never have gone to a country music concert—so Marshall's life was just a vague picture in her mind.

Without turning on the lights, she woke up her

computer and typed his name into the search bar. Apparently, every entertainment media outlet had carried the accident in detail, and now those reports popped up on the screen. She skimmed the first few articles. A motorcycle accident. Few details released by Harry Santino, his manager. That must be the Harry he'd mentioned who made the arrangements at the resort. Marshall had been in the hospital on and off for five months. He'd mentioned surgeries. More than one. Images of his face and scarred hand flashed through her mind.

What had his life been like before the accident? She added an arbitrary date a month before the accident to his name in the browser. A new string of articles appeared. A nasty divorce. A photograph of Marshall, his young daughter in his arms, her face buried in his neck, his one arm out, fiercely fending off the paparazzi. Then Marshall in leather, his hair stylishly long, a gorgeous blonde model on his arm outside a Hollywood restaurant. Drool-worthy in a tux, accepting the CMA album of the year award.

She shook her head. *Wow.* She'd had no idea. It was hard to reconcile these pictures with the man she knew. Imagine having your every move followed by the press. How intrusive that would be. She could see how it could push you into hiding away.

Back in the browser, she deleted the date and quickly typed *Follow Me* after his name and a string of YouTube videos popped up. She settled back in her desk chair in the darkened office and clicked on the trailer for the song. Cuts from a concert were interspersed with scenes of him and the blonde model on his motorcycle. It struck her as ironic—his biggest hit and the bike. A portent of his downfall.

But man, he was gorgeous. And sexy. Guitar slung

low on his hips, he brushed the dark hair off his forehead. Hips swaying, fingers giving the 'come-on' signal, he egged on the crowd until the fans roared. Every woman's bad boy dream. The superstar every man longed to be.

She sat in the dark watching video after video and when finally, she'd had enough, she continued to sit in her chair, pressing her fingertips in an arch in front of her chest while she thought. This was the man he had been, but was he still the same man? Sexy idol or depressed recluse.

Which was the real Marshall Mason?

Chapter 15

The next day, Lily pushed the cart along the path to Marshall's cottage, her heart fluttering. "No reason to be anxious," she told Sweetie who, as usual, trotted at her heels. "He's still the same guy as all the other times."

But now the sexy singer in the YouTube videos seemed to be beckoning to *her*.

She slowed at the sight of a brand-new Mercedes parked at the back of the cottage. She'd bet her first paycheck it wasn't local. Marshall had only mentioned one friend who visited—his manager, Harry.

Lily left the cart on the path and walked quietly up onto the porch. She could have turned back—the cottage didn't really need to be cleaned right now—but she was curious to meet Harry.

The front door was open, and men's voices drifted out, Harry's insistent tones and Marshall's mumble, but she couldn't make out their words. She peeked around the corner and saw a man with a large, square frame through the screen, his sport shirt a bright spot in the dim interior. So obviously not Marshall.

The man's eyes locked with hers. "Hello."

She backed away. "I'll come back later."

She was pushing the cart full speed down the path when she heard footsteps pounding behind her. "Wait up."

The man's face was flushed, and he was breathing hard from the ten-meter sprint when he caught up with her. She slowed her pace but kept walking.

"You must be Lily," he said.

She stopped and faced him in surprise. "How do you know?"

He waved a hand. "Marsh has told me all about you."

"Well," she said thoughtfully, "if you're Harry, he's mentioned you, too."

A corner of Harry's lips twitched. "It's always, 'Lily says this,' and, 'Lily says that.'"

"Really?" she said, a little bit pleased. "Are you here for a visit?"

"A visit, and to try to talk some sense into him. A break is one thing, but he needs to go back." He shook his head in obvious frustration. "He's always been a stubborn bastard. And I should know. We've been friends since we were kids."

Go? The idea shook her more than it should have because of course she'd always known he'd go at some point. "Why does he have to go now?"

"He needs more surgery, but he says he's not ready."

"Well maybe he's not. Is there any medical reason it has to be now?"

"It's scheduled for two weeks from now."

She looked down at the cart, not registering the pile of white towels or the box of individual soaps. She couldn't see Marshall in his current state on a plane or walking into a hospital.

She shook her head and looked Harry in the eye. "I don't think he's ready. He can barely leave the cottage—and then, only if it's dark or to sit on the porch. I'm no doctor, but I'd say at this point his problems are more emotional than physical."

"If he had the surgery it might help."

"Would he be able to play again? Perform again?"

Harry's face went blank. He stuffed his hands in his pockets and studied the ground.

Lily softened her tone. "You say you've been friends since you were kids. Do you really think he's ready to go back to his old life?"

Harry seemed focused on the rough path. After a moment he looked up and Lily was shocked to see tears in his eyes.

"He was always *the man*, you know? The top guy, the guy everyone wanted to be with, just to bathe in his aura of greatness. He was never arrogant about it. Always kind to fans and strangers. He didn't deserve this."

Lily put a hand on his arm. "But is he *ready*, Harry?"

Harry pressed his lips together and shook his head. "I just thought—hoped, I guess—that if he could have these next surgeries, if his hand and face were even a bit better, he'd find it reassuring. It might give him hope."

His voice sank to a whisper. "He thinks his career is over, and that his life is over. He may not be able to perform again, may not want to perform, but that doesn't mean it has to be over. There are other things he could do." He shook his head. "He just doesn't see it."

"Yet. Give him time. He's already so much better than when I first met him, but he still won't go out where people might see him. He thinks his face is horrifying, even though it's really not that bad anymore. I think he's depressed."

"Maybe I should bring his doctor—get him to prescribe some pills."

Lily shook her head, memories of disasters on the

suicide line raising their gruesome heads. "I don't think that's a good idea. Antidepressants can be fatal if mixed with the anti-inflammatories he's still taking."

Harry cocked his head. "You seem to know a lot about this."

"I clean his rooms. I know what he's taking. And I've had experience with depression. And suicide." She frowned thoughtfully. "Does the surgery have to be in L.A.?"

"That's where his family is. His kids really miss him."

Lily pressed her lips together, remembering the heart wrenching pictures she'd seen online the night before. "Right. His kids."

"It's one of the worst parts of this whole thing. He loves his kids. Fought for joint custody after the divorce and was devastated when he lost. But since the accident, he won't talk to them. He's worried they will be afraid of him, you know, with the scars."

"That's ridiculous."

Harry shrugged. "Well, like you said, it's more emotional than physical at this point." He looked down and scuffed the ground. "I'll tell him I'll try to get a surgery postponed." Then he looked at her and smiled. "He told me you put him on the meal plan. Thanks for that, I should have thought of it. Can you come for dinner? I could have it delivered out here for us all. I'd like to give him a sort of normal evening, just a couple of friends having dinner together. Will you come?"

She looked down at her tee-shirt and shorts and frowned. "I'd like to get changed first."

Harry shrugged. "Marshall likes you just the way you are."

Lily laughed in protest. "Thanks, Harry. I'm sure

you meant that as a compliment, but I still want to change clothes. And I have more work to do. I'm on the clock here."

"More rooms to clean?" Harry asked innocently.

Lily frowned. "What? Oh, yeah. I mean no. I do a lot of different jobs around here. Marshall is a special request. His is the only cottage I clean."

Harry looked embarrassed. "I didn't mean—"

Lily waved it off. "No shame in cleaning. It's not my main job, though. Listen, I'll order dinner for seven and be back before then. Anything you need in there?" She motioned to the cart.

He shook his head. "No. We're good."

She smiled. "Then I'd better get back to work."

"Okay. See you later." Harry started back to the cottage.

"And Harry," she said. He stopped and turned to face her. "Thanks for looking out for him."

He cocked his finger at her. "Back at you."

At six o'clock, Lily let herself into the cabin. Today had been one emergency after another. She had changed back into her office clothes but was hot and sweaty and not looking forward to going out again. She'd told Harry she would come, though, and sensed Marshall might need some back-up. So, marching into the bathroom, she stood under the shower until she felt human again.

She hated the thought of him leaving now. For his sake. He was making progress, but she didn't think he was ready to go back to his old life. Not yet. She could imagine him holed up in some mansion in L.A., totally isolated. Lonely.

She'd be lonely too, if he left. *But he is leaving so get used to the idea.* There was no way he'd stay in

Fortune Bay forever.

Her eyes blurred and her image in the pitted mirror seemed to glow. The air sweetened and a breeze brushed her cheek. He might not be here forever, but she'd make good use of the time she had. Tonight, she'd show them she was just as good as anyone in Hollywood. But *Holy Guacamole,* what on earth would she wear?

She held up first one dress then the next. Too revealing. Too tight. She'd put on a few pounds over the last year and not lost them all yet. The next one was too young. Then a cobalt blue, silk sundress slipped off the hanger and onto the floor. She had bought it for a party last summer and had never worn it when Troy had gone out of town at the last minute.

She stepped into the dress, pulled it up and like magic all the bumps and bulges disappeared. It was casual yet elegant, showing just the right amount of cleavage. She blew dry her hair and piled it on top of her head in a loose knot, added dangly silver earrings and, looking in the mirror, felt a surge of confidence.

The feeling carried her out to the car and all the way to Cottage Four. When she pulled up behind the cottage, the bottom fell out of her stomach. The thing was, now that Harry was here, would it be the Marshall she knew waiting inside, or the L.A. music idol. People could change, depending who they were with. Troy did it all the time. Like a chameleon, he blended into his surroundings. But she'd promised she'd come so, shoulders back, chest out, she got out of the car and marched up the ramp toward the sound of clinking glasses and voices: Harry's, Marshall's, and—was that a woman?

She glanced through the screen and saw a woman sitting on the couch, holding the hand of someone that had to be Marshall who sat just outside of Lily's view. The woman was looking at him beseechingly, saying, "It's not over. You have to come back to L.A."

Whoa, Nellie. Lily was barging in where she didn't belong. She tried to back up, but Harry had appeared in the doorway, ultra-urban in suit pants with a blue button-down shirt, sleeves rolled up to the forearms.

"Lily," he said.

She took a step back. "I'm early." She wanted to get out of there, but Harry had opened the door and, taking her hand, drew her into the room.

The woman holding Marshall's hand looked familiar. Then Lily remembered. She was the woman from the video who'd been straddling the motorcycle, clinging to Marshall's waist. Now she sat with him on the couch, full breasts spilling over a tube top, long legs sticking out of a very short, shiny skirt.

The old, ravaged look Lily remembered was back on Marshall's face. She could almost see him physically withdrawing. Could see his progress slipping away.

His face lit up when he saw her and he stood, pulling his hand away from the woman's grasp. "Lily. I'm glad you came. This is Lola, an old friend."

Lola was sitting on the couch with her legs curled beneath her. She stood up, unfolding like a gazelle, and extended her hand. She was gorgeous, tall but with more curves than a model. More like a chorus girl or aging starlet.

Flipping her long blonde hair over her shoulder, she said, "Nice to meet you." Then looked questioningly from Harry to Marshall.

Marshall said firmly, "Lily's a friend."

"Oh, good. Maybe you can talk this hard-head into going back to L.A. for his treatments."

"I don't want to," Marshall said stubbornly, showing more vigor than Lily had seen from him yet. "I'm just getting settled here. I need more time. Can't we postpone it until the fall?"

"The surgeon I've lined up is the best there is," Harry said. "He's not going to be at your beck and call. If you drop off the list, I can't promise when you'll get back on."

"I don't see what the rush is," Marshall retorted. "It's not like I'll be performing again."

"Maybe not, honey," Lola said, putting a proprietary hand on his arm. "But whatever you do next, you'll want to be in the best shape you can be."

"It's not just the surgery," Harry said. "There is business you need to see to."

Marshall laughed harshly. "Like what?"

"Well, for one, there's a young singer interested in recording your material. He's good. I think you should hear him. And your children have been asking about you."

Marshall winced and ground out, "Not now." Lily sensed that was a low blow.

Harry turned to Lily. "What do you think?"

Marshall's eyes locked on hers, begging her to back him up. Harry might mean well, but she really didn't think Marshall was ready. "It's not for me to say, but I don't see why it has to be now, either. There is more than the physical trauma to deal with, and he is dealing with it. At his own pace."

"The peace and quiet is what I need now. I was a wreck when I left L.A."

"But what about your kids?"

"I'll talk to my kids, dammit, when I'm good and ready."

Silence pulsed in the room. Marshall's breath came

in pants. Finally, Harry said, "Okay. I'll try to postpone the surgery. But I can't promise he'll take you at your convenience."

Marshall visibly deflated. Lily could see what the battle had cost him.

Harry turned to her. "Lily, you look lovely. Would you care for a martini?"

Marshall smiled with relief as the subject was dropped and despite her own discomfort, Lily was glad she'd come. She took the empty living room chair and Harry made her a martini from the bar that had magically appeared on the kitchen counter. Marshall, she noticed was drinking bottled water.

Lola curled up on the couch beside Marshall again, telling him a story about a hilarious misadventure at a recent award ceremony where Harry had apparently picked up the award for best album for Marshall. Lily cringed inwardly, feeling the pain in Marshall's grim smile. The award had to be bittersweet, possibly the last album he would put out.

Lola finally got the message that he didn't want to talk about his old life, and she turned to Lily. "So, how long have you been working at the resort?"

"Just since it opened a month ago."

"Are you local?" Lola's smile seemed genuine, if a trifle condescending.

"No, I'm from Seattle."

"Lily works in the office. Her father owns the resort."

Lola looked startled. "I thought you were the maid."

"She's just helping out—to preserve my anonymity."

"Oh." Lola took a sip of her martini and Lily could see the wheels inside her head turning.

Just then the waiter arrived with a large tray of

covered dishes. Lily had told the chef to go all out, and the waiter to wear one of the dress uniforms they had in stock rather than the informal white tee-shirts they wore most nights in the restaurant. After he unloaded the dishes onto the kitchen counter, he quickly set out plates and cutlery and napkins, and Lily saw Harry press a roll of bills into the man's hand as left.

Lola got up and went into the kitchen and lifted the lids. "Smells wonderful. Asparagus with Hollandaise, roast beef with mushrooms and onions. I'm starving. Let's eat."

She'd slipped a short, sheer kimono over her tube top and the wide arms billowed around her as she served the plates, a giant ring on her finger flashing like a beacon. She served Marshall first, and he handed the plate to Lily. Lola smiled, flashed a look at Harry and served up another. Lily followed Marshall out onto the porch where dusk had fallen, and the air was pleasantly cool. They put their plates on the coffee table and he took her hand, guiding her onto the two-seater beside him. "I'm so glad you came," he said softly.

Moments later, Harry and Lola came out. Lola stopped in mid-sentence when she saw Lily on the couch next to Marshall. She took one of the chairs, and her eyes flashed to Harry who returned a deadpan look.

They ate in silence for a few minutes, then Lily said, "Lovely ring."

Lola brightened, extended her hand and wiggled her fingers. "I forgot to tell you. I'm engaged."

"Really?" Marshall said. Had he seriously not noticed? The ring was as big as a gumball. "Do I know him?"

"I don't think so. He's a producer. I met him years ago when I first got into acting." Lola turned to Lily and added, "I used to be an actress, before I became a back-up singer. Marsh and I met when I sang on one of his tours.

She turned back to Marshall. "Gerry's a sweetie. A little bit older." Harry guffawed into his napkin and Lola gave him a swat. "But he's wonderful to me."

The corner of Marshall's lips twitched. "Well, I'm happy for you."

"When's the wedding?" Lily asked.

"September." Lola turned to Marshall. "And you better be there, you big lug."

Marshall pulled his lips back in a pseudo-smile, but didn't commit.

After the meal, everyone was quiet, relaxed and replete. "I feel like I ate a cow," Lola said, patting her flat stomach. "I have to watch my figure if I'm going to fit into my wedding gown." She yawned. "I'm going to turn in. Harry had me up at the crack of dawn."

Lily wondered if that was her cue to leave. Where were they sleeping? She couldn't imagine Lola and Harry in the twin beds in the cottage guest room. Her discomfort must have shown on her face, because when she glanced at Marshall, he took her hand in both of his. "Lola and Harry have rooms in the main building."

Lily was embarrassed by how thankful she was for his answer. Of course Lola was not sleeping with him, not if she was getting married to someone else in two months.

They cleared away the plates and Harry and Lola said their goodbyes. "We'll drop by in the morning before we leave," Harry told Marshall.

Lola wrapped herself around Marshall and went for a full-on kiss. Lily warmed to her for being so natural, not appearing at all distressed by his scars. That was what he needed, more interaction to convinced him he wasn't disfigured. Still, she was glad Lola was leaving in the morning.

As Harry and Lola walked away down the path, Lily turned to Marshall and before she could make her own goodbyes, he took her hand. "Don't go. Not yet."

She smiled, but her pulse was pounding as he pulled her back into the shadows of the porch. They had always sat on separate chairs before, but that seemed artificially distant after sharing the two-seater for the past hour, so she sank back onto the love seat.

"Would you like a drink?" he asked. She hadn't been drinking during dinner, wanting to keep her wits about her even though the evening had turned out to be very pleasant. But now... "Sure. Is there any wine left?"

"I'll check. Lola was really going at it."

He came back a moment later with two glasses, gave one to Lily and sat next to her on the sofa. He leaned back and put an arm along the back, playing with the tendrils of her hair that had fallen. "You look lovely tonight. Although I like the Daisy Duke look too."

She laughed, aware of the heat of his body next to hers and the tickle of his fingers on her neck. "I do my best. I like your friends. Have you known them long?"

"I've known Harry since we were kids. When I got to high school and started playing in garage bands, he arranged our local gigs. Parties, school dances, that sort of thing. He has a real knack for managing people, difficult people, and we've just stuck together ever since. He's made my life bearable over the past few decades."

"And Lola?"

He laughed. "We dated for a while about fifteen years ago. Stayed friends. What can I say? She's Lola."

Lily smiled. "I like her."

Marshall's eyebrows pulled into a frown. "Harry brought her to try to talk me into going back. I'm glad you were here to back me up or I'm afraid I'd be getting on that plane with them tomorrow. I'm not ready to leave."

They were sitting very close, his arm, now clearly around her shoulders, pulling her closer still. She felt his breath tickle her ear, causing a physical reaction in nether regions she'd never realized connected to the ear at all. It had been so long since she'd been on a date, since a man other than her husband had put his arm around her, that she'd lost any *savoir faire* she'd ever had. And even that had never been much.

She looked down at her glass. "I'm not ready for you to go yet either."

He turned her to face him with the gentlest touch with the back of his hand. Sitting this close, in the shadows, his dark brow, sharp cheekbones and strong jawline melted her insides and she wondered why, exactly, she had thought it was such a bad idea to kiss Marshall. Why she had thought it couldn't work out for them.

His lips were gentle, giving her the option of pulling away, but she fell into the kiss as if she'd been waiting for him all her life. And maybe she had, marking time with that other guy, whose name escaped her. Now that she was kissing Marshall, her head spun, and her thoughts were scrambled. She felt like the wine had gone to her head, although she'd had only a sip.

He pulled away and held her transfixed with his eyes for a long moment. She took a ragged breath. He smiled with a tinge of sadness, picked up his glass and drank. "I've been alone for a long time." He put down his glass and rested his arm again along the back of the sofa.

She settled lightly into the curve of his arm. "Me too."

"What's your story?"

She stiffened. "What do you mean?"

"Your story. Everyone has a story. Mine is out there—you just have to google me to get it."

She smiled. "You wouldn't get much if you googled me." She took a nervous sip of wine. "You know my story. My husband dumped me for his secretary." She groaned and covered her face with her hand. "What a cliché I am."

"You're not a cliché. *He's* the cliché. What a jerk."

She thought she might as well get it all out there. "She's pregnant."

He shook his head. "What a douche." His lips were gentle on her ear, her neck, and a soft buzz ran down her arms. He whispered, "You deserve better than that."

His lips found hers, gently, but she wanted more. She pulled away to put down her glass, and when she did, she felt him stiffen. His head tilted down an inch, so the hair fell more fully over the injured side of his face. She wasn't going to play that game and looked at him until his eyes came up to meet hers, then she put both arms around his neck and softly kissed first one corner of his lips then the other. She felt his smile beneath her lips, and his mouth hungrily descended on hers. She felt a tightness inside her uncoil, warmth flow through her body. This was what she'd been waiting for.

Chapter 16

He'd kissed her.

Lily had been up half the night, that thought running in a loop through her head. She hadn't felt this gut-churning, all consuming, mind blowing crush since she'd been in high school.

She grinned at herself in the bathroom mirror. Although gentle and sweet, the kisses had definitely moved their relationship up a level to, well, to a relationship.

It may not last, really, could not last because they were from two very different worlds. But for now, it was exciting. What thrilled her most was that this proved without a doubt that there was more to life than Troy Brewster. That she deserved more than someone who didn't respect her and—truth be told—wasn't good enough for her.

Oh no. She could do much better.

The aroma of ground coffee went straight to her head as she spooned it into the percolator basket. She hardly had to drink it, just had to inhale it. Usually, she hurried into the resort in the morning and had coffee and breakfast there, but today she wanted to savor this moment.

She had been given a reprieve; she could have spent her whole life with Troy. A grin bloomed as she realized she was off the hook for a marriage she hadn't known she desperately wanted to escape. How could she have been so self-deluding?

Or, when he left her for Melissa, she could have stayed in the city. If she'd gone to Carmen's instead of to her dad's, she'd probably still be at her old job that, to be honest, wasn't nearly as exciting as working at the resort. She'd probably be living in a hole in the wall apartment in Seattle, working even more hours at the crisis line and generally grinding herself deeper into the same hole she'd already been in. Instead, here she was in Fortune Bay, reunited with her father and immersing herself in the exciting business of running a resort. Not to mention having a summer affair, because, after all, that was all it could be.

She'd been given a second chance at life—and maybe at love—and this time, she was not going to settle for a man who wasn't crazy about her, or for a life that wasn't full of joy and excitement.

And what was more exciting than a clandestine friendship with a famous rock star? Hell, the man was a *sex idol.* Marshall Mason was her friend, and maybe could be more. She raised her hand to rub her lips. When he'd brushed his hand down her cheek, his touch left a tingle of awareness, waking her up like the prince in a fairytale. And then, he'd kissed her. A soft, melt-her-a-puddle-of-lust kiss. No question. He'd woken up body parts that had been comatose for years. She had a feeling there was a lot more to making love than she'd experienced with Troy. And she couldn't wait.

Pulling Sweetie up onto her lap, she gave her an exuberant squeeze. "I kissed Marshall Mason!"

But the attraction wasn't just that he was famous. They'd gotten to know each other in the past few weeks and she really liked him. She wanted to help him. Help him accept the new restrictions his injuries would place on his life. They hadn't talked about it, but his condition had probably caused his depression. After all, this could mean the end of his career. His life wasn't over, but it was irrevocably changed. He wouldn't be going back to his old life of playing music and touring again any time soon. If ever.

Could he cope? What else could he do? These questions must be running over and over in his mind. And what about his family responsibilities? Why didn't he see his children? He obviously missed them. He could hardly mention them without choking up. Maybe they could visit him here in Fortune Bay.

Oh, yes. They had plenty of things to talk about.

Lily paused for a moment on the porch. She could count on the fingers of one hand the number of times she'd sat on this porch and just to enjoy the view, the way the watercolor brush strokes of spring green along the opposite shore contrasted with the rocky, peach-colored cliff above.

Now she realized why she'd never sat here, why she'd kept so busy since she'd arrived in Fortune Bay. She hadn't wanted to think. But now she wanted to take a moment, breathe in the clean air and embrace her new life. The rosebush that twined along the porch rail was showing its color. She'd hardly noticed it until now. Any day it would burst into bloom, and she'd be here to see it.

She didn't have to go back to Seattle. She could stay indefinitely in Fortune Bay, if she so chose. She could live in the cabin, at least for a while, and work with her dad at the resort. Her life here felt real in a way her busy day-to-day in the city hadn't felt for years. That had been filling the hours in the day. This was living. She didn't know what lay ahead, but it would be new and different and of her choosing.

The cabin was an oddly soothing place to live, with

its yellow table and turquoise stove, and the calendar that, strangely, always showed the right day of the week even though it was years out of date. She felt warmed in a way that might have been the sun, or the sweet smell of cookies baking that she always seemed to notice here. Like right now. She felt her blood pressure dropping and, as if she was going into a trance, sank down onto the faded couch on the porch.

This is home. The voice was not her own—it was Augusta's voice—yet the words were there inside her head.

She nodded. *Home for now.* She'd been moving at one hundred miles an hour ever since she'd come to Fortune Bay. In some ways, moving even faster than she had in Seattle, trying to outrun her thoughts. Her fears.

A warm breeze raised a light chop on the bay and the brilliant blue sky outlined the snowy peaks. The lake glittered like blinking diamonds in the morning sun. It was early in the season for the sun to be so strong and she could tell it was going to be another hot day.

Slapping her hands on her knees, she surged to her feet, went into the cabin and dug out her one-piece bathing suit. Tugging it on, she grabbed a towel from the bathroom and quickly, before she could change her mind, hurried down to the pebble beach.

The stones cut into her feet as she approached the shore and she stood for a moment on the large flat rock that sloped into the water, feeling it cool and smooth against the soles of her feet. Then she stepped into the water, fresh as a spring tonic, and before rational thought could interfere, splashed a few freezing steps into the lake and dove under.

Like a baptism, the shock washed away the

remnants of her trance-like state, the iciness soothing her ravaged heart. She shot out of the water a new person, starting over, vowing she would live her life differently, feel every emotion honestly, starting today.

Freezing and laughing at the insanity of swimming when snow still clung to the mountain peaks, she splashed her way to the shore. Her skin was red and tingled as if she'd rubbed her body with a stiff towel. She felt alive, and determined to hold onto the feeling.

Change was good. No more sham of a marriage to keep her on edge, no more lying to herself. It still hurt horribly, the betrayal most of all, but like the pain after a bad tooth has been pulled, the underlying ache was gone; an ache she'd barely known she'd been harboring because it had grown slowly, relentlessly, for so many years. Its absence was the source of her new-found calm.

As she rubbed her body with the big bath towel trying to restore the circulation, Frankie emerged from the path through the trees. "Are you insane? That water's freezing."

Lily laughed. "But invigorating."

"I bet. I'll wait another few weeks before I go in though, thank you very much. I just came by to tell you we found a dress for Louise. A full length, white maternity gown. It should be perfect."

Lily toweled the dripping tendrils of her hair. "Where did you find it?"

"Online. They're sending it by express post so we should get it in time for the wedding. I hope." She held up both hands, fingers crossed. "Louise is so excited. I guess I'd feel the same way if it was my wedding."

"Any news on that front?" Lily asked as she wrapped herself in the towel.

"No. Not yet. I'm thinking August. Get Sean and

Amber moved in before school starts, while Amber and I are on vacation. I'm hoping it will give us a chance to bond a bit, decorating her room, letting her help finish the family room. I'm just on my way to school, now. Classes are finished but there are still exams and the final wrap-up. I can't wait for vacation to start, although, I can see I'll be spending the first month painting."

Despite her words, Frankie looked radiant at the prospect of her new family. And for the first time Lily believed it could happen to her, too. That miracles really could happen.

Lily had been watching the town Facebook page all week, fighting down the hope that Sweetie was hers, dreading the possibility that someone would claim her. She had checked the notices for lost dogs stapled to power poles in town, but this week they were looking for a Rottweiler and a Beagle—not Sweetie.

The small bag of food she'd bought at the general store was almost empty. She'd check the Facebook page one more time, then buy more food. Surely a week was long enough to wait for her owners to step forward, if they were out there.

The page wasn't very active; someone giving away a kid's swing set, someone else complaining the squirrels had dug up their tulips. No comments on the post about Sweetie. But what was this? A new post asking, who was this mysterious stranger in town.

Lily's heart sank when she saw the dark, blurry, unrecognizable photo that was probably Marshall, sitting on his shady porch. Luckily, there was only one comment from someone who thought it looked like Darth Vader. Hopefully there wouldn't be any interest and the post would sink to the bottom of the Facebook pile, but she planned to keep an eye on it.

She'd smuggled Sweetie into her office again, although she knew no one was fooled. Chloe always brought a little treat from home for the pup, and one day, Lily had caught her dad getting a facewash from Sweetie. The dog seemed happy to sleep the day away, so for these first transitional days it seemed to be working out.

On her lunch hour, with Sweetie trotting at her heels, Lily went down to the resort dock. Four canoes lay in a row, overturned on the shore. Small motorboats and paddle boats were tied to the dock, with the rowboats tied down at the end.

Tonight, the moon would be almost full. She was hoping to tempt Marshall out on the water in one of the boats.

Johnny, a good-looking Native American guy she'd met at team meetings and stealing pastries in the kitchen, was responsible for the boats and swimming gear. He was in one of the motorboats, his long shiny hair falling seductively over his forehead as he wiped down the leather seats. Two young teenage girls sunbathed on the dock under his nose, pretending not to notice him. Lily stepped carefully over the girls, but when Sweetie pranced by, they sat up, hastily adjusting their bikini tops.

"Hey, Lily," Johnny said. "What can I do for you?"

"Can I try out one of the rowboats?"

"Sure. Have you rowed before?"

"A bit, as a child. I might need some instruction."

He climbed out of the motorboat and walked down to the rowboats at the end of the dock. As he passed, the girls erupted in bubbles of stifled giggles.

"Your fan club?" Lily whispered with a smile.

Johnny laughed. "I guess. They've been lying here every afternoon for the past few days."

The rowboats were tied to the dock, their overlapping, ship-lap sides painted white with blue stripes at the gunnel, the colors of all the resort's aquatic equipment.

"Can you get in yourself?" he asked. "They can be tippy. You have to face the stern."

Lily sat on the dock and Johnny gave her a hand as she stepped down into the boat. Tippy barely described it, and she was glad to hold his strong arm. She plunked down on the seat facing the end where the gunnels swooped together in a gentle arc. "This is a lovely boat."

"The pointy end is the bow," he explained gently, hiding a smile. "It cuts the water more easily than the flat end."

Lily's cheeks burned, and she swung her feet around until she was facing the flat end. "I know that." Sweetie jumped in without hesitation. It seemed wherever Lily went, the dog was happy to follow.

Johnny untied the ropes from the bow and the stern, setting her loose, and gave the boat a push away from the dock. The oars were hinged in oarlocks on the gunnels, halfway down the sides of the boat, the blades resting on the stern. She took hold of the handles and the oars seemed unnecessarily long and awkward, the handles hitting her in the chest as she dropped the blades into the water and pushed. They dug into the water, but she seemed to be moving backwards, plowing the flat end through the water. "This can't be right."

She glanced at Johnny over her shoulder as she drifted away from the dock. "It's harder than it looks."

Johnny called out, "Lift the oars out of the water and reach forward. Now drop the blades into the water and pull back."

She felt the resistance of the water but managed to pull the oars to her chest. The boat stopped moving forward—or was it backward? —and she lifted the blades out of the water, reached forward and dug in again. The rowboat glided backwards through the water. She quickly glanced over her shoulder and realized she was heading straight into the dock.

Johnny got down on one knee and caught the bow of the boat and gave it a shove away from the dock again. "Use only one oar to turn," he called.

She dropped one blade into the water and let it drift, using both hands to crank on the other oar. The boat turned in a tight circle until she was facing the dock and the pointy end, the bow, was pointing across the bay. Not in the direction of Marshall's dock, but she wasn't planning to go there until dusk. And she obviously needed to practice, first. She spent the next half hour weaving back and forth across the bay, turning awkwardly at each end. Finally, looking over her shoulder to navigate, pulling a bit on one oar then a bit on the other, she managed to land back at the dock. Johnny got down on his knees and caught the nose of the boat to prevent a crash landing.

"It's harder than I remember," she said, climbing out onto the dock while Johnny steadied the boat. "But then, I always went with Dad."

She looked at the rocks at the point, suddenly unsure about rowing to Marshall's dock alone at dusk. "Could you take a boat over to the dock at Cottage Four before you finish this evening and leave it there for the night? Dad will okay it."

"I can do that," Johnny agreed, reaching down to tie up the boat and then climbing in to arrange the oars with the blades resting on the stern. She'd have to remember to leave it like that tonight. She hoped

Marshall knew more about boats than she did, or this could prove to be a disaster.

"And if you have a light, that would be good too," she added.

He winked. "Will do."

Chapter 17

That night at dusk Lily returned to the resort, left her car in the parking lot and took the lakeside path around the point to the cottages. Sweetie trotted happily at her heels, up for a nighttime adventure. The sun had dipped below the mountains half an hour ago and darkness was falling fast. At the boat dock, white and blue boats glowed in the fading light, bobbing on the gentle swells. Lily blushed to remember Johnny's conspiratorial wink when she left him at the dock and wondered if he thought she was having a romantic tryst.

And maybe she was. Excitement bubbled inside her. Marshall was surprisingly sweet, and she needed this. Needed confirmation that at thirty-eight she was still a desirable woman, not a washed up, uninteresting ex-wife.

Was a summer fling between consenting adults wrong?

Well, yes, she had to admit, it may be a bad idea between these particular consenting adults, one just getting out of a long-term relationship and one struggling with depression. She stopped in her tracks and closed her eyes. What was she thinking?

Then she opened her eyes and started walking again. But nothing wrong with helping a fellow human being, *a friend*, take the first steps out of a lonely dark place.

She hadn't been able to stop thinking about the difference between the man on the videos and the man

Marshall had become since the accident. Or had that man—the boy who played with his brothers on the raft on the lake—always been there, lurking beneath the Nashville and L.A. glitter and glam? The glitter and glamor were intriguing, but she wanted to know about his childhood, too. And what had happened in the accident that had brought him to where he was now. She wished they could talk about it. Keeping the past bottled inside wouldn't help him heal. She picked up her pace. Maybe they would start tonight.

An almost-full moon rose at the end of the lake, reflecting on the water as the stars began to glimmer overhead. The perfect night for a moonlight row. As she passed the eight-plex condo pods, sounds of a family settling their children down for sleep drifted out the open sliding doors. It was only the beginning of the season. More families would arrive in force in a few weeks when the kids were all out of school.

She was curious about Marshall's children. She didn't think of him as a family man, but he'd sure looked like it in the pictures. In one, he'd been throwing his daughter up in the air. What would she have been? Four? Maybe five? And that heart wrenching photograph of her crying on his shoulder. That had been taken during the divorce, one short year ago. What a terrible year for those children—for that family—having their world blow apart. He must miss them so.

Moonlight lit the path and as she took the last turn through the trees she saw the rowboat bobbing on the water. *Thank you, Johnny.* Walking up the flagstone path to the cottage, her stomach suddenly started churning and she reminded herself that this boating excursion was for Marshall. It did kind of feel like a date, though. The full moon and the soft summer night were certainly romantic.

Her footsteps slowed as she approached the cottage door. What was she thinking? He wasn't in any shape to be...probably wasn't thinking about... She put her hands on her burning cheeks. *Pull yourself together.* He was definitely thinking about it last night when he'd kissed her.

She shook her head and knocked on the door. "Marshall, it's me."

The fact that he wouldn't open the door to a stranger was evidence enough that he wasn't ready for any kind of relationship. And even if he was ready emotionally, why would a guy like him, handsome, rich and *famous*, pick her. *Don't get ahead of yourself.*

The door swung open and he was silhouetted against the dim light of the interior, his hair covering half of his face, the other half radiating sex and danger. She shivered. Lately she'd caught glimpses of the underlying magnetism that had made him a star, that made women fall at his feet.

Then he turned on the porch light—and the moment passed. He was Marshall again.

Quite the imagination.

"Lily. What are you doing here?"

"I just thought you might..." *This was a bad idea.*

He opened the door and Sweetie launched herself at him. He knelt to pat her. "Might what?"

He stood up and stepped out onto the porch. In the moonlight she could see he was smiling. In fact, he looked happy to see her, and she took the courage she needed to continue from that. "I have a boat. I thought you might want to go for a row."

He grinned. "You what?" He looked around her down to the dock. "How did you manage that?"

She smiled. "It's a resort, Duffus. We have boats.

That's why people come here. Although most of them go out on the water in the daylight..."

"No. This is perfect. Just let me get changed."

He was wearing sweatpants and a torn black t-shirt. "It doesn't really matter."

"Don't go anywhere. I'll be right back." He darted into the house, closing the door behind him.

Lily turned and looked out at the lake. She licked her dry lips. So far so good. He seemed excited. Her heart gave a flutter. *She* was excited.

She hoped he knew how to row better than she did.

Moments later, he stepped out onto the porch. He had changed into cargo shorts and a clean white t-shirt that outlined his shoulders in the dim light. For the first time, she was aware that he was quite tall, at least six feet. He'd always seemed stooped and withdrawn before, but now his shoulders broadened on top of a long, lean swimmer's body.

He tipped his head in question. Right. He was waiting for her. "Okay. Let's go," she said, and turning abruptly, started down the steps. "It's a great night for a row, with the full moon. I had Johnny bring the boat by earlier. I hope he put in life preservers." She was babbling. As they walked onto the long dock, she bit her lip to force herself to stop talking.

He got down on one knee to examine the boat. "Nice boat. I've been watching them out on the lake."

She sat on the edge of the dock resting her feet on the gunnel. "I hope you know how to row. I'm pretty pathetic."

He was still for a moment, then cleared his throat. "I do know how, but I don't know if I can. My hand." He rubbed his bad hand, hiding it with the other.

"Oh. Wow. Sorry." *Who's the Duffus now?* "Well, I can row. I rowed this afternoon, just badly. You can give me instructions." She stepped into the boat, causing it to rock wildly. Last thing she needed was to go into the drink. His hand was warm and firm when she reached for him, and she gripped it tightly, longer than needed, until finally the boat stopped rocking and she had to let go.

He untied the ropes and threw them into the boat. Sweetie jumped in and raced up to stand with her paws on the bow. Then, causing barely a wobble, he dropped onto the seat in the stern, facing Lily, and pushed off. She took hold of the oars. They were secured to the oar locks with pins, the blades resting on either side of Marshall on the flat transom behind his seat. Again, like earlier in the day, they felt long and cumbersome and she couldn't remember which way to push—or was it pull? —the handles.

In trying to get them into the water, she whacked him in the shoulder with the blade. She giggled. "Sorry. I'll try not to knock you into the water."

Using his hands, he moved the oars out of the danger zone. "I'd appreciate that."

She suppressed her laughter as she tried to remember the sequence she'd learned earlier in the day. "Now, oars in the water, push, lift."

The boat moved—the wrong way. Marshall put out a hand to stop the gunnel from banging into the dock.

Lily couldn't stop giggling. "You think this is bad. Getting away from the dock isn't half as much of a problem as getting back. We may have to swim."

"Having me in the stern doesn't help. The balance is wrong, the bow too high out of the water. But I want to ... talk."

Talking was good, but what he really wanted was to do was look at her. The moon behind him lit up her face. She was still laughing, a careless, girlish laugh that warmed his heart and made him smile.

"Brace your feet on this board on the bottom," he said.

She put her feet on the bracing board he indicated, the moonlight caressing her long, perfect legs, from the trim ankle up to where her rounded thighs disappeared into the crisp, tiny shorts. Womanly hips narrowed to her waist and with each pull back on the oars, her rounded breasts thrust forward, straining the buttons on her sleeveless blouse until he thought the buttons might pop. He hardly dared to breath.

Even when she was rowing in the right direction, she was a disaster with the oars. She reached forward again and on the next pull, one blade dug in but the other one didn't, skimming the surface of the water, hitting him with a cold spray. The laughter bubbled up again and although she tried to hide it, she couldn't stop.

And Marshall couldn't stop smiling. "Make a big oval shape with the handles," he said, demonstrating with his hands. "Hold them high when you're pulling back, to keep the blades in the water. Then when you get to your, ah, chest, push down to bring the blades out of the water. Keep your hands down as you push forward. That'll keep the blades high and not splash us, then drop them into the water..." he stopped demonstrating as she started to row in time with his words. "Pull...hands down, blades up, lean forward, and drop."

She had it now, rowing more smoothly over the moon-dappled surface of the bay.

"Johnny said there were running lights," she said. He felt around at the stern for the switch and a small white light flashed on at the bow.

Marshall stretched his legs wide in front of him on

either side of hers and leaned back to look at the stars. "I love this. The stars are so bright. There's Orion." He pointed to the sky. "And wow, that must be a planet."

"I think I saw in the paper that it's Jupiter."

"So bright." Lily was rowing smoothly now, so he put his hands behind his neck to cushion his head and let his thoughts drift, carried away on the soft summer air.

"So, how old are your kids," she asked, out of the blue.

Marshall froze. A reasonable question. She couldn't know what a sore spot it was for him. "A girl, five, and a boy, eight."

"You must miss them."

There was no sound but the dip and plop of the oars. The transom was digging into his back, but he didn't want to sit up and face her. "I do."

"What are their names?" Her voice was languid. Just making conversation.

"Emily and Boston."

A pause, then she giggled. "Boston?"

He sat up. "Their mother's idea. It was a thing a few years ago to name your kids after cities. She thought Boston sounded like a boy's name. I was never a fan."

"Do you see them much?"

No, and it's tearing me apart. He looked into her eyes, soft and compassionate. "Not as much as I'd like."

"Maybe now that school's almost over they could come for a visit."

Even if their mother agreed, could he risk seeing the horror in their eyes when they saw his face? Risk having them pull away from the touch of his clawed hand? "Maybe."

They'd rowed around the rocky point and into a large bay. Marshall wracked his brain for safer topic. "Where are we going?"

Lily stopped rowing, put down the oars and let them drift. "This is Fortune Bay. You see that little white cabin over there, with the light on over the steps? That's where I live. For now." She paused for a beat. "It's haunted."

He let out a whoop that echoed into the darkness across the bay. "Seriously?"

Her nose wrinkled. "Apparently. Although she hasn't appeared to me yet. Her sister, who lived there last month, and my friend Louise have seen her. I guess we haven't been roommates for long enough yet. Maybe when she gets to know me better... I do think she talks to me though. Inside my head. It's hard to explain... And she turns on the porch light for me at night."

She flipped her head sending her ponytail over her shoulder as she looked behind her at the cabin, then back to the point from which they'd come. Marshall flexed his hands. He wanted to take the elastic out of her hair and run his hands through the silky strands. How would she react if he did? What was she thinking, bringing him here? Was it an act of charity? A friendly gesture? Or was it more? The kiss on the porch had him voting for more.

"How do you turn this thing around?" she asked, grinning and flailing the oars in the water. "Something about 'one, one way and the other, the other way'." A laugh bubbled up that made him want to laugh, too.

He reached forward and put his hands, both hands, on hers. She looked up quickly in surprise. His heart froze, then she smiled. The iciness in his core began to thaw. She didn't pull away, didn't even look away, or at his bad hand, just smiled into his eyes. So he pushed with one hand and pulled with the other, showing her how to turn the boat around on the spot.

"Oh, that's fun," she exclaimed. As she finished the turn, over-turned and managed to get them more-or-less on track, he took his hands off hers and laughed out loud.

A charge went through him, sharp and metallic, part fun, part fear. It was the first time he'd laughed in over a year. A real laugh that felt warm and good in his stomach, not one of the alcohol-induced, *you can't hurt me* laughs that had been so common during the divorce, or the *everything's really all right* laughs he'd put on for the sake of the children. And since the accident, he was pretty sure he hadn't laughed at all.

"So, tell me this," she said, looking over her shoulder, the bow of the boat heading first too far out into the lake, then too far into the shore. "How do you know where you're going? You can't row looking over your shoulder. How do you stay on course?"

"Get the bow pointed where you want to go."

She looked over her shoulder and he pulled on one oar until they were headed to a spot just out beyond the point. "Now look straight ahead, past me. Find the spot on the land that's dead center on the stern and keep it there as you row."

"My cabin," she said, and started to row. Slowly they began to move and as he watched the swoop and strain of her muscles with each pull, the desire to feel that power in his own limbs again began to grow.

As they rounded the point, she dropped the oars again, letting them float on the water. "I really don't think I can get the boat into the dock without crashing."

He looked at his hands, did an experimental flex. It was only about a hundred feet, and his claw-like hand might actually be the right curve to hold the oar. "I'll take us in."

Her eyes widened. "How do we switch places?"

He felt warm inside to know that that her only question was, *how do we switch?* Not, *can you do it?* He smiled and put a hand on each gunnel. "We just switch. Can you swim?"

She laughed. "I don't want to."

He shifted his weight forward onto his hands. "Sneak under my arm. We used to do this all the time when we were kids."

She giggled and dived for the bottom of the boat.

"Slowly. Move slowly or you'll tip me over the side."

She slid up beside him and he turned lightly on his feet, keeping his center of balance low, and sat on the center seat. The boat wobbled, so he put his hands back on the gunnels and leaned forward. She did the same, bringing them nose to nose as the boat slowly settled.

She smiled and whispered, "We did it."

She was so close, lit only by the moonlight, her eyes and lips inches from his. Her eyes were smiling, and he knew, just knew, that he wasn't a damn project. She really liked him and, wonder of wonders, didn't seem put off by the scars on his face. He grinned and felt the stiffness in his scarred cheek begin to give.

He reached for the oars. The shafts fit intimately, like an old friend, into the palm of his good hand—and adequately in the other. He could do this. It wasn't far. He pulled on the oars and the boat shot past the point. He had to adjust, the left hand wasn't as steady or strong on the oar, but it wasn't bad either. He squeezed it tighter and felt some response.

The dig of the muscles in his shoulders, the stress on his thighs as he pressed his feet into the brace on the floor left him wanting more. Wanting to take the boat for a lap around the lake, but his time was up. They were already pulling up to the dock. Probably enough for the first time anyway, he thought as he pulled on one oar and the boat swung in nice and tight to the edge of the dock.

"Perfect," Lily said, raising her eyebrows, obviously impressed. He felt a foolish burst of pride. It was only a landing, but he'd always been a show-off. He knew who he was, and suddenly he saw that one of the hardest things about this recovery was just that. He'd lost his pride.

She grabbed the side of the dock and held the boat there. Sweetie gave a yip, jumped on the empty seat and up onto the dock. Marshall lifted the oars out of the locks and stored them lengthwise on the seats, then hopped out onto the dock feeling lighter than he had in months. Reaching down, he took Lily's offered hands and helped her step up onto the dock, then kept her hands in his, not wanting to let go.

"Thank you. It was wonderful to get out on the water like that."

She beamed. "I remembered you saying how you and your brothers had a boat."

He was still holding her hands. "You know, I'd like to do a bit of rowing every day. Maybe early in the mornings. I need some exercise to get these muscles back in shape."

"You could walk down to the main dock and borrow the boats any time."

He stilled. That was...too much. "Could I rent a boat? Keep it here at the dock?"

Lily smiled. "I don't know. I'll ask."

He couldn't just let her go. Not without knowing what she was feeling. If he was imagining the heat between them. If she was just being kind.

Keeping his good hand in hers, he brought up the other hand, tingling now from the unaccustomed use, to brush a loose strand of hair back from her face.

Her eyes were focused on his. Apparently unconcerned about the state of his fingers, she reached up and rubbed her hand down his jawline, rasping the five-o'clock shadow. He wanted to lean into it like a cat, suddenly realizing how much he'd missed the human contact, loving her for accepting him as he was.

She left her fingertips gently touching his cheek, a clear signal in his book. Once it had been second nature to kiss any woman who stopped in his path for more than a minute. That was usually what they were after, and it meant squat. But this time he felt truly grateful and his lips were tender when they found hers. The air shimmered as she relaxed into the kiss. Possibilities blossomed in his chest.

He was back.

Chapter 18

"Sorry I'm late," Lily said to Chloe as she hurried into the resort lobby.

Between calls, Chloe smirked around the headphones. "I think someone got lucky last night."

"Who, me?" Lily tried to get her face under control and brush off the comment. "With whom?"

"Your secret guest in Cottage Four."

Lily turned her back to the room and shushed her friend sternly. "You know we're trying to keep that quiet."

"I know, but who is it? Do you know? You'd think it's the President of the United States or Harrison Ford with the hush hush around here."

Lily tried not to smile. "Nothing that exciting. Just someone with personal problems who likes his privacy."

Max walked into the foyer from the dining room.

"Dad, can I talk to you in your office for a minute?"

"Certainly, honey."

Lily followed her father into his office and closed the door. "It's about Mr., ah, Morris in Cottage Four. And just so you know, I know who he is."

"Well, I guess you had to figure it out sooner or later. How is he doing?"

"Pretty well," she said brightly. "I took him out for a row last night and—"

"*You* took him out?"

"Yes. He told me he used to love going out in the

boats at his family cottage and I thought he might like to get out on the lake."

"Well." Max thought this over. "Good."

"We've gotten to be friends." She tried to suppress a blush but wasn't sure she succeeded. She cleared her throat. "Anyway, he asked if he could rent one of the boats for the length of his stay." *Because, right, he isn't here permanently.* When they had both been temporary visitors to Fortune Bay, she hadn't really thought about the future, but now that she was planning to stay for a while, it was uncomfortable to think that at some point he'd have to leave.

But her dad was talking. "—only the two rowboats so I don't want one of them permanently tied up. We have more guests arriving every day and soon we'll be running at capacity. But you could call Alex at the marina. He might have a boat to rent or know where you could get one."

So that's what she did. Alex had one and said he would bring it round later in the day. Marshall could rent it for as long as he was at the cottage.

"And who should I make it out for?"

"Marshall...Morris." It was getting hard to think of him as anyone other than Marshall Mason. She had to be careful if she was going to protect his identity.

* * *

Later that afternoon, Marshall sat in the seclusion of his porch with his headphones on, listening to music on his laptop. Seduced by the sultry air, he was in a private world with his eyes closed and his hat pulled low on his forehead. He'd been in self-imposed exile for months now and suddenly needed to know what was happening in the industry. Little Big Town had a new song out that sounded good, and Keith and Carrie had teamed up on one that he was sure was going to be a hit.

Something whacked him in the shoulder with enough force to propel him onto his feet, his heart pounding. He ripped off the headphones, dislodging his hat in the process. He was alone on the porch, but a frisbee lay at his feet. The patter of feet on the stairs had him searching for his hat, but it had flown across the porch and there was no way he could reach it before two young kids, about the same age as his own two, charged up onto the porch.

The girl was the older of the two, probably around ten, and immediately took charge. "Hello."

He looked anxiously over the railing, hoping their parents were hot on their heels, but no luck. He looked back at the girl who was waiting expectantly.

"This your frisbee?" He bent to pick it up, letting his hair fall over his cheek.

"Yes, thank you." She tilted her head to one side and studied his face. Her brother took the frisbee and with a quick, *thank you,* ran back down the stairs, calling, "Come on, Lindy," over his shoulder.

Please, just go, Marshall begged silently. But instead, she openly scrutinized his face, interested but seemingly not upset. Finally, she asked, "What happened to your face?"

He couldn't move, his throat was dry, but he managed force out the words. "An accident."

She nodded seriously, thinking it over. "Does it hurt?"

He shook his head. "Not anymore."

She smiled. "That's good. Thanks for getting our frisbee." Then she turned and raced after her brother.

He watched as she ran back to the small yard

behind the cottage next door. Her brother fired the frisbee at her. She didn't look back.

Kids were so honest. They hadn't screamed, hadn't shrunk away. She'd just asked the obvious question, considered the answer and accepted it at face value. The little boy hadn't seemed to notice at all.

Marshall went inside and looked in the mirror, pulling the hair away from his face and scrutinizing the scar in a way he hadn't for months. It had actually healed quite well. Wasn't blazing red like a wound anymore. In fact, it was almost the same color as the rest of his face. Another surgery would open it up again and, for a while, he'd be back to square one with a wound on his face stitched up like Frankenstein. The doctors had said every subsequent surgery would heal better than the last, but he didn't know if he could face that. Yet.

Lily didn't seem to mind it the way it was, and her disinterest made him wonder if he hadn't blown it out of proportion in his mind. She didn't cringe when he'd kissed her. He'd been trying not to think about the kiss all day because he didn't know what to think. Maybe he shouldn't have done it—it just confused their relationship and he counted on her so much these days. He hoped he hadn't ruined their friendship, that his hunger for human contact—for her—hadn't scared her away.

Although, as he recalled, she hadn't shrunk from his kiss. Instead, she had softened into it, not brazenly like so many of the women he'd known in recent years, as if their response was some sort of competition. As if they had something to prove.

Refreshingly sweet and womanly, she seemed to genuinely care.

The sound of a motorboat brought him to the door.

It was putt-ing toward his dock and as it approached he could see it was pulling another, smaller boat. A rowboat. He smiled. Lily had come through again.

The driver expertly docked the launch and climbed out. He pulled the rowboat in by the tow line and tied it up, but then, instead of getting back into the boat, he came toward the cottage, lifting his hand in a casual greeting. Marshall grabbed his hat and put it on his head, tugging it low.

"Hi, there," the man said as he reached the porch. "Are you Marshall Morris? Did you order a rowboat?"

Marshall nodded. "That would be me."

Now the man was up on the porch and holding out his hand to shake. Marshall felt backed into a corner, but took a deep breath and shook the man's hand.

"I'm Alex Porter. Run the marina across the lake. Lily Brewster called and asked me to bring the boat by. How long are you planning to stay in Fortune Bay?"

"I...I'm not sure. A couple more weeks at least."

"That's fine. There are two life jackets in the boat. Just let me know when you're ready to leave. Lily said I could bill you through the resort."

"Yes, good." Did he even have a credit card with him? He'd been in such sorry shape when Harry had settled him in, and with his food and beverage needs billed to the resort and the general store, he hadn't needed a credit card before now. His wallet was probably in the bedroom. Was he supposed to tip this man? Harry handled that too when they were on the road. The man was still stand there, looking at him. He held out his hand again. "Thank you for bringing it by. I'll take good care of it."

"No problem," Alex said, and shook his hand, his eyes narrowing slightly. "Just let me know when you're done with it."

Marshall smiled back stiffly, waiting for him to figure out who he was. "I'll do that."

With a wave, Alex headed back to his boat and Marshall let out a huge sigh of relief. He hadn't figured it out. Or if he had, he hadn't acted on it. Nothing weird had happened. It had felt kind of...normal. More normal, in fact, than any encounter he'd had with anyone in years. Except for Lily.

A smile formed on his lips. *I like this place.*

But meeting Alex raised a bunch of new questions. Should he be tipping the waiter who left his meals for him on the porch each evening? Should he be tipping Lily? No. That would be insulting. She wasn't really a maid and now that he knew that, he was kind of embarrassed to have her cleaning for him at all. He could take care of himself, and maybe he should.

He'd have think of some other way to thank her for all she had done.

The next morning the sky was bright, but the sun had not yet risen over the hills at the head of the lake when Marshall carried the oars down to the dock. He'd gone down the evening before and inspected the rowboat. It was an old one, hand crafted, even nicer than the boats the resort owned. The oars had a curve to the blade and were loose in the oar locks which gave you greater control of the angle of the blades in the water—or less control, depending on your degree of expertise. He smiled at the thought of Lily struggling to maneuver the much simpler set-lock oars. She'd be flailing with these.

He'd taken them up to the cottage for the night, old habits from his youth kicking in. This one was a lot like the boat they'd had at the cottage when he was growing up. Like the Olympic Peninsula, the lakes in Minnesota were cold into July, but that never stopped him and his brothers from swimming and horsing around in the water.

This morning, the lake was smooth. Clear as glass. Every stone on the bottom looked like it was just below the surface, until it all dropped away into unfathomable darkness. His chest constricted with exquisite excitement as he stepped carefully into the boat. Except for the other night with Lily, it had been at least twenty years since he had rowed. Settling himself on the seat, he tested the foot brace on the bottom and decided it was set at just the right distance. It must have been Alex, or someone his height, who'd rowed it last.

He flexed both of his hands, not sure how far he'd get, but the row with Lily the other night had broken the spell of lethargy he'd been under since leaving the hospital. He'd remembered what it felt like to feel the fresh night air on his face and the rewarding burn of using muscles in his thighs and arms and shoulders. And what it was like to spend time with a woman who made him feel like a man.

One at a time, he dropped the iron pins into the oar locks and gripped the shafts. Checking the angle of the blade, he thought he had it just right, and pushed away from the dock, far enough for the oars to have room to arc over the water. Leaning forward, he dipped the blades into the still water and pulled. The boat shot ahead. He adjusted the grip of his left hand and pulled again.

Between pulls, he rolled his stiff shoulder, enjoying the burn. He'd always worked out, both at home and on the road. It centered him, preserved his sanity in the crazy world of entertainment. He loved the writing, the playing, performing in front of the crowds, but the constant travel had gotten old. Maybe he didn't need the glory anymore, certainly not as much as he had when he was thirty and couldn't get enough of screaming fans. Now the entourage had grown into an unwieldy machine that controlled his every move, on the road and off. It interfered with his family life, had destroyed his marriage and had turned his children into virtual strangers.

To counteract the stress, he'd taken the time to work out and to ride his motorcycle. On the open road, he could be any guy—and it had felt like freedom. Kind of like this.

His muscles strained against the resistance of the water and, engaging his core, he sent a surge of power from his legs to his arms and out through the shaft to the blades.

The boat flew across the water and as the sun rose above the eastern hills, his body came alive.

Chapter 19

Lily had lunch with her father the following day.

"So, how are you doing, honey?" Max asked as they sat at a table in the restaurant. "I hardly see you. I have to thank you for the load of work you've taken off my shoulders, but what about you? You doing okay?"

"I'm fine. I keep taking on more—but I love it. Just keeping the books would be dull compared to the work I do now. I really enjoy working with Frankie on Louise's wedding preparations, and helping Sean get ready for the fishing derby."

"And you're okay about Troy?"

"The painful part is over and now I'm kind of glad it happened." Marshall's face flashed through her mind and she hoped she wasn't blushing. "It's time to start over." She looked out the window. "I'm just still trying to I figure out what that's going to look like."

Max straightened in his chair. "I know what you mean. I'm starting over here, too."

Lily smiled. "I guess you are."

He nodded. "It takes a while to make new friends. To start a new life. Don't rush it. Take your time. See what comes your way." His cheeks turned pink and he cleared his throat. "How is it going with Marshall?"

Lily busied herself with her spaghetti. "I don't know. We're friends."

"Good friends?"

She nodded at her plate. "Good friends."

"Just be careful, honey. I know you're a grown

woman and everything, but he's not like other men you've known."

"I know. I've seen the YouTube videos, but the funny thing is, he really is just like other people. Maybe he wasn't before, but his life has changed since the accident. And, well, I think I'm helping him come to terms with it."

"But what about when he goes back? You know he has to go back sometime."

Her eyes felt dry and she held them open unnaturally wide. She looked back out the window. This was something she'd been trying not to think about, that Marshall could walk away at any time. She tried to smile brightly at her dad. "I know. He might go back. Will go back." She closed her eyes and ran her hands through her hair. "I don't know, Dad. I'm trying to keep my distance, be smart, but we really seem to have a connection."

Her father frowned. "In his world, you don't make connections. Or at least not lasting connections. When the gig's over, you move on. That's what he's used to."

She bit her lip. He was right. She could be setting herself up for heartbreak because she was afraid she was falling for Marshall Mason.

* * *

Max took the shoreline path to the cottages. Everything looked ship-shape. The gardeners were doing a good job of grooming the trail, leaving the wild look but keeping it safe. Couldn't have someone tripping and suing.

Who was he kidding? This was neither a supervisory inspection nor a casual stroll. It was time to put a face to the name—Marshall Mason. Max had checked him out online when he had moved into Cottage Four, hoping he wasn't making a mistake letting a big star like that who probably liked to party move into his quiet family oasis. But the bottom line was, they needed the money in this crucial start-up period.

You couldn't believe everything you read online, but his years in the hotel business had taught him that musicians had a well-found reputation for partying. He'd told Mason's manager right up front that this wasn't a party place, that if he had too many guests or made too much noise, he'd have to leave. His manager, Harry, told Max he didn't have to worry, that Marshall was looking for peace and anonymity. And he'd been right. So far, Max hadn't heard a sound from the last cottage and hadn't caught a glimpse of the guy. No problems at all. And the steady income had been welcome.

Max appreciated Lily's help and discretion in overseeing the needs of their special guest, but since she told him she'd befriended the star, he'd begun to worry. He didn't want to overstep his bounds, jump in and try to father his grown daughter when he'd never been there for her before, but she was vulnerable, getting over a nasty break-up that looked like it was headed for divorce.

Over the years he'd done stints at hotels in Nashville, New York and Los Angeles, and he'd seen the way entertainers 'entertained'. He didn't want Lily getting in over her head. Didn't want her getting hurt.

He rounded the bend that set the last two cottages off from the rest of the resort. A boat bobbed in the water at the dock. A man sat quietly on the porch of Cottage Four. Max had heard about the accident—horrific from what Stephanie had said—and he didn't want to intrude. But there was nothing out-of-place with the manager checking in with his guests. In fact, it was kind of crazy that Marshall had been here for two whole months and Max hadn't met him yet.

As he walked up the flagstone path to the front steps, he noted the porch looked in good shape. Of course, Lily would have reported if there were any problems—excess drinking or underage guests.

The man saw him and rose from the chair. He was tall and lean, wearing a broad brimmed hat even in the shade of the porch. His laptop was open on the coffee table in front of him.

"Hello there," Max said, climbing the stairs and extending his hand. The man hesitated for a second then put his hand out to shake. Firm grip. A good sign.

"Hello." His voice was carefully neutral, neither welcoming nor rude.

'I'm Max Finster, owner and manager of the resort." Max used his hearty, friendly-host voice. "Just thought it was time we met."

The man nodded. "Is there a problem?"

"No problem. Just a courtesy call. I would have come when you moved in, but your manager said you wanted total seclusion. I hope everything has been to your satisfaction, Mr. Mason."

Marshall visibly relaxed. "Yes. Thank you. Have a seat. Can I get you a drink?"

He held his head at a strange angle, pretty well hiding the facial injury Max had heard about. "Thank you. That would be nice." As Marshall passed him to go inside, he caught a glimpse of the too-smooth patch of skin that stretched from his jawline to his nose and from the corner of his lips to his eye socket.

While Marshall was inside, Max glanced at the computer screen and was surprised to see a chess game in play. Marshall reappeared with two bottles of water in one hand and handed one to Max. The other hand was shoved in his pocket.

"This cottage is nice and peaceful," Marshall said. "I'm enjoying the lake."

"I've loved this location since I first laid eyes on it. It was just a patch of forest then, but right away I knew I wanted to build here."

"Have you been in the hotel business long?"

"All my life. It was a good life, except it kept me on the road too darn much. Hard on the family."

Marshall hesitated for a moment, then said, "You're Lily's father."

Max smiled. "I am." An awkward silence followed. Then Max said, "I hope she's been taking good care of you." *But not too good.*

Marshall nodded. "She's been very thoughtful. Putting me on the meal plan—your chef is fantastic, by the way—and facilitating the rental of the rowboat for me."

"Have you been getting out in the boat much?"

"Some."

Not an easy man to talk to. Max wondered what he was like with Lily, if she had the magic touch. "I see you're playing chess. I like a good game myself. Never tried it on the computer, though."

"It passes the time."

"Interested in having a real game sometime?"

For a simple question, Marshall gave it serious thought. He turned and Max could see the extent of the damage to his face. The scar wasn't that bad, but the lack of expression on that side of his face that might have been the result from muscle damage was slightly disconcerting.

"I'd like that. Do you have a set?"

"I do. That would be great. I haven't found anyone to play with since I moved to Fortune Bay. How about tomorrow evening? I could come by after work."

Marshall stood up and Max took that as his cue to leave. As they shook hands, Marshall said, "I'll look forward to it."

Max had a lot to think about as he walked back to his office. Marshall wasn't the man he'd expected, but he'd reserve judgement until he got to know him better. You can learn a lot about a man over a game of chess.

Chapter 20

The next day, Lily was staring at the computer screen, indulging in her guilty pleasure of watching YouTube videos of Marshall, when Louise stuck her head through the office door. Her face was flushed with excitement. "It's here. The dress is here."

Lily quickly turned off the screen. "What? Where?"

"Frankie picked it up at the Majestic post office. I can't wait to try it on. I'm going over now. Want to come for the 'unveiling'?"

Lily glanced at the clock. Three o'clock. "I'd love to. Meet you at Frankie's."

Max had given her *carte blanche* to work on the wedding, so she logged out of her computer for the day. It was something they all agreed was a good direction for the resort, especially in the off season, and this would be a trial run. Louise had talked over a menu for the reception with the chef and would be getting an in-house discount.

Lily drove home in her own car, parked at the cabin and walked next door to Frankie's through the narrow slice of forest. The sun was bright, and she found Stephanie on Frankie's back deck, but there was no sign of Frankie or Louise.

"I couldn't miss this," Stephanie said as she poured Frankie a glass of iced tea. "I'm kind of Louise's substitute mother. I've known her all my life and have been watching over her since her mother died when she was a teenager."

"Where is she now?" Lily asked.

"In the bedroom with Frankie, trying on the dress."

Lily sat back on a lounge and smiled. "She's really been looking forward to this dress. It's been fun to watch."

"Did you have a big wedding?" Stephanie asked.

"Yes." Lily took a sip of her tea. "But it wasn't much fun."

A howl sounded from inside the house, preventing her from continuing.

Stephanie's brows contracted low on her forehead. "That doesn't sound good."

"Should we go in?"

"Mmm. Maybe we should wait out here."

A moment later a vision in white, the size of a circus tent, came barreling out onto the deck. The dress had a high waist and plunging neckline, and tiers of white lace cascaded over Louise's belly to the floor.

"It doesn't fit," she howled. "We can't even do up the friggin' zipper."

Stephanie was on her feet. "Maybe we can alter it. I'm pretty handy with a—" She broke off when Louise turned around and they saw a surprisingly slim, bare back through the six-inch gap in the back. "Hmmm. Maybe not that handy."

"It's a *disaster.*" Louise slumped down on the foot of the lounge and put her head in her hands.

Frankie slunk out of the house. "It sounded so good. What are we going to do now? There's only four days until the wedding."

The deck was silent, with only the sound of Louise's heavy breathing.

"You can always wear the black dress." Frankie said tentatively.

"It's not a frigging' funeral," Louise said, jumping up and trying to shake loose the dress. Frankie had fastened the top hooks at the back and Louise was ready to tear it off.

"Be careful," Frankie said. "We want to get your money back." She led the furious Louise back into the house.

Lily and Stephanie sat in silence for a few moments, then Stephanie said, "She can't be the only pregnant bride—"

"With twins—"

"With twins, in history. There must be a dress out there somewhere."

"It would have to be close by for us to get it in time. Are you thinking second hand?" Lily asked.

Stephanie nodded; her eyes narrowed in thought. "I'm thinking Facebook."

* * *

Ms. Bowden the town Facebook page master was watering her English cottage garden in the last house before the Hall when Stephanie and Lily pulled up.

"Betsy," Stephanie said. "We have a delicate problem and could use your help."

"Come inside ladies and tell me all about it."

Ms. Bowden's parlor smelled of lemon oil and once they'd settled on the antique chairs, Stephanie began. "We need a special wedding dress, quickly. It's for Louise."

"Ohhh." Ms. Bowden's eyes widened with understanding. "But the wedding is just—"

Lily nodded. "Four days from now."

"We thought possibly someone who had been in a similar condition, or who was just really big, might have a gown tucked away. She's dead set on white, but this is Louise, she's always been fine with gently used clothes."

Ms. Bowden nodded. "I remember those crazy retro clothes she used to wear when she worked at the diner. There are some big ladies in the valley. Maybe one of them could help out."

Stephanie nodded. "I'll leave this in your capable hands."

* * *

The next morning, when Lily got to the office, she logged onto the town's Facebook page. There was a post from the night before. *"Needed: one previously-loved wedding dress to make this mother-to-be-of-twins dream come true. Must be VERY full. Call Stephanie Murphy IMMEDIATELY."*

That should do the trick.

* * *

The following day, Sean greeted Lily when she arrived at the resort. "The guys and I are going into Bremerton to pick up the tuxes." He grinned. "How's *Operation Wedding Gown* coming?

"Ms. Bowden has put out the word, but I haven't heard anything yet."

"Blue says Louise has been baking non-stop. It's a sure sign she's anxious. She's baked six freezer pies since yesterday, and in her condition..."

"I'll let you know the minute I hear."

* * *

The next day, Louise stuck her head into Lily's office. Her eyes sparkled like a child on Christmas morning. "Someone called Steph with a dress."

"That was quick."

"I don't know what it looks like and at this point I don't really care—as long as it's white and I can zip it up."

They met Stephanie at Frankie's.

"Is Maddie coming?" Lily asked.

"She was cleaning like crazy, and complaining about an aching back," Stephanie said, eyebrows arched. "Nesting," she added with a nod, as if that explained everything.

"Well, she is due any day," Frankie said. "I'm glad she bowed out of being in the wedding party. Too unpredictable. And then we would have had to get a dress for her, too. But who volunteered the wedding dress?"

"Doreen Davis. She's bringing it by," Stephanie said. "I know Doreen from way back. She was pregnant when she got married and although she didn't have twins, she was still always much bigger than you, Louise. It will probably be big enough; I just hope it's the right shape."

"The problem is, I'm so out of proportion now. My shoulders are still small, my boobs are bigger than before but not huge compared to some people, but my waist looks like I'm giving birth to a killer whale."

"We have two days," Stephanie said. "If you can zip it up, we can make it work."

"What does it look like?" Lily asked.

Stephanie pressed her lips together and shook her head. "I have no idea."

The doorbell rang. "What if it's hideous?" Louise whispered.

Frankie giggled. "That never stopped you from wearing anything before."

Louise gave her the squinty-eyed *you-think-you're-so-funny* look and Frankie stuck out her tongue as she hustled to the door. A portly woman with very short black hair and chocolate brown skin stood on the front porch, a giant garment bag over her arm with a froth of white lace hanging out the bottom.

"You must be Doreen," Frankie said.

Stephanie was right behind her. "Hi, Doreen. Thanks for coming to our rescue."

"Hi, Stephanie. I hope this works for your bride."

Doreen kept the black bag clutched to her bosom as Stephanie introduced her to everyone. "When I saw the notice in Facebook, it reminded me of my own wedding. That was twenty years ago. My lord, how time flies. So, I went up to the attic and got out the dress. I'd had it dry cleaned before I put it away, but I hung it out on the line for the day to air it out. I don't think moths have got to it or anything. Of course, in those days it wasn't done nearly so much, the big church wedding with all the trimmings when you already had a bun in the oven, but I'd always wanted a white wedding and thought, the gossips be damned." Tears came to her eyes. "I hope, if you wear it, it brings you luck. My Marty and I have had twenty wonderful years together, and we're still going strong."

"That's wonderful to hear," Louise said. "Can I see the dress?"

Doreen seemed to have a bit of trouble unhinging her arms and letting go of the dress, but finally she handed the bag to Louise. "I hope you like it. It might be kind of dated, but feel free to alter it if you need to. It's yours now."

Louise's eyes sparkled. "I can't wait to try it on.

Frankie?"

They disappeared into the bedroom.

Lily could hear whispering behind the closed door, and a few minutes later Frankie emerged, looking tentative.

"Could you do it up?" Stephanie asked.

"Yes. That wasn't a problem."

"I carried a little extra weight in those days," Doreen said, almost proudly.

"Louise, let's see," Stephanie called.

There was a rustle as Louise fought her way through the bedroom door, the bouffant skirt of the dress brushing both sides of the hall as she walked into the living room.

It was white, all right, and big. The mound of shapeless lace hung on Louise's tiny shoulders like a piñata. Her bust didn't fill out the bodice, leaving her décolletage looking sunken and bony. She could have fit two arms in each of the puffy sleeves. She looked like she was going to cry.

"Oh my," Doreen said, her face dreamy. "Such beautiful lace."

Lily looked at the dress again. *So much* beautiful lace. Doreen must have been seeing her own wedding when she looked at the dress because it looked farcical on Louise.

"Thank you so much, Doreen," Stephanie said, taking her arm and gently tugging her toward the door. "I'm sure we can make it work."

Doreen finally came out of her dream world. "Right. You must have a thousand things to do. I'll just be on my way. Nice to meet you all." She waved two pudgy fingers at Louise. "Congratulations, dear. I'm sure you'll be a beautiful bride."

The door closed behind her and Stephanie hurried

back to the group. Louise's shoulders drooped as forlornly as the dress. "I feel like a little girl playing dress up. A fat little girl."

"Well," Stephanie said, assessing the dress with a critical eye. "At least Doreen is tall, so length won't be a problem. We can always make it smaller, where need be."

Louise shook her head, tears in her eyes. "I don't think this can be saved. There isn't time to make a whole new dress—that's what I should have done in the first place. I'll be wearing black to my wedding after all."

"How good of a seamstress are you?" Lily asked Stephanie.

"I'm not bad, but my mother is a whiz. I think it's time for a visit to Motley Manor."

"There's no time to lose," Louise said, hiking the skirt up to her knees in a billowing cloud, and heading for the door. "I'll just wear the dress."

They trooped out to the front porch, Lily thinking it might be time to absent herself, but when they surveyed the four cars in the driveway, her Impreza was the only one faintly big enough to take all four women and the dress.

Once they were inside, all Lily could see of Louise in the back seat was her face and cropped blonde hair poking out of a froth of white meringue.

"Do you really think your mother can fix this," she whispered to Stephanie who shared the front seat.

"I'm sure of it. Mom's a wiz with pinking shears and a measuring tape."

Dorothy was thrilled to see them, tut-tutting over Louise and the dress. "My, my," she said, pinching the bodice here, the puffed sleeves there, lifting the skirt to examine the voluminous crinolines.

"Stephanie, you put on the kettle. Louise, take off that dress and give it to me. Did you bring other clothes? No? You can borrow a robe. Lily, there's a clean one of Howard's in the laundry closet."

When she had the dress in her hands, Dorothy examined the underside of the skirt. "At least it has an empire waist. But what was she thinking with all these crinolines? They have to go. Seems to me these days young mothers like to show off the baby bump, not hide it."

With a large pair of shears, it took her only a minute to remove the underskirts. "It's not like pregnant brides are anything new. There," she said as the tiers of netting fell away. "That will be better already. Now, let's see about the sleeves. I think I'll have to take them off completely, for now."

The women drank tea in Dorothy's cramped, crowded sitting room as Louise tried on the dress inside-out and Dorothy pinned it in place. While it still wasn't clear what the final gown would look like, Lily could see it taking shape. Louise's shape.

"I could take in three inches right up the center of the bodice, but that will destroy the sweetheart neckline," Dorothy mused.

Stephanie's phone rang, *Here Comes the Bride,* and everyone laughed. She answered and her face lit up in surprise. "When did you leave? Where are you now? We're at Mum's. We'll stop by on the way home."

She closed the cover on her phone with a snap. "Maddie's at the hospital. Jake took her in two hours ago. She was having contractions. I knew it. Nesting is always a sure sign."

Dorothy put in a few more pins and promised the dress would be ready by the morning of the wedding.

"Talk about cutting it close." Louise said as she headed out to the car, still in Howard's dressing gown. "I hope we don't get stopped on the way home."

"I want to go the hospital and sit with Maddie and Jake,' Stephanie said. "You can just drop me there on our way by."

"My clothes are at Frankie's, if you don't mind going back there." Louise giggled. "You sort of have to, I guess. Howard's dressing gown hardly closes over my belly."

"That's okay," Lily assured her. "I'm not going back to work anyway. I'll just go home."

When she got back to the cabin Lily was too wound up to concentrate on doing anything. She poured a glass of white wine and went out to sit on the porch.

She was excited for Louise and Maddie, but also a little bit down. It wasn't that she was jealous of the other women. Envious might be a better word. From what she'd been learning about her new friends, they'd all paid their dues and deserved the happiness they had. While she was with them, she got caught up in their plans; the drama of the wedding, the excitement of a new baby. It was only when she was alone that she wished she had someone to talk to about it all. Wished something like that would happen for her.

But they were a family, she admonished herself, and thoughtful to include her in their celebrations.

She was an outsider, and alone, and would be for a while.

She still wanted children. Had always dreamed of having more than one. As an only child herself, she wanted to experience living in a house full of childish laughter. And tears. There were bound to be tears, and arguing and yelling, but she was ready for it. She still had time.

She just had to figured out how to make it happen.

Chapter 21

As Lily set out for Cottage Four the next morning she felt anxious. No, excited. No, anxious. She'd hardly seen Marshall since the night they'd gone for the row. Her steps slowed. So, what was their relationship now? Not guest and maid anymore. Or maybe they were. It was just a kiss, not a date. He must have stayed in a thousand hotel rooms. Maybe this was business as usual, kissing the maid. That's what her father would say.

She'd told her father they were friends and if sharing secrets made them friends, that's what they were. And anyway, how could they date if he wouldn't leave the house? It wasn't only that she wanted to go out with him -which of course she did—it was that his life from here on out would be empty if he stayed in the house all the time. There had been some improvement though—getting out in the rowboat, standing outside listening to the open mic. She told herself to be patient.

Marshall was hunched over the coffee table on the porch. *Outside. That was progress right there.* And the boat was still tied up at the dock. Another good sign.

"Been out for a row yet?" she called as she walked up the steps.

He grinned when he saw her. "A couple of times. I can't go for too long; my hand gets kind of numb and then later it's sore." He rubbed it hard with the other hand. "But it's coming. The therapist said to rub it to loosen up the tendons, try to get some movement back. I guess I've been kind of slack about that." He studied the palm. "A glove might help. Protect the new skin."

This was much more information about his injuries than he'd been willing to share with her before and she didn't know whether to encourage him or just be cool. "New skin?" she asked.

"Plastic surgery." He turned away.

Okay. Enough for now. "I'll start in the living room," she said, and turned to the door.

His hand shot out and captured her wrist. "Lily. You don't have to clean for me."

She didn't know what to say. How to tell him she liked coming over, liked taking care of him. "Well somebody has to," she said, adopting a teasing tone and easing her wrist from his grasp. "And you don't seem to want many people around."

She went into the living room and threw open the curtains. "I don't know who else I'd trust to keep your secret. You should hear how the cleaning staff gossips about the guests." She laughed. "It's terrible. I wouldn't want to send any of them out here."

"I met Alex. He dropped off the boat."

She nodded. "He's cool. Actually, he's one of the family."

"Your family?"

"Well, no. Part of the Murphy family." She started tidying, noticed there were music magazines on the table and wondered if Harry had been there. Marshall leaned in the doorway, watching her work.

"My dad and Alex's wife's mother are seeing each other," she continued. "The Murphy's are a big, ungainly mess of family. I'm just starting to understand everyone's connection to each other. One of the women who I've kind of become friends with went into labor last night. I'm just waiting to hear. And another, Louise—well she's not really family either but you'd never know it—is getting married tomorrow here at the resort. She's eight months pregnant. With twins. You wouldn't believe the time we've had getting her a dress."

"It sounds like you're having fun." He was still watching her work. Just—watching. His gaze tickled like warm fingers on the nape of her neck.

Slowly she became aware that something in the room was different. The dust cover was off the electric piano. She walked over and even though it was turned off, put her hands on the keyboard, forming a few chords, just to feel the action of the keys. It was obviously a far superior instrument to hers.

"Do you play?"

She pulled her hands off the keys and looked at him over her shoulder. He was smiling. She laughed self-consciously. "A bit. But not like you."

Lily put a hand back on the keyboard and formed a G minor chord, hearing the sound in her head, although nothing emanated from the speakers. "Have you been playing?"

"I won't really be able to play again," he said softly.

Why then did he have the piano as a horrible reminder? She reached for the cloth cover. "Shall I cover it up?"

He didn't answer so she glanced at him before laying it over the keys. Her hands hung in the air for a moment, then he said, "I was working on a tune."

Her heartbeat sped up. "Really? Can I hear it?"

He looked at her for what felt like minutes, her mind racing through the possible responses. *No, I told you, I can't play,* or maybe, *Yes, I wrote it for you.*

Then he reached for a piece of paper on the shelf

by the TV. "You play it. I'd, well, I'd like to hear it." He held up his clawed hand and the reality hit her. He could only play with one hand. Only hear it in his head.

"I'd love to," she said, and held out her hand for the music.

She flipped the switch on the piano and the lights above the keyboard lit up. Settling herself on the bench, she looked over the sheet music in her hands. The notes were written in pencil, some obviously erased and rewritten. He could hear it that clearly in his head. *Lento,* he'd written at the top. *Slowly.* Good.

So slowly she started to play the chords. It wasn't like other songs of his that she'd heard. They were anthems that caught the spirit of the times with a driving beat and stirring words that often bordered on political. This one was soft and slow and, she'd just bet, personal.

When she reached the bottom of the page, she stopped and turned to him. He was staring out the window, arms crossed on his chest. "It's beautiful. Are there words?"

He looked at her and she knew there were. But did he trust her enough to show them to her?

"Not yet."

"Well," she said softly, rising from the piano bench. "I'd love to see them when they are finished."

"You'll be the first." His gaze was intense. The blood rushed to her cheeks, and her chest and her loins and had her doing Kegel crunches to ease the arousal.

"I'd better get to work," she said, grabbing her bottle of all-purpose cleaner and hustling into the bedroom.

The bedroom. She had such intimate knowledge of him for two people in their position. She made his bed and changed the sheets that were infused with the scent of Marshall. Over the weeks it had changed from a musty, sick room smell to something clean and fresh and masculine. She didn't know what else to call it, but when she stood over his bed and inhaled deeply, those Kegels started all by themselves.

Enough! She grinned as she smoothed the clean sheets on the bed and moved into the bathroom. There were no beer bottles or water bottles in the bedroom anymore. Again, not a sick room. He was taking care of a lot of the jobs himself.

But she still felt he had to get out more. Had to get out *at all.*

When she went back to the living room, he was at his computer and looked up at her as she stood over him.

"Why don't you come over for dinner tonight?" she said.

His brows shot up in surprise.

"To the cabin."

He smiled broadly. "I'd love to."

"I could come and get you."

He stood up, suddenly close, towering over her. "If the weather holds, I can get there on my own. Do you have a dock?"

"You'll row?"

"Sure. Why not. The moon's pretty full."

"I do have a dock, but it's really just an old raft that floated in over the winter. Sean, a friend of mine, tied it up at the shore."

His face softened into a smile. "It'll do."

When Lily got back to the Lodge, Sean was at the reception desk computer. She sat on the stool beside him at the counter. "I'm thinking of leaving a little early."

"Sure." He glanced up and shot her a grin. "Hot date?"

Suddenly she wanted to tell him about Marshall. After all, he was a manager of the resort. He probably already knew.

"Do you know about our 'special guest'?" She just blurted it out.

Sean turned to her, excitement in his eyes. "Yes." He lowered his voice. "Marshall Mason." He breathed the name with respect. "Max told me yesterday that you were taking care of him. Apparently, they've been playing chess together." He shook his head. "I don't think Max really understands how famous he is."

"My dad doesn't have much respect for musicians. I guess he's seen the worst of their behavior over the years he spent working in hotels. But I've gotten to know Marshall and he's not like that," Lily said earnestly. "He's nice, and quite down to earth. A recluse, really. At least he is now, since the accident. I've been trying to get him out of the cottage but for various reasons, he's afraid to go out in public. I invited him over to the cabin for dinner tonight. Just to get him out," she added hastily. "Maybe you could drop by. I'd like him to meet a few people, see we aren't all going to rat him out to the media."

"Is that what he's afraid of?"

Lily nodded. "Can you drop by tonight?"

Sean's face lit up. "I'd love to meet him."

"Maybe you and Frankie could join us for dinner. Just drop in, make it seem casual, last minute. I don't want him to think I'm setting him up."

"You got it."

Chapter 22

At seven o'clock, the allotted time, Lily stood in the cabin looking out through the screen door. Sweetie sat quietly at her feet, but by the quiver of her ears, Lily could tell the pup knew something was going on.

Lily had made a run into Majestic for chicken and veggies, a bottle of wine, and picked up a little smoked salmon for an appie while she was there.

One burner on the turquoise stove didn't work, but she was able to prepare a chicken curry and rice on the others. She prepared enough for Sean and Frankie too, if Sean came over in time. She liked to cook when there was someone besides herself to cook for. It had been a long time since she'd cooked a real meal. For a man. In Seattle, between her and Troy's schedules, she usually grabbed take-out on the way home. Heaven only knows what he did now. She was pleased to find that the thought of her ex-husband didn't bother her anymore. Not when Marshall was coming for dinner.

Did he like sweets? She didn't know, and there was nothing in the house to serve for dessert. She looked like she was waiting, just standing there, so she walked outside and plunked herself down on the couch.

The evening was perfect, warm, a light breeze, a few clouds, nothing that should prevent him from rowing across the bay. In fact, it should only take him fifteen minutes or so. Unless he was trying to call her to say he couldn't come, or that he'd changed his mind and wanted to be picked up. She charged into the house and found her cell phone in her jacket pocket. No messages. Good. But that didn't stop the butterflies in her stomach. She went back into the bedroom and peered into the mirror.

"Are you sure?" she murmured. She was wearing the sundress and cardigan that had been laid out on the bed when she got home. It wasn't the first time Augusta had "suggested" an outfit for her to wear. The dress was perfect for a casual, early-summer dinner. She got what Sean meant about Augusta leaving him messages. It seemed Augusta was a matchmaker at heart.

When she stepped outside, Marshall was pulling the rowboat up to her rickety dock and tying it to a big iron ring on the side. Her pulse sped up at the sight of him, but she stood on the porch, hands clasped in front of her, looking—and feeling—like a teenager waiting for her first date. And wondering what to do.

Sweetie knew just what to do. She raced to the dock, ears flapping, and jumped on Marshall as he climbed out of the boat, covering his face with kisses. Lily wished she could do the same, but instead, she walked demurely down the flagstone path to meet him.

He stepped off the raft as she approached, put a hand on her waist and pulled her close, kissing her on the cheek. "Hi."

She was too flustered to think of any better answer than, "Hi."

He held out a bag. "Hostess gift. My mother taught me to never come empty handed."

She pulled a bottle of wine out of the bag, recognizing the label as one they served at the resort. She smiled. "One of my favorites. Come on up."

"Cute place. Did you say you were renting?"

"I am. It belongs to Stephanie Murphy, my dad's girlfriend, mother and matriarch of the Murphy clan."

He laughed. "So, it's all in the family."

"More or less."

On the porch, Marshall absently touched a tiny pink rose blooming there. "My mom grew roses. Geeze, that's the second time I've mentioned my mom."

She took the bottle out of the bag and held it up in question. He nodded, and she got two clunky wine glasses out of the cupboard. "Do you speak to your folks much?"

His mouth tightened. "They died last year."

She stopped and turned around. "Oh, Marsh. Both of them?"

He nodded.

"How did it happen?"

"Car accident. They think my dad had a stroke while he was driving. They were both killed at the scene."

She walked over and put her arms around his shoulders. He resisted for a moment, then softened and wrapped his arms around her ribs, allowing the hug, allowing her to comfort him, just a bit. After a moment she released him and, without comment, poured the wine.

Marshall said, "I met your dad. Nice guy. We've played chess a couple of times."

Lily handed him his glass and led him out onto the porch. "He loves chess."

"He's a shark," Marshall said with a grin, taking the seat on the far side of the couch that allowed him to shield the scarred side of his face. Lily tried not to feel frustrated that he still felt he had to do that. It was probably just habit now, but it really didn't look that bad.

A twig snapped in the forest and Sean emerged

from the path to Frankie's house. He held up a hand in greeting.

As Lily said, "Hi Sean," she felt Marshall stiffen beside her. She took his hand.

Sean came around to the front of the porch and put one foot up on the step. "How are things going?"

Lily smiled. "Great. This is my friend, Marshall. Marsh, this is Sean, I think I've mentioned him to you. He's the marketing manager at the resort."

Sean took another step up and held out his hand. Marshall rose stiffly and shook, then, head down, retreated to his seat again.

"Marshall's staying at the resort," Lily said brightly. "A long term guest."

Sean nodded amiably. "We have a few of those, including Frankie's father and his girlfriend. They're in Cottage One."

Marshall didn't respond, so Lily said, "Marshall's in a cottage, too."

"How are you finding it?" Sean asked.

"Very nice," Marshall replied.

Sheesh! Lily suddenly wondered if inviting Sean and Frankie for dinner was such a good idea. But surely Marshall would unwind as the evening went on.

"Why don't you and Frankie join us for dinner? I made plenty." Her voice sounded too perky, even to her.

"Why thanks. Maybe we will. I just came over to borrow a hammer, but then I'll go and get Frankie."

"You know where the tools are," Lily said. Sean lifted a hand and walked around to the back of the cabin.

Marshall hadn't moved a muscle by her side. Her heart was pounding in her chest. Too pushy. Too much too soon. When would she learn? She just hoped she hadn't blown it. Hoped he wouldn't jump in the boat and row away before Sean and Frankie got back.

She stretched her fingers wide and rubbed her palms on her thighs. "Sean's the lead guitarist in the band that hosts the open mic," she said, trying to fill the uncomfortable silence. "He can play anything, really. Many different instruments and lots of different styles. He lived here, in the cabin, last year."

A warm breeze blew through the porch, brushing her cheek and ruffling Marshall's hair. He took a deep breath and she saw his shoulders relax to a more normal level. Her heartbeat slowed down, and her muscles relaxed as the aroma of cinnamon cookies drifted past.

"You baking cookies?" Marshall asked, the warmth back in his voice.

"No, but that smell of baking happens quite often." She lowered her voice. "I think that's the ghost. At least, that's all I've been able to figure out."

A smile crinkled his dark eyes. "Really. You believe that?"

"The family all swear she's here. It's Stephanie's Aunt Augusta. I do sort of believe it. More so the longer I live here. I often feel her presence, particularly when I'm anxious. A warm breeze drifts through that smells like cookies. Or baking bread. It makes me relax."

"Well, *I* certainly feel relaxed," Marshall said, sinking further into the sofa. "I thought it was the wine."

Lily giggled. "Come inside, I'll show you her picture."

She pulled him up and they walked into the cabin, over to the staircase and looked at the photograph of the young woman driving the antique car.

"She's got a real air about her," Marshall said, studying the photo.

A knock rattled the screen door. "Hello?"

Lily felt Marshall stiffen beside her. Better get the evening rolling.

"Hi there." She gave Marshall a bracing smile before turning to greet her guests.

Frankie came in first, her toothy smile barely hiding her excitement. Lily gave her a hug, holding her for an extra moment hoping to calm her down. Frankie seemed to get the message because when she pulled away her face looked more composed. She held out a covered plate. "Desert. Unless you already have something planned, in which case you can freeze this."

Lily took the dish. "What is it?"

"Pie. First cherries of the season. Sean made it."

"That sounds wonderful. This is so spur of the moment, I have nothing planned for dessert. Luckily I made a lot of the main course, though. I'm so glad you could join us." She gave Marshall a smile which he didn't return.

"This is my friend Marshall. He's visiting Fortune Bay for a while."

Frankie briefly shook his hand and gave him a smile. Just like she would to anyone. *Good job.* "Nice to meet you." She turned to Lily. "What's for dinner? It smells amazing."

Lily smiled. "Curry. Not too hot, just lots of lovely spices."

Sean stepped forward and shook Marshall's hand. "Nice to see you." The two men contemplated each other, Sean all easy charm, Marshall stiff as a board.

"Just so you know," Sean said. "I know who you are."

Lily's head snapped around to look at Marshall. He didn't move for a moment, then, wonder of wonders, seemed to relax.

"But don't worry," Sean continued. "Your secret is safe with us. Now," he said, rubbing his hands together. "What are we drinking? I brought a bottle of wine."

Lily kept an eye on Marshall, but he seemed to relax more and more as the evening progressed. They ate at the yellow Formica kitchen table and Lily's curry and rice was a hit. Since no one was driving, the wine flowed, and talk moved from the resort to the rowboat to the best fishing holes on the lake.

"I've got a little fishing boat," Sean said. "If you'd like, we could go out sometime. I like to go first thing in the morning, though."

"That's good for me," Marshall answered. "I've been getting up early lately to row." He smiled at Lily and her heart swelled, both at how much he seemed to be enjoying the evening and fact that he had special smiles just for her.

After they finished the main course, they took their desert out to the porch. The sun was just dropping behind the mountains across the lake. Sean pulled a couple of chairs out from the kitchen to augment the seating on the couch.

"I love these long evenings," Frankie said, licking the cherry juice off her fork.

"I remember fishing in the evening at my childhood cottage," Marshall said. "Great pie, by the way."

"Sean's the cook," Frankie said. "Although, I'm learning."

"Amber must take after you," Lily said to Sean, remembering that his daughter was Louise's assistant baker at the resort this summer.

Sean puffed up with pride. "She does." He turned

to Marshall. "You have any kids?"

"Two." Marshall concentrated on the pie. "Haven't seen them in a while."

"That must be hard," Sean said. "I didn't see Amber for fifteen years, but I thought about her every day."

Before Marshall could respond, a gruff voice sounded from down the path. "I hear voices."

"Dad," Lily exclaimed as Max and Stephanie rounded the corner of the cabin. "What are you doing here?"

"Just out for a walk. Sean, Frankie." He nodded at each in turn while Stephanie came up onto the porch and gave them each a hug. "Marshall, nice to see you. Steph, this is Marshall. You know, the guy I'm playing chess with. Marsh, my girlfriend, Stephanie."

"My mom," Sean said helpfully.

Stephanie turned to Marshall with a warm smile and held out her hand to shake. "Max is thrilled to have found someone who can challenge him in a game."

Marshall shook her hand. "Nice to meet you. I'm enjoying the mental exercise myself."

Lily wasn't sure what to do next. "Want to join us?"

"No, no. We are just out for a walk," Stephanie said, rejoining Max on the path.

"My constitutional," Max said. "She's determined to whip me into shape."

Stephanie laughed, low and easy. "After all day in the studio I wanted some fresh air. Let's go, Max. Enjoy the evening," she said as they continued around the other corner of the cabin and down Frankie's driveway.

"Dad lives across the road in the big log house," Lily said to Marshall. "But maybe you haven't seen it. We'll have to go for a drive some time so you can see the area."

"Where does your mother live?" Marshall asked Sean.

"She lives between here and town. This path runs from the point," He pointed in the opposite direction to town, "past Frankie's house, past here and Mom's place, all the way to town."

Marshall nodded. "Nice."

Sean laughed and squeezed Frankie's shoulders in a hug. "It'll be nicer when I'm not living with my mother anymore."

Marshall's eyes widened. "Awkward."

Sean nodded. "Right. I was living here last year and moved back with Mom when I found my daughter—long story. But now we're putting an addition onto Frankie's house next door and soon Amber and I will move in there." Sean and Frankie smiled at each other in blissful understanding that made Lily's heart tug with envy.

Sean turned back to Marshall. "Want to see it?"

Marshall perked up. "Sure."

The two men set off together, Sweetie at their heels, Sean explaining the work they'd already done, leaving Lily and Frankie grinning at each other on the porch.

"That went well," Frankie whispered.

Lily nodded. "Better than I expected. I was worried there for a minute, but it must feel good to have a normal conversation with normal people after months of being virtually alone."

"He's nice. You've got a good one there," Frankie said.

Lily suddenly felt flustered. "I don't know if I've 'got' him."

"I think you might," Frankie said knowingly.

Lily stood up, eager to change the subject. "Let's go

with them. I want to see how the addition is coming along."

They followed the men along the path through the trees. "Progress has actually kind of ground to a halt," Frankie said. "Sean's been so busy—"

Lily nodded. "We are getting busy at the resort."

"Right, and Jake's totally preoccupied with looking after Maddie, who's already had one false alarm and could pop any day, and the same with Blue, who's trying to get his own house ready to absorb two babies."

"I see the problem."

"Amber is busy taking Louise's shifts—I don't think Louise judged correctly how much work she'd be able to do at this point. So that leaves me sanding drywall and painting alone all summer."

"I'll try to give you a hand sometimes," Lily said. "I've never done that kind of work before, but it's probably a good skill to have."

They found the men up in the master bedroom, which did look pretty much like it had the night when, after the work party, Lily had stood up there looking out at the water. Sean pulled Frankie away to show her a new problem downstairs, leaving Lily and Marshall alone together on the tiny balcony, admiring the view.

"I could be happy in a place like this," Marshall said softly, leaning forward on the new wrought iron railing.

"I think I could, too," Lily agreed. "I wasn't sure when I got here, it was just a place to go to get away from Seattle. And my marriage. But now I'm thinking of staying. At least for the foreseeable future. I like my job, I like being close to my dad, and I'm making friends." She turned to him and smiled. "What else is there?"

He looked into her eyes, and she could see thoughts were going through his head, but she couldn't read them.

"What else indeed?" he said, putting an arm around her waist and pulling her close to his side. It was perfect, the way they fit together so easily, and as they looked at the view Lily couldn't help wondering, *what if?*

Marshall turned his head and kissed her temple. "You're lucky to have this." Then taking her hand, he led her downstairs.

Frankie and Sean were ensconced on lounges on the deck, and after saying their goodbyes, Lily and Marshall walked through the soft dusk, back to the cabin, hand in hand.

The porch light was on. Marshall was pretty sure it hadn't been when they left. They'd been sitting out there, eating pie and...no. He was sure it was off.

"Did we leave that on?" he asked in confusion.

Lily shook her head and smiled.

"Is it...?"

She shrugged, keeping her shoulders high in fun, her grin broadening. "Augusta? I guess so. And look, she cleaned up the dishes."

They stopped at the bottom of the steps and he took both her hands. "Too bad. I was going to offer to help clean up, but maybe she's suggesting I should go."

He tugged her hands gently and she floated into his arms. He kept his lips soft as they explored the taste of hers. Cherry pie and good wine. An intoxicating combination. He trembled, holding back, although, after months of being alone, he wanted to bury himself in her soft, lush curves.

"You don't have to go," she whispered, her lips a millimeter from his, so close he could feel the warmth of her breath on his lips.

He shook his head. "My life is a mess. I can't drag you into it."

One of her eyebrows went up. "My husband asked me to leave so he could move his pregnant girlfriend in. Beat that."

He let that sink in for a moment, then laughed. "Okay, you win. For today." He became serious. "But I mean it. I can't promise anything."

Her eyes travelled down his body and back up, smiling coquettishly. "You can be my rebound guy."

"Rebound, eh?" He leaned forward and took her face in his hands, pausing an inch from her face, giving her a chance to pull away if she was only being nice. "I can live with that."

She closed her eyes and the tip of her tongue made a slow arc across her lips leaving them slightly apart with an inviting sheen.

A tremor went through him and he hardened instantly. He pressed his lips to hers and her mouth opened, not with heat or aggression, just with a tender invitation to taste. He held himself back, accepting her offer, gently sweeping his tongue over her lips and teeth, then withdrawing.

He rested his forehead on hers. She sighed deeply, her eyes still closed. Then she opened them and looked into his. "It's been a long time."

He chuckled. "Me too." He ran his teeth over her bottom lip. "Your call."

Then she kissed him, and the burning edge of his passion spilled over as he pulled her tight against him with a hand on her lower back. Running the other hand up her side, he took the weight of her breast in his palm and brushed his thumb over the point. It peaked under his hand.

The ache in his groin was going to be painful if she

turned him away. And she might. This was new territory for him.

She began to pull away and his hopes fell. *Okay, too much too fast. Here it comes, the big goodbye.*

Instead, she smiled, not sultry or seductive, but genuinely happy, and grabbing his hand—the stiff hand but she didn't seem to care—she tugged him up the stairs, straight through the cabin, thrusting aside the flowered curtain on the rear wall and into the bedroom.

Okay!

She stood expectantly between him and the bed and he looked at her, the pretty sundress, the little blue sweater. He started with the sweater, quickly pulling it off.

Then she stepped up and put her lips on his, her nimble fingers undoing his shirt buttons as he devoured her mouth. Her lips opened to him with the slightest pressure, but he felt like she was distracted by his buttons, so he stepped back and whipped the loosened shirt off over his head.

She put both hands on his chest and sighed, the sound reviving a pride he'd lost somewhere along the way. He stepped back into the kiss, letting her feel his passion. She was all in, too, giving, exploring as hungrily as he. He slipped the thin straps of the dress off her shoulders, but the bodice stayed tight over her breasts. Confounding construction of women's clothes. He preferred stretchy ones that slipped right off. Finding the zipper on the back, he felt a sensuous rush that went straight to his groin as he slowly pulled it down.

The fabric loosened over her breasts. He glanced down and—mercy! —she wasn't wearing a bra. He stopped unzipping the dress when he got to the waist, taking some time to peel off the top and explore the soft beauty of her skin, the pearly color, the pink tips, hard for him. Then with one quick pull the dress was unzipped and fell, leaving her in just a lacy thong. He practically exploded out of his pants.

She put her hands on her hips. "Not fair."

My pleasure. His pants were gone in a second.

He'd been wanting this for weeks and walked her backwards until her knees touched the edge of the bed. They fell onto the soft bouncy mattress, that was probably hell for sleeping on but now promised fun times ahead.

"I want to feel your hair," he murmured. She pulled out the elastic and her silky hair spread over the pillow. His body was on fire. He hadn't felt like this in years. It was different than the itch any woman could scratch. This was a yearning, a pressure he couldn't explain, but he would do his best to share with her. The woman who was bringing him back to life.

Sometime later, Marshall groaned and rolled onto his back, keeping Lily pulled tight to his side.

"Is that a good groan or a bad groan?" she asked, her lips pressed to his collar bone.

"Definitely a good groan. The groan of a starving man taking his first bite of a juicy hamburger. With all the trimmings."

She giggled. "All the trimmings?"

He rolled on top of her. "You bet." And kissed her again. Then he rested his forehead on hers. "And thanks."

She smiled. "You don't have to thank me for that."

His face remained serious, and his voice deepened. "No, I mean it. Thanks for inviting me over. For getting me out of the cottage and introducing me to your friends." *For renewing my life.*

"Happy to oblige."

He couldn't get enough of her. His eyes scanned her face, the creamy skin of her neck and shoulders, trying to memorize every inch of her. She was a ray of sunshine in his bleak life, ushering in a world of possibilities he'd imagined were closed to him forever. She made him feel wanted, not as Marshall Mason the star but as Marshall the man. It had been many years since he'd felt that, and he wasn't sure it could happen in the world to which he had to return.

Chapter 23

The morning of Louise and Blue's wedding, rain poured from the sky. Lily was the first of the wedding crew to arrive at the resort and was standing on the long stone veranda outside the double French doors that led to the dining room when Frankie arrived.

They stood together in the damp cold air and looked out at the waves crashing against the boat dock, where Louise and Blue had hoped to take their vows.

"It's not going to happen," Lily said. "We can't risk setting up on the dock."

Frankie shook her head in agreement. "It might let up, but we can't count on it."

Lily looked at the imposing stone pillars that held the veranda roof. "This area looks kind of like a church," she observed.

"We could put a long table there at the end," Frankie said, thinking aloud. "The tall vases of white flowers would look striking against the stone wall."

Lily flicked on the lights. "It would look great. I just hope it warms up a bit by mid-afternoon."

"If not, we might have to move it all into the dining room."

Lily groaned. "I hope not. I was planning to have the reception dinner set up in there before the ceremony began. Let's set up here and hope for the best."

Fiona's lanky son Matt had been hired for the day and with his help they set up rows of chairs on each side of a central aisle for immediate family and friends. The ceremony would take place at one end, with the three sets of double French doors left open for the overflow of guests to watch from inside the dining room. Both Louise and Blue were local and well-liked, so Lily expected a crowd.

They'd barely finished the setup when Sean arrived with the flowers. Stephanie had contributed a white damask tablecloth which they used to hide the utilitarian table on the veranda. The tall urns of white Gladiolas and Lilies, sprinkled with sky-blue Forget-me-nots, looked stunning against the grey stone wall. They attached white satin bows to each chair on the aisle to line the processional route and draped satin bunting between the pillars.

When they were finished they stepped back to admire their work. "It looks lovely," Lily said. "I definitely want a picture of this for the resort's website."

Frankie's cheeks were pink from exertion and excitement. "I always forget when I volunteer for the planning just how rushed the actual wedding day will be. I'm sorry, I can't help with the rest of the flowers. I have to run. I still have to pick up the wedding dress from Dorothy, then go home and shower—"

"I'll get the dress," Lily said.

Frankie's eyes widened in surprise. "Would you? That would help so much."

Lily grinned. "I'd be happy to." It was fun being part of the excitement, and she was dying to see what Dorothy had done with the dress.

Frankie headed out right away, but before Lily left, she helped Sean move the flower arrangements and tablecloths for the guest tables onto the head table. It was set up in front of the windows at the end of the dining room with the backdrop of lake and mountain views beyond. Matt would help her set up the dining room for the reception after the resort guests had finished lunch.

As Lily drove to Majestic to pick up the dress, she ran through the plans in her mind. Max had taken care of ordering wine and champagne. Louise had dropped off the cake, a magnificent confection with white icing, and pink roses and green leafy vines cascading over the top layers. Gorgeous. It was a shame to cut into it. She would have to get a picture of that, too.

She was getting the dress—check. She'd have to find a moment to stop at the cabin and get ready herself. She was glad she'd brought all her clothes from Seattle after all because this was the perfect chance to wear a red and black dress that she'd bought and never had an opportunity to wear. Another failed date with her husband. In retrospect, she was surprised she hadn't seen the pattern. The dress had been a tiny bit tight when she bought it and she had been pleased to discover it fit better now. That was progress. It would look perfect with her fancy red cowboy boots. Wouldn't Troy have a fit if he saw her in those.

Rain bounced off the pavement as she pulled up at The Manor in Majestic, adding *'find space for the guests' wet outerwear'* to the still-to-do list.

Dorothy had obviously been waiting and met her at the door. "I thought Frankie was coming, but never mind." Her softly lined cheeks were pink with excitement as she took Lily by the arm and pulled her into the sitting room, barely giving her time to kick off her wet shoes.

The dress was hanging from the top lip of the doorframe. Lily sucked in a breath. "You're a miracle worker, Dorothy. Louise will be thrilled."

The white tent had been fitted for Louise's much

smaller frame, with tucks below the bust to leave the fullness where needed. Dorothy had reduced the sleeves from puffy balloons to sleek, and the delicate lace skimmed lightly over it all.

Dorothy smiled and clasped her hands to her chest. "Do you really think so? I was quite pleased with how it turned out, myself. I went to the drugstore and looked through some bridal magazines for inspiration. This dip in the back," she turned the dress around for Lily to see, "is quite the thing this year."

Lily gave Dorothy a hug. "Louise will love it. Do you have something we can cover it with? I'd hate to dip the train in a puddle."

They bundled the dress into two large, clean, plastic garbage bags and Lily carried it carefully out to the car and drove to Blue's cabin where the bridal party was assembled.

Louise was overwhelmed when she saw the dress and tears flowed down her cheeks. She laughed and wiped them away. "Darn hormones. But it's beautiful. Thank you."

"I didn't do anything," Lily said. "Thank Dorothy."

The two bridesmaids were there, Frankie and Louise's sister Brandy. At nine months pregnant, Maddie was not part of the wedding party, but she was there too, stretched out on one couch, lending moral support along with her daughters, Sarah and Jen, prepared to take pictures when the time came.

"False alarm the other night?" Lily asked her.

Maddie nodded. "They kept me at the hospital for two hours the other day, then sent me home. I'm getting too old for this. I just want it to be over. Just not today." She laughed. "Please, not today." Then she got serious again and lowered her voice so Louise wouldn't hear. "But the way my back is aching, I wouldn't put money on it."

"Oh dear." *Add that to my things-I-can't-possibly-prepare-for list.*

"I love weddings," Sarah said in a wistful voice. "I was the flower girl at Daddy and Mommy's wedding last year." She smiled up at Maddie and Lily's chest tightened. Another happy, blended family. Who knows, maybe it could still happen for her.

By four o'clock, when Louise walked down the aisle on her father's arm, the clouds had parted, the wind had dropped and promising beams of sunlight shone through the stone arches of the veranda adding a final touch of magic to the ceremony.

The men all looked gorgeous in their tux's. The groom, big Blue, had trimmed his woodsman's beard for the occasion. Sean as best man stood beside him, along with Jake as the groom's man. Stephanie had dug a white fur wrap out of the depths of her closet for Louise to wear over her shoulders to hold off the chill, adding the final fairytale touch to the gown.

As the music started again, and the beaming bride and groom walked triumphantly back down the aisle, Lily was surprised to find tears in her eyes. Maddie was not in the crowd surrounding the blissful couple on the porch, but Lily found her in the dining room, sitting in one of the arguably more comfortable dining room chairs, rubbing her lower back.

"Still bothering you?" Lily asked.

Maddie forced a weak smile. "I'm sure it's nothing. Just the effect of the extra weight. I'm glad I got most of the photographs finished before the ceremony, though."

Lily pointed a finger at her. "I'm keeping an eye on you. No heroics tonight. You can't fight mother nature. I don't want any babies born on the dining room floor tonight."

"I'll try," Maddie said, but Lily worried about the weakness in her voice.

Add 'watch pregnant mothers' to the list.

Matt was in charge of a group of local young people who were serving trays of hors d'oeurvres and glasses of wine and sparkling water. Lily was on her feet for the next few hours, in and out of the kitchen, making sure the resort guests were greeted and included when they came for dinner, or served in the bar if they preferred.

Her father caught her in a quiet moment. "Hi, honey. How's it going?"

"Oh, Dad." Lily blew out a breath. "It's been non-stop all day."

"Well, you're doing a great job."

She grinned. "It is pretty fun, but if we were going to do more weddings we really need an extra room."

Max nodded. "I've been thinking of adding a big all-purpose room to the plan. Then we could host weddings and conferences." Another group of surprised resort guests poked their heads through the door, catching Lily's eye. "I'll let you get back to work."

Sean had been working the room as host and best man. As he passed Lily, he grabbed two wine glasses from a passing tray and held one out to her.

She took it gratefully. "I think things are finally under control. Everyone's seated. Most of the food is served. We should have a few quiet moments to catch our breath."

Sean studied the room thoughtfully. "Second time in as many years I've been the best man."

Lily smiled. "Always the best man, never the groom?"

"It'll be my turn soon," he said, tossing back the

wine. "We might need your help again in a few months."

"I'll be happy to help," Lily said cautiously, thinking back to Frankie's comments, not wanting to get in the middle of whatever was going on.

Chapter 24

After the toasts came the cutting of the cake. Lily was surprised to find tears in her eyes again, but to her this part of the ceremony was the second promise, the first step they took together, his hand over hers. Then the doors were thrown open to the covered veranda which the crew had transformed into a dance floor for the evening. The wedding gods were on their side. The night had turned clear and a balmy breeze had followed the front, something the locals called, "the pineapple express."

A local band had set up at the end of the veranda and they started to play. Frankie gave Lily an exuberant high five as she walked by to join the bridal party for the first dance.

So far so good, Lily thought. Tomorrow she would add 'wedding planner' to her ever-growing job description.

Crossing her arms on her chest, she leaned on the stone column by the steps going down to the grounds and watched the first dance. Blue was very gentle for such a big burly guy, taking Louise by the hand as if she was his princess, which indeed was what she looked like in the re-designed lace dress. Lily caught Dorothy's eye across the room, a teary eye she was dabbing with a lace handkerchief and sent her a thumbs-up.

Sean and Frankie joined the happy couple on the dance floor a few moments later and soon the veranda was filled with dancing family and friends. People, Lily realized, she was beginning to consider her friends, too. She was beginning to see what a future in Fortune Bay could look like—working at the resort, planning weddings for friends and neighbors and out-of-town guests, and, who knows, maybe meeting someone special herself.

A few dances in, Jake crossed the floor toward her. Dark and tanned against the crisp white shirt, he looked gorgeous in his tux. "Maddie says you are responsible for making this happen."

"I just helped Frankie and Louise." Lily laughed. "Which I have to admit sometimes felt more like a mediation."

Jake chuckled and held out his hand. "Care to dance? My partner is down for the count." He indicated Maddie who was squirming uncomfortably in a chair on the sidelines.

Lily took his hand as he led her to the dance floor. "Think she'll make it through the night without having the baby?"

They both looked over at Maddie, whose twenty-year-old daughter Jen had sat down beside and was holding her hand. Jake's forehead wrinkled in a frown. "She's trying. She doesn't want to disturb the wedding, but I don't know if she'll make it."

Jake was a good dancer, but Lily's thoughts went to another man, also tall, dark and broad shouldered, who she couldn't help wishing she was dancing with tonight.

Jake suddenly stopped moving and stepped back. "If you don't mind I think I'll just go and check." And the next thing Lily knew, she was alone on the dance floor. She sighed. Nice of him to think of her. She hadn't really been in town long enough to have guys lined up on her dance card.

Louise had also sat out the last few dances, but now she and Colleen were out on the floor in all their glory, side by side, clapping their hands over their heads along with the music.

"Come on, you all," Colleen called. "I know some of you know how to do this. I've seen you in class. And those of you who don't, then just stumble along with us anyway."

As the women started to move, the dance floor began to fill up. Star ran over and grabbed Lily's hand. "Let's go, girl. You can do this." And next thing she knew, Lily was clapping and stomping and grape-vining her way across the floor in a happy mass of dancing people. Star was behind her and Louise in front, then *stomp, clap, turn,* and there was Sean right behind her. "Is *Busted Muffler* going to play tonight?" she asked.

"We're thinking of doing a few numbers later on." And *clap, turn,* she was facing the other way again.

When the song ended, Lily felt pink-cheeked and breathless. Glancing out through the stone arch into the gathering night, a movement in the shadows caught her eye. She put a hand to her chest as her heartbeat increased even more and slipped down the steps onto the dark path to the lake.

Before she'd gone more than a few feet, a shadow separated itself from the dark trees.

She stepped into the shadows to meet him. "Hi."

"Hi." Marshall thrust his hands into his pockets and rocked back on his heels. Obviously uncomfortable, though she wasn't sure why. "You look lovely tonight."

She looked down at the flowered silk sheath, glad she'd had something special to wear.

"The wedding?" he asked.

She nodded, and sighed deeply, relaxing for the first time all day.

"How's it going?" he asked.

She smiled. "Really well. The wedding dress actually fit—did I tell you Louise is pregnant with twins?"

In the gloom, she saw him smile and nod.

"But she's not the only one. Maddie is past her due date and I'm afraid she won't make it through the evening. It's exciting, really."

"You really want children, don't you?"

His quiet question stopped her in her tracks. She pressed her lips together to control the emotions that threatened to spill over. "Yes. I really do."

They watched the dancing up on the porch as the band swung into a bouncy beat. "Not the same band as the other night," Marshall observed.

"No. That band *is* the wedding party tonight. They might play a few songs later, though."

"They're better than this."

Lily nodded. The beat was contagious, and she took his hand. "Come and dance with me."

He didn't move.

"Please?"

The song ended just then and another, slower number began. He moved toward her and took her in his arms, weaving to the music. "Dance with me here."

She felt his hand on her back, warm and firm through the thin silk. He seemed so much taller and stronger than just a few weeks ago. He must be rowing every day. Why did she feel so nervous with him tonight?

He pulled her closer and his chest was hard under her cheek. She could feel the sinewy muscles in her shoulders and arms, his thighs pressed against hers as his hand went to the small of her back, pulling her close. A fire leapt to life low in her belly and she melted her curves to his. She felt the beat of his heart, strong and even, against her cheek and wondered if he felt the magic too.

The song ended on a whisper, but she didn't want to stop. She raised her head and stared into his eyes. His hand moved from hers, sliding up her bare arm to her neck. Then his fingers were in her hair, pulling her closer to his until she could feel the warmth of his breath on her lips. He paused there, and she knew he was waiting for her to say yes. So she did, leaning forward a fraction of an inch, and when their lips touched, a moan ripped from her chest.

He changed the angle and his tongue stroked hers. The hand on the small of her back pressed her into his heat, until she could feel him hard against her.

He stepped back further into the darkness, pulling her with him, pressing her against a tree. As she fell into his kiss, she knew she was falling for him.

The revelation terrified her. This wasn't a casual summer affair anymore. She pulled away and he kissed her temple and then as she looked away, her cheek.

He rubbed his cheek against hers, rasping her soft skin. She wanted to feel that rasp in more intimate places. The top of her breast, her inner thigh.

But she was going too fast. Too far too fast. It was dangerous to go that far with him. Dangerous to want him this much. They were worlds apart. She had too much to lose.

His voice sounded gruff in the darkness. "I want you to see me as a man."

She laughed a painful laugh and ground lightly against his erection. "I see you as a man all right. But I can't go there with you."

He stiffened and his hands fell to his side. *Oh no.* The last thing she'd wanted to do was to hurt him. He didn't understand.

She dropped her head onto his chest. "You could hurt me."

He took her by the shoulders and pulled her back, so he could see her face. "That's not what I'm trying to do."

She tried not to let the depth of her feelings show, but the truth was, it had already gone too far. He *would* hurt her when he left. She shook her head and tried to smile. "You won't even have to try."

She put her hands on his, and he let her go. She stepped back. "I'd better get back to the party."

He thrust his hands into his pockets again. She tried to read the look on his face, but he'd done that Marshall thing, tilting his head so his features were hidden by the darkness.

She backed away, into the light, then she turned and ran back up the steps, to the party.

*   *   *

Just after midnight, Lily was lying on the bench in the gazebo out on the point. She could see the full moon through the arching filigree woodwork that held up the roof. The dance had wound on and eventually Sean and Jake and Blue had thrown off their ties, rolled up their sleeves and taking the stage in their rumpled tuxes, *Busted Muffler* cranked out the few final songs of the night.

Lily had tried to enjoy herself, but couldn't stop thinking about Marshall, alone somewhere out there tonight. Finally, she had left to see if he was still there and ended up here, in the gazebo. She was trying to decide if they'd reached the summer solstice yet, but she'd had a few too many drinks to figure it out.

Apparently so had Frankie and Star. They stumbled together up the two steps into the gazebo.

"There you are." Frankie said. "We were wondering if you needed a ride. Sean's a designated driver." She lay down on the opposing wooden bench and put her feet up on the railing. "Oh my god, I've been dancing for hours."

"Where did you go?" Star asked Lily, her gossamer gown sparkling like a fairy's wings in the moonlight.

"I've been around."

"Did you see him?" Frankie said.

"See who?" Star asked.

Frankie wiggled her eyebrows. "Her mystery man."

"I did," Lily said. "We danced in the dark."

"Oh my *god*, that's so *romantic*," Star said. Then in a theatrical aside to Frankie, she asked, "Who's her mystery man?"

Frankie whispered back, the wine showing, "I can't tell you, he's a *mystery*."

"He was a god," Lily said dramatically, her own wine consumption having gotten the better of her. "Adored by millions, struck down in his prime. He's still a god. A creative genius who's lost his muse. I want him, I think I love him, but I know he's not going to stay."

"Who *is* he?" Star asked.

"I can't tell you."

Star put her hands on her hips. "You can't tell us what you just told us and not tell us who he is."

Frankie tilted her head to look at Lily. "She has a point."

"Can I trust you?" Lily asked Star seriously. She knew Frankie wouldn't tell, but she wasn't sure about Star's discretion.

"Brownie's honor," Star said, holding up her left

hand with the middle and pointer fingers crossed.

"That's not the Brownie salute," Frankie said. "Crossing your fingers means you're lying. Three fingers is the Brownie salute." She demonstrated, trying to hold the baby finger down with her thumb and struggling to straighten the other three. "It was easier when I was eight."

"I was never a Brownie," Lily said, losing patience.

"That's too bad," Star said sympathetically.

"Pinky swear," Lily said, holding up both her baby fingers, suddenly wanting to tell Star her secret.

Frankie and Star leaned forward and linked baby fingers with Lily and with each other, so the three women were joined in a ring.

"He's Marshall Mason," Lily whispered.

"Marshall Mason!" Star shrieked.

Lily clapped a hand over Star's mouth. "Quiet! You pinky swore!"

"Okay," Star whispered, pulling her face away. "But, OH MY GOD," she whispered.

"I know," Lily said dismally.

"What's the problem?" Frankie asked. "I'd think you'd be over the moon. I mean, the guy's a sex god."

"Who's going to break my heart."

Star drew in a deep breath and blew it out. "Right. That's probably true."

"Have you slept with him?" Frankie asked.

Lily sent her a morose look.

Frankie drew in a breath. "And?"

Lily nodded dejectedly. "It was great. I'm falling for him. Far too fast. He's obviously not here for good, and I'm not good with short term. Especially not right now. Probably not ever. He's kind of vulnerable too, right now. Barely over the accident. And the divorce."

"Hmm," Frankie said. "I see what you mean."

"You couldn't just be each other's rebounders?" Star asked.

Lily shook her head. "I don't think that will work. At least not for me."

The women sat in thoughtful silence for a moment, then Frankie suddenly said, "I almost forgot. We have news. Jake took Maddie to the hospital. She'd been sitting at the reception in labor all evening and not telling anyone."

Lily sat up suddenly, then grabbed her spinning head. "I told her, I didn't want any babies delivered in the dining room."

"Well, I'm pretty sure they made it to the hospital. We'll get the details in the morning. She'll probably come home tomorrow."

The three women sighed in unison.

"I think this is the first in a string of babies," Frankie said.

Lily agreed fervently, "I hope so."

Chapter 25

Marshall could feel the depression pressing in like a black cloud on the edges of his consciousness, threatening the fragile reality he was rebuilding.

What did Lily mean, he would hurt her? Was that what she said, or that he *could* hurt her? Could he? Would he? Certainly not on purpose.

He was deep into his own recovery—he could see now that's what this was—and seeing her interest was a boon to his ego, but he hadn't thought about what it would do to her. He had to remember that she was just getting over a major hurdle too—her own marriage breakup—and it sounded like her jerk of a husband had done a pretty good job of stomping on her self-esteem.

Sometimes, like now, when he was wrestling with his own demons, Marshall forgot how distorted his image was in the outside world. The power of the media was so strong that women fell for him without even meeting him. Lily could be a victim of the hype, too. Hell, she may not even like him at all.

In recent years, finding footing in the real world had been increasingly difficult. He was just beginning to realize what a relief it was to be out of the hype and submerged in this new reality of the lake and the wind and a community of people who seemed to like him for himself, something he realized he hadn't felt for almost twenty years.

Lily did like him; he was almost sure of it. He could

feel it in the way she melted when he touched her.

He wouldn't hurt her for anything.

Braced by this renewed grasp of reality, Marshall fired up his laptop and opened his email program for the first time in months, wincing as hundreds of emails streamed into his inbox. Mostly garbage, he glanced through the list in case there was something important, from Harry or his family. He hadn't heard from his family, and Harry phoned on the burner he'd bought for Marshall when he brought him up north.

Marshall skimmed down the list, not ready to dive in and delete the obvious, but he stopped at an email from his ex-wife, Mignon. It was short and sweet.

Well? I have to know soon or I'll have to make other arrangements for the kids.

What about his kids? Marshall skimmed down the list of emails, way down, to a message from two weeks before.

Hi Marsh

I hope you have recovered enough to take the children for July. They are dying to see you and to be honest, hurt that you haven't even chatted with them online since the accident. I think it would ease their minds to spend some time with you.

July was supposed to be your month anyway and I have a job lined up for the month and need you to take them. It's a big chance for me to get back into television. The pilot for a new weekly drama. This would be BIG for me if it's a success. Nanny also has plans for July. If you could keep them for August too that would be great. Let me know A.S.A.P.

Mign

July. That was—In one week. When was this letter? .... Oh, shit. A month ago.

Marshall closed the laptop and stared at nothing.

He wasn't ready for this.

* * *

The day his children were due to arrive, Marshall faced his reflection in the mirror. If his face didn't scare them, his caveman hair would. He'd always worn it slightly longer than the fashion, but now it looked like he lived in a cardboard box on the street.

He picked up a pair of scissors but just stared at them in his hand. He had no idea where to start.

"Marshall?" The sound of Lily's voice snapped him back to reality.

The screen door opened, and she walked in. Saw him in the kitchen and smiled—then her gaze dropped from his face to the giant sheers in his hand. Her eyes widened. "Oh my god, what are you doing?"

She held out a hand, palm up. "Is everything okay?"

He looked at the giant scissors that looked more fit for cutting a chicken in half than for cutting hair, blew out a breath and handed them to her. "I need a haircut."

Lily nodded as if talking someone off a ledge. "I know someone who can do it."

"No. I don't want to see anyone. I thought I could do it myself."

Her laugh sounded hoarse. "Not with those hedge trimmers. Let me help."

More help that he was sure was not in her job description. God, he was a sorry case. But he did need her help—now more than ever. "Thank you."

That set her in motion. Lily always seemed happiest when she had a job to do. She bustled into the bathroom and returned with a towel, dragged a stool into the middle of the kitchen floor and tapped it, indicting he take a seat. She picked up the scissors and looked them over. "Quite the shears. They look like they're for shearing sheep. Don't move too suddenly or you might lose an ear."

He smiled and took his seat. She wrapped a towel around his neck like a smock and made a *snip, snip* sound with the scissors. "What do you want? Buzz cut?"

"Just neaten it up a bit."

She walked around him studying his head like a sculptor. He immediately regretted asking for her help. He shouldn't have dragged her into his problems, again.

"Not too short in the front?" she asked.

"Yes. Although," he sighed. "It doesn't really fool anyone."

"Not really," she said softly and beginning at the back, started to cut. "What's the occasion?"

"My children are coming."

"What?" She stopped cutting and flew around until she was staring him in the face, her mouth and eyes wide in surprise. "Really? When?"

"Today."

That seemed to please her. She grinned and went back to work with new energy. "Well then, we'll have to do a particularly good job."

He couldn't bring himself to tell her it wouldn't matter, that nothing she could do would hide the scars. He couldn't sound so vain. And it wasn't all vanity. Not anymore. He just didn't know who he was anymore without the music and the life he'd always known.

"You're lucky you got the two-bedroom place. How long are they staying?"

"A month."

"What?" she shrieked. "That's fabulous."

He shook his head and she stopped him with a hand on the top of his head. "I don't know if it will work. I mean, I love them so much, but I haven't seen them in a long time."

"How long?"

"Eight months." She stopped cutting for a moment, then blew away the fallen hair that tickled his neck. Her breath was warm on his ear. Did she know what she was doing to him?

"That's a long time."

"I've never gone that long before without seeing them." He wanted her to understand. He was a good father. Wanted to be a good father. "Even while touring, I never went more than a month without seeing them."

"What happened? Why so long this time?"

"Well, there was the accident."

"How did that stop you from seeing your children?"

"We thought, my wife, my ex-wife and I, that it might be too traumatic for them to see me right after the accident."

"But that was what, eight months ago."

She didn't see the problem, and he was embarrassed to admit how he felt. "I know, it's time. But to have them come and stay? How am I going to take care of them?"

He didn't have to spell it out. Not to her. Lily would know right away what he meant. If they came, he was going to have to go out of the cottage, in the daylight. "This is just so different from anything we've done together."

"What did you used to do with them?"

"You know. Just hang out. I was on the road most of the time before the divorce. I never had them to myself for more than a few hours at a time."

"And their mother trusts you to take care of them for a month?"

He ran a hand over his face, digging his fingers into his eyes. "I can do this."

"Of course you can. It's time to man up. You're in a friggin' kids' paradise here."

He looked out the window at the lake. "I guess."

"How old are they?"

"Five and eight."

"Great ages. There are tons of things to do." She stopped talking for a minute while she cut around his ear. "But you're going to have to get out and do it with them."

His heart sank. *And that's the problem right there.*

She came around in front of him and squatted slightly so she could look him in the face. His cheeks burned and his head drifted to the left.

"Stop that," she said, and put one hand on each cheek to turn him to face her.

"I don't want it to... disturb you."

"What? This?" She patted his scarred cheek, her eyes dropping to his. "It doesn't disturb me. I think it disturbs you more than anyone. You think it's worse than it is. It's just kind of... smooth."

Her eyes went back to his hair, but she kept her hands on his cheeks. Her palms felt cool on his cheeks, both cheeks, and his heart seemed to stutter as he realized that the feeling had returned to his scarred cheek. He could feel the weight and contour of her palm. It felt so good to be touched that he closed his eyes and leaned into it.

Lily stood directly in front of him. "Don't move," she said, and raised both hands to pull up the hair in the front and snip, giving him a chance to really look at her. Two small vertical lines of concentration ran between her brows, and faint freckles sprinkled across her nose. "I didn't realize you had freckles."

She swiped a hand absent-mindedly across her face as if she could brush them away. "Only in the summer. I've been riding my bike to work lately."

Her honey-gold hair swung to her shoulders, shiny and smelling like fruity shampoo. He wanted to bury his face in it. Or in her neck, the length of which was exposed as she stretched first one way then the other to check the cut around his ears. Her collar bone was delicately outlined through her pale skin, a few more freckles leading his eye down to the V-neck of her t-shirt.

His mouth went dry and his arms vibrated. He wanted to hold her but didn't dare. He didn't know where they stood after what she'd said at the wedding, a disorienting feeling for a man who'd always, in the past, known exactly where he'd stood with women. The groupies didn't know him and any fooling around with them had just been a game. No real feelings involved. Or so he'd thought. Then came Mign, and his days on the road had ruined whatever they had had together. But with Lily he had a fresh start. She knew him, showing she cared for him in hundreds of ways.

He realized he was staring. She chewed on her lips, her eyes scanning the room. "Kids, huh? You've got to get some kid's stuff for them." She looked at her watch. "I'm supposed to be cleaning. I tell you what. You make a list while I run through the place, then later I'll go to the store and pick up a few things." She got up and started bustling around the living room, straightening cushions and his papers on the coffee table. "You should change your meal plan, too."

Marshall felt like a weight had been lifted off his chest and energy flowed through him like honey. He could do this. He could take care of his kids.

Chapter 26

What had he been thinking? He couldn't do this alone.

Christina, the nanny, had brought the children as planned, but now she was getting back into the car to drive away. Just like that.

"I'm sorry, Marshall," she said in the clipped tones she saved just for him. "But as I think Mign explained, I have made plans for this next month. July is your month, and I will meet you—or at least the children—back in L.A. in August."

He'd walked her out onto the porch and now looked back inside at his children. Boston sat slumped on the couch and, already at eight years old, his eyes were glued to his phone. Probably playing a game, but still, Marshall wasn't sure what he thought about him staring at that screen at such a young age. Emily was sitting on a kitchen stool, swinging her legs, banging her heels against the frame, the backs of her sneakers lighting up with every bang. The phone pissed Marshall off, but at least it kept Boston busy. Emily, at five, didn't have one yet. What on earth would he do with her for a month?

Christina walked stiffly away, not sparing a glance at the children. If he had his way, he'd replace her in an instant. Fortifying himself with a deep breath, Marshall went inside.

"I'm hungry," Emily whined, pushing her long black bangs out of her face. When had she turned into a whiner? She'd given him a spontaneous hug when they'd arrived twenty minutes ago, but that happiness seemed to have evaporated.

"Me, too," Boston grunted from the couch. He was carrying extra weight around his middle, probably from spending too much time on the couch with his phone, or tablet, or whatever his game addiction was this month. But at least it kept him occupied. Marshall winced at the thought. *Great parenting.*

"I have some pretzels," he said, pulling an almost empty bag out of the cupboard. He'd added two kids' meals to the meal plan, but obviously that wasn't going to be enough.

"I hate pretzels," Emily said, pushing her hair back again.

Boston didn't look up. "I'll take 'em."

"Do you have any yogurt shakes?" Emily asked.

"Or Twinkies," Boston said. "I really like Twinkies."

Emily brightened. "I *love* Twinkies."

There weren't going to be any Twinkies, that was for sure, but as Marshall stared into his empty cupboard, he had no idea what to offer instead.

He heard clattery taps on the porch and a familiar yip, then Sweetie burst into the room. She stopped just inside the door, looked at the kids and barked again. It was game on.

Emily flew off the stool, Marshall barely getting a hand on her arm to prevent her from flying headfirst into the floor. "A dog. You've got a dog!"

Boston rolled off the couch with the first smile Marshall had seen since he'd arrived. "Cool."

Sweetie put her front paws and chin on the floor, stuck her haunches in the air, then yipped and ran in a tight circle, ready to play.

Lily stood in the doorway, her arms full of grocery bags. Marshall's anxiety evaporated in a sigh. *My savior.* Hurrying to the door, he gave her a heartfelt kiss on the cheek, pleased when she blushed. "The cavalry. Just in time."

She cracked a smile. "I don't have any Twinkies, but I did bring a few snacks and kid cottage essentials."

Marshall peered into the bag he was holding. Floaties, hot dogs and marshmallows, two board games. He grinned at her. "Got it. Essentials."

"There are some granola bars in there too, for a snack."

He found the box and pulled it out.

"I wanted Twinkies," Boston said from where he was rolling on the floor with Sweetie. Any mention of food was right on his radar.

"Sorry, they were all out," Lily said with a straight face.

"I guess that will be okay," Boston said holding up a hand for a granola bar. Emily jumped up and took one from Marshall too.

Lily grinned over their heads at him. He could have done more than kiss her. Lily to the rescue again.

"Yahtzee!"

At nine o'clock that night, the kids were still playing in the cottage when Marshall and Lily went out onto the porch.

"We had that game at the cottage when I was a kid," Marshall said. "Where did you find it?"

"In a box in the attic at the cabin," Lily said, sitting on the two-seater. "Sean said he remembered it from when he was a kid visiting his Aunt Augusta. He thought it might still be there, so I braved the cobwebs and went up. There was a box of games right beside the trap door, almost as if they'd been left there on purpose."

"Really?" Marshall pulled her close and nibbled her ear.

"I'm just saying."

"Well, I'm just saying this." He kissed her, a real kiss, satisfying an urge he'd been fighting since he'd seen her standing in the doorway that afternoon.

When they came up for air, Lily snuggled into the warmth of his arms. "The kids are adorable. They obviously take after their mother. What is her nationality?"

"Vietnamese. She grew up in Paris though. Her family escaped in the late sixties and Mign was born in Paris."

"She must be exquisite," Lily said, wincing at her obvious fishing attempt.

"She is," Marshall said, but without feeling. Of course, he'd been surrounded by beautiful women all his adult life. Had beautiful women *throwing* themselves at him. Lily had never been sure what he saw in her, except for the fact that she was the *only* woman he'd seen since he'd been in Fortune Bay. She pulled away slightly, but his fingers on her shoulder pulled her back.

"Yahtzee!" Emily's sweet little voice called out in excitement from the living room. She was holding her own against Boston.

Marshall closed his eyes and shuddered. "A whole month? I don't think I'm up to the task."

"Sure you are," Lily said, giving him a gentle elbow in the ribs. "Don't worry, Dad. I'll be here to help you. Starting with lending you Sweetie tomorrow."

"Really? I could kiss you again for that."

She smiled and wrapped her arms around his neck.

"What's stopping you?"

* * *

The following afternoon after work, Lily hurried over to Marshall's cottage where she'd dropped Sweetie off that morning. Emily had been sitting in the living room, watching cartoons, and Sweetie had jumped up and settled in beside her. Lily's heart had softened at the sight. They'd both have more fun this way together than spending the day apart.

There'd been an emergency in the kitchen that morning and Lily hadn't been able to check on Sweetie at noon as she'd planned. She told herself that was the only reason for going to Cottage Number Four, although she knew it was a lie. Yesterday she'd had so much fun with the children, she would have loved to spend the day with them and Marshall again. She just hoped he was coping on his own.

The afternoon was gorgeous, bright and hot, and she was surprised to see no one on the dock. She tapped on the screen door and looked inside, but it was hard to see into the dim interior. Marshall came to open the door his hair standing almost straight up, as if he'd been running his hands through it all day. Sweetie lay on the floor, in the middle of a mess of plates and bowls, too exhausted to give Lily more than a passing thump of her tail.

"Is everything okay?" Lily asked. "Where are the children?"

"Boston's in my room and Emily is in theirs. I had to separate them for a time out. They were at each other's throats all day."

Lily's eyes widened as she imagined the scene. "Didn't they like what you had planned for them?"

He looked confused. "Planned? When we were kids my mom never planned anything for us. We just went out and did stuff all day. These two just want to sit in the house and watch TV. When I finally turned it off they started fighting over who would play with Sweetie. Poor pup. She's exhausted. She was great with them, but I couldn't stand the noise. Finally, I sent them to their rooms. I don't think they are speaking to me right now." His shoulders slumped.

Lily sucked in a breath that hissed through her teeth. "They can't be inside all day. They're kids. But we have to remember they are city kids. They probably don't know what to do here."

"What do you mean, don't know what to do? You go out and play."

"With what? They are probably not allowed to go out on their own in L.A. And with the lake right there, it might not be a good idea here, either. Do they know how to swim?"

Marshall scratched his head. "I'm not sure."

"They're probably all hot and out-of-sorts. Let's all get into bathing suits and go for a swim."

Marshall looked out at the lake, vaguely horrified.

Lily laughed. "Come on, Dad. Put on your trunks and get those kids out here." Lily went to the guest room and tapped on the door. "Emily? Sweetie wants you to go swimming with her."

There was a squeal from inside the bedroom and Emily threw open the door. She had on pink leggings and a Dolce & Gabbana t-shirt that hung coquettishly off one shoulder. "I want to wear my new bathing suit," she said, diving into her giant suitcase.

"Okay. Girls change in this room, boys in your dad's room." Lily dug around in the other case and found shorts for Boston. Sweetie was running in circles in the living room adding to the level of excitement.

Lily had been hoping to go for a swim with the kids, so she'd tucked her suit into her purse on her way out the door that morning. Turned out it wasn't nearly as stylish as Emily's bikini, but it covered more skin and that was a good thing.

They all met in the living room, Boston literally dragging his feet. "I don't want to go in the water," he said. "I hate swimming."

"Well, Sweetie loves it," Lily said. "Maybe you can throw some sticks in for her."

Boston brightened up. "Where are the sticks?"

"You've got to find one."

His face twisted up in concern. Had the boy ever been outside in the city? She sent Marshall a telling look.

He dropped a hand on Boston's shoulder. "Let's look behind the cottage."

Emily jumped on the balls of her feet. "Let's go. Let's go." She raced out the door.

Lily grabbed a few towels from the bathroom and the floaties that were still in the shopping bag and followed her down the flagstone path.

Emily obviously had no fear of the water and was already in up to her waist, clapping her hands at Sweetie, encouraging her to come in. The dog ran back and forth on the shore, whimpering. She wanted to go in, but Lily wondered if she had ever swum before.

"Can you swim?" she asked Emily.

"Sure." Emily threw herself prone onto the water, thrashed for a few seconds, and came up coughing and choking.

"O-kay." Lily grabbed her around the waist and set her on her feet. "I think you'll get the hang of it in no time, but for now, why don't you try these floaties?"

She tossed one to Emily and showed her how to blow them up. Marshall and Boston came out of the forest beside the cottage with a couple of sticks. Boston threw one in the water and Sweetie went into a frenzy, racing up and down the shore. She really wanted to go in but was afraid.

"Good throw, Boz," Lily called.

"Yeah, Boz. Good throw," Emily echoed.

"Maybe not so far," Marshall advised. "Until she gets used to it."

Boston threw the next stick a yard out and Sweetie tentatively walked out, paddling the last foot and triumphantly bringing it back to the shore. Everyone went crazy praising the pup who pranced and barked for more.

Lily pulled the floaties onto Emily's skinny arms and she took off like a porpoise, her straight black hair slick and shiny on her head. Lily followed close behind her. After a couple of moments, she felt confident enough about Emily's ability to glance at Marshall who was back on the shore. He was staring at her and smiled when their eyes met. She felt her heart expand and a warmth rush down from her chest.

Then Marshall let out a war whoop, raced to the end of the dock and cannonballed into the water.

Emily paddled back and forth between her father and Lily, confident in water way over her head. Boz didn't venture out past his knees, but Lily thought she caught a few interested, even wistful glances in their direction.

That night after a dinner of barbequed hot dogs, something Marshall was horrified to learn neither of the children had ever had before, he sat with Lily on the dock watching the sun sink behind the mountains.

"Quite a day," she said.

He groaned. "I did a horrible job. Until you arrived."

"It's a learning curve," she said generously, hiding a smile.

"Where did you learn to deal with children?"

"I worked at the YWCA in Seattle, mostly counselling adults, but I loved helping out with the kids' summer camps. It was very urban, but we did our best to get them active and out into the parks."

"Well," he said, his eyes softening. "You're a natural."

She laughed. "You just need to have stuff for them to do. They can't really manufacture fun out of thin air, regardless of what you think you and your brothers did."

He laughed. "The floaties were genius."

"Emily is a natural. She'll be swimming on her own in a week."

He frowned. "But Boston is another story." He paused. "Boz. I like that."

She smiled. "Let's give the kid a fighting chance."

"He probably feels too old for floaties. Maybe he'd like a tube."

"Or a boogie board."

A motorboat rounded the point, and Lily felt Marshall stiffen as it headed right for them. The driver sat up on the top of the seat and looked over the windscreen as he brought the boat in to the dock.

"It's just Sean," she said and started down to the dock, happy to see Marshall followed her down. Lily recognized Sean's daughter Amber in the boat with him, a Mariners ball cap holding her long blond hair back in a ponytail.

"I thought you and the kids might want to go fishing," Sean said, cutting the motor. "I know a few good spots nearby."

Marshall glanced toward the house. "I don't know. The kids are pretty bagged from swimming."

Just then, Boz raced out of the house and down to the dock. He had on board shorts and a tee-shirt, and his feet were bare. A touch of sun-pink highlighted the bridge of his pug nose. Lily grinned to see how quickly he'd changed into a regular cottage kid.

"Wow. A boat. Can we go for a ride?"

"What's Emily doing?" Marshall asked.

"She's asleep on the sofa." Boz couldn't take his eyes off the boat.

"I don't know," Marshall said, obviously torn.

Lily put a hand on his arm. "You go. I'll stay with Emily."

"We won't be long," Sean said. "We'll be back by dark."

Marshall frowned. "I don't have any rods."

"That's okay. I have extras."

Boz was already clambering into the boat, holding Amber's hand for support. Marshall turned to Lily and took her hands in his. "You sure it's okay?"

Lily nodded. "If Emily wakes up, I'll put her to bed. Just go and have fun."

He gave her a quick peck on the cheek and climbed down into the boat. Amber was already getting Boz into a lifejacket, so Marshall settled into the front seat beside Sean. He gave a wave as the boat came to life and roared away, Boz grabbing his seat and laughing in the back with Amber. Lily smiled as she raised her hand in response, wondering if Marshall and Boz had ever had this much fun.

An hour later, Lily was sitting on the porch with Sweetie exhausted at her feet, when she heard the faint sound of the motor starting up across the lake, from under the shadow of the mountain.

Emily was asleep in her bed. She hadn't stirred when Lily carried her in and pulled off her shorts, leaving her to sleep in her tee-shirt and SpongeBob underpants. She'd pulled the blanket up to her chin, marveling at the girl's delicate features. She could see some of Marshall in Boston's still-pudgy features—something about the eyes and eyebrows—but Emily must be pure Mignon. Lily had checked the covered portion of the picture on Marshall's dresser and seen his beautiful wife. She puffed out a sigh. When she had kissed Emily on the forehead, the little girl had smiled in her sleep. Lily's arms ached to hold her, but she covered her gently with a quilt instead.

It was almost dark when Sean's boat pulled up to the dock. She could hear the calls of *thank you,* and *good night,* and then the guys made their way up to the house.

"We've got fish for breakfast," Boz said, his voice shrill with excitement.

"That's right," Marshall said, holding up a string with two tiny fish hooked to it. Lily held back a smile as Boz stifled a yawn. "Good for you. Who's going to clean them?"

"I'll clean them this time," Marshall said. He ushered his son into the house. "I'll show you how next time."

Boz went to bed without argument. Marshall put the fish in the refrigerator and came back onto the porch.

"I'll have to get some fishing rods," he said, taking a seat beside Lily. "And maybe rent a motorboat. I'd love to teach the kids to waterski."

Lily patted his arm. "Let's take this one step at a time. I think they should learn to swim, first, or at least feel comfortable in lifejackets in the water."

"Of course," he said. "What was I thinking? But I think I'll call Alex and see if I can rent one."

"The kids would probably love that," she said carefully. "But first things first. You have to be able to take care of the basics."

"I'd do anything for them," he said passionately.

"I know," she said gently. "But you have to take care of them on a basic level."

He blinked, processing. "What do you mean?"

"The first step is a visit to the store."

Marshall's stone-face came up.

"I know how you feel about being 'discovered'," Lily said. "But I think you've blown this out of proportion. This is Fortune Bay, not Memphis or Nashville. Yes, someone might recognize you, but if they are brave enough to approach you, just smile and say hi. After a while the interest will die down. I swear it will."

He did not look convinced.

"And if any of the local women try to throw their undies at you, they'll have to contend with me." That finally got a smile. "If you're going to take care of your kids, you have to be able to get them what they want."

"I'd give them anything they want."

She gave him a minute to think about that. "I mean, *go and get it,* yourself. Ice cream and hot dogs at the General Store."

Chapter 27

The following afternoon Lily put Marshall's hat on his head and, staring him down, called to the children. "Who wants ice cream?"

The predictable chaos ensued as the kids raced out of their room. "My treat," she said, still holding Marshall's stony gaze. She was beginning to recognize his pattern; he'd stubbornly hold this unyielding posture until she'd proved him wrong. Then he'd relax. If she could hold out that long. She just hoped that this time she was right, that there wouldn't be a scene at the store. Surely fans weren't that crazy. Surely they'd respect his privacy. Wouldn't they? There was no way to know without trying. But one thing was for sure—he couldn't spend the month in the cabin with the kids without going into town. This was his new world order and she hoped it worked.

They followed a trail behind the cottage through the forest until they came to the main road. The general store was one hundred feet away, across the road. The parking lot was humming with cars coming and going. Well, three cars, which constituted a crowd in Fortune Bay. After they crossed the road, she took the lead and left Marshall to keep the kids safely on the gravel shoulder. They marched up the steps in single file. She pushed open the door and stepped inside.

Fiona looked up from her regular spot at the cash. Her eyes narrowed behind her fuchsia glasses but all she said was, "Lily."

Lily waved. "We just came for ice cream." She led the way into the café. Luckily it was empty, except for two men reading newspapers at a table by the window. They didn't look up. So far so good.

Behind the counter, Star's eyes lit up. Lily sent her a hard look and Star pressed lips into a straight line.

"Hi, Star. We're here for ice cream."

Emily's black eyes grew round. "Is your name really Star?"

Star smiled. "Actually, it's Starlight."

Emily's eyes grew wistful and she glanced at her father. "I wish I had a pretty name like *Star*."

"What's your name?" Star asked, heading to the ice cream cooler at the end of the counter.

Emily's lips turned down at the corners. "Just Emily."

"No!" Star said, feigning surprise. "That's *my* favorite name."

Emily's eyes widened. "Really?"

"Really. Now, what kind of ice cream cone do you want, Emily?"

Star gave her a scoop of chocolate as requested, then Boston stepped up. "My name's Boz," he said, chest puffed out, obviously not immune to Star's fairy charms.

When Boz had his cone, Lily introduced Marshall. Star took a deep breath and her eyes sparkled, but all she said was, "And what size cone for you?"

When they were all licking their cones, Lily said to Marshall, "I saw boogie boards in the store the other day." As Marshall and the kids trooped through the arch into the store, Star called, "Bye, kids."

They answered, "Bye, Star."

Lily lagged behind and grinned at Star, who mouthed, *OH MY GOD,* and reached out and gave

Lily's shoulders a silent but hearty shake.

She found the others in the toy section, where Marshall was talked into getting the boogie board for Boz and a bubble kit for Emily. Marshall seemed more relaxed, thanks to the ice cream and the fact that there was only one other person in the store at that moment and she was concentrating on the meat selection.

"We'd better get a few other things," Marshall said.

They got Oreos and apples and a loaf of whole wheat bread.

"We have white bread at home," Emily complained.

"This is what we have here," Marshall said. She seemed to accept his answer and went back to licking the drips on her cone.

He took the kids up to the cash to pay.

"Will that be on your account, Mr. Morris?" Fiona asked, deadpan.

Marshall shot Lily a surprised look. She shrugged in reply. "Ah, sure," he said.

As he held the door for the children, Lily stayed behind and bought some gum, an excuse to take a minute to say to Fiona, *sotto voce*, "You really do know everything, don't you."

Fiona just gave her a rare, enigmatic smile in return.

Marshall and the kids were waiting in the parking lot, finishing their cones. As they started down the road he said, "What are you doing tomorrow?"

"Oh, that's right," she said, suddenly remembering the conversation with Stephanie and her dad that morning. "It's the Fourth of July. I've been invited to Stephanie's for a family party."

Marshall frowned and concentrated on his dripping cone, but after a minute he said, "So have I. Me and the kids."

She smiled. "That's great. The kids will love it. Steph has tons of grandchildren. It'll be a chance for them to meet other kids their age."

He didn't say anything.

"What's the problem?" she asked.

"You know what the problem is," he replied tersely.

"It's time to get over yourself," she said, not trying to hide her exasperation. "You saw what happened in the store. Nothing. And—news flash—both Fiona and Star *knew who you were.*"

Marshall looked surprised and then looked away, taking a moment to let that sink in. Then he said, "Who do you think will be there?"

"Family. You've met some of them already. Sean and Frankie. And Amber. Jake, Sean's brother and his family – he has a daughter about Emily's age, and a brand-new baby. Probably Louise and Blue, the newlyweds, if the babies don't arrive that day. I heard something about baseball. You know, family."

Emily tugged at her father's shirt. "Can we go swimming?"

"Okay," Marshall said. "But wait until we get there," he called as the children ran down the trail through the fir trees to the cottage.

"So, are you going?" Lily asked as they came out at the water. Emily was dancing from foot to foot on the dock.

"I can cannonball too," she shrieked, then ran to the end of the dock and hurtled through space into the water. She went down like a rock.

Boz was standing on the dock. His mouth fell open and he looked helplessly at Marshall and Lily.

"Get her," Lily screamed as she raced for the dock. Emily was still underwater, and Lily felt like she was running in slow motion. She'd never get there in time.

Marshall passed her like a bullet and real time was restored. Later, she'd have sworn that his feet never touched the dock. He was in the air when Emily came up, eyes wide in terror, thrashing and gurgling. When she went down again, Lily was sure she'd taken in a mouthful of water.

When Lily reached the end of the dock, both Emily and Marshall were under water. She held her breath for what felt like an hour—until Marshall's head broke the surface and he gasped for breath.

A split second later Emily's head emerged beside him. Lily could see his arm wrapped around his daughter's chest. Emily gave a choking gasp and started to cry. It was the most beautiful sound Lily had ever heard. She crouched on the dock and as Emily's pathetic little arms reached up for her, she took her from him.

Marshall grasped the dock with two hands and surged up out of the water. A moment later he was beside them, and grabbed his daughter and held her tight.

Boz was inching his way toward them and Lily held out her hand to him. Tears of fright ran down his cheeks. He shook his head as he took her hand and said, "I didn't know what to do."

Lily put her arm around his shoulders. "Water can be very dangerous if you don't know how to swim. We make it look easy, your dad and I, because we both learned to swim when we were kids." She knelt beside him and looked Boz in the face. "You could learn too. You'd have fun and be able to help if someone's in trouble."

"I can swim," Emily blubbered. "I just forgot my floaties."

"No, honey, you can't," Marshall said, now also on

his knees, holding her close. "Not yet. But you'll learn.

"Okay," Marshall said, taking a deep breath. "That's enough excitement for today. I think I see Buddy coming with dinner."

Boz took off with Emily right behind him as the waiter emerged from the forest trail with a tray of covered dishes.

Marshall flopped on his back on the dock, his breath uneven. "Christ. I thought I'd lost her."

"You were amazing. You saved her." Lily put a hand on his heaving chest.

"I never want to be that scared again." He reached out and grabbed her ankle, running his thumb along the arch of her foot, sending spirals of delight up her leg.

"It's dinner time, Dad." Lily said with a laugh, pulling her foot away.

"Can't we get away some time together? Just you and me? Isn't that what babysitters are for? So grownups can have sex—I mean, some adult time."

Lily giggled and stood up. "You've recovered pretty quickly."

"Haven't you heard? Extreme danger is an aphrodisiac." Still flat on his back on the dock, he ran his hand up her leg to the loose hem of her shorts.

She stepped away and took his upstretched hand in hers, pulling him into a sitting position. He leapt to his feet beside her.

"Amber might babysit," she said, amazed at her boldness. But she'd been having the same thoughts herself. What with the danger and all.

He pulled her to his chest, and she shrieked as his wet body imprinted on hers. "Is it too late to call her for tonight?" he asked, his cold chin nuzzling her neck, his evening shadow rasping her sensitive skin.

"You're soaking wet," she said, giving him a push. It was useless, though. His arms were like bands of iron, holding her to him.

"I know," he said, kissing the *really* sensitive spot just above her collar bone.

Despite his being soaking wet, she could feel his arousal and pressed herself closer. Heat radiated from his core. "Let's give Amber a call."

Chapter 28

They rowed over to the cabin with bottle of wine and enjoyed an evening of laughter and loving. She tried not to think how nice it would be if this could be their regular routine. If this could be their life.

"Why didn't we think of this babysitter thing before," Marshall said, pulling her to his bare chest, their legs entwined beneath the sheets.

They'd told Amber he'd be home by eleven, so all too soon he was kissing Lily goodbye on the dock and climbing into the rowboat.

She kept her eyes on his as he rowed away.

"Pick you up tomorrow at two for the picnic," he called. She raised a hand in acknowledgement and watched as, a moment later, his face was obscured by the darkness. Lily stood on the beached raft, feeling a light breeze lift the heat from her skin, and watched as the light on the rowboat diminished in size until it was just a speck on the water across the bay.

Finally, the light on the boat disappeared around the point and the warm feeling in her chest burnt out like the flash of a spent bulb. When they were together she tried not to think about where they were going, or how fantastic it felt. Tried not to think about how ephemeral this time was, a classic summer romance, fleeting and probably doomed. Fortune Bay might turn out to be her permanent home, but it was just a blip on the screen for Marshall Mason.

And, she thought, turning back to the path to the

cabin, if that were true, she wanted to enjoy every minute they had together.

They'd left her car at his place, so at two the following afternoon he arrived at the cabin, just like another date, except for the two excited children in the back seat and Marshall's white knuckles on the steering wheel.

"It's just family," she said softly. "You already know most of them. It'll be cool."

He nodded, keeping his eyes on the road.

A dozen cars were already parked in Stephanie's yard when they pulled in, more than Lily had expected. She saw Marshall scan the front yard, his brows contracting, probably doing the same mental calculation. He looked ready to make a U-turn and head right back home again.

She pointed to the old Jaguar parked next to the front steps. "That's Dad's car," she said, hoping for a distraction. All she got in reply was a grunt.

Then Frankie appeared on the front steps and waved, so Marshall grudgingly pulled into an empty parking spot. Tugging his wide-brimmed hat further down on his head, he climbed out of the car.

"Glad you could make it," Frankie said. Lily had spent the morning making a tray of devilled eggs, and Marshall had ordered a case of beer, and a box of ice cream bars from Fiona for the kids.

"Let's just take those into the kitchen," Frankie said. "They should really go into the freezer."

Inside, they passed a pile of shoes in the front hall— "Leave yours on," Frankie told them—and went into the kitchen where Stephanie was running herd over a crew of people, including Amber and Sean and half a dozen people whose relationship to the Murphy family Lily didn't quite catch during the quick introductions.

None of the cooks had time to pay any extra attention to the new guests.

Stephanie shooed them out into the yard— "Too many cooks," she laughed—and standing on the back steps looking over the group of twenty or so *more* people, Lily got a whole new idea of what family could mean. Her own family had consisted, at most, of her mother and father, and in her early childhood years, her paternal grandparents and Uncle Matthew, her mother's uncle who smelled...funny. Like he washed with a kitchen cleaner that didn't quite mask the underlying body odor.

To the Murphys, 'family' meant uncles and aunts and cousins and their children, as well as a few old friends from down the shore. They were sitting on lawn chairs and blankets thrown on the ground, and there were kids and dogs causing chaos everywhere. Lily felt Emily's hand slip into hers, and she looked down into the girl's sparkling jet-black eyes.

A tall man with curly black hair sticking out from under a Porter Marina cap approached with a rolling, long legged gait. He had Marshall fixed in his sights and Lily thought, *oh no, this is it.* Too bad someone had to recognize him so soon, and in such a public way.

Before she could formulate a plan, the man stuck out his hand and said, "Hi Marshall. These your kids?"

"Hello, Alex. They sure are." And wonder of wonder, Marshall was smiling. Who was this man and how on earth did Marshall know him?

Then it clicked. Porter Marina. Alex Porter. Lily had called him herself to arrange for Marshall's rowboat. She remembered that somehow, he was related to the Murphys, so she shouldn't be surprised he was here. With Colleen, right, who was *very* pregnant, sitting right over there with Maddie and the new baby.

When she zoned back in to the conversation, Marshall was introducing the kids to Alex, who said to Boz, "My boys must be about your age," and to Emily, "I have a niece about the same age as you."

"Can I meet her?" Emily asked, dropping Lily's hand in favor of a new friend.

Lily smiled and shook hands with Alex. "Hi, I'm Lily Brewster. I called you from the resort about renting the boat for Marshall."

After shaking her hand and saying hello, Alex returned his attention to the children. "Come on, I'll introduce you to the kids."

"I was thinking of calling you," Marshall said as they all wandered off together. "I want to rent a motorboat..."

Well, look at that. Lily couldn't stop grinning as the men walk over to a group of children who were playing a game that vaguely resembled soccer.

"What's put that smile on your face?" Frankie said, coming out of the house behind Lily. Then she followed Lily's gaze to where Alex and Marshall were standing in the shade of an old maple tree, arms crossed on their chests, watching the children play. "Oh, I see. Nothing sweeter than big strong men bonding over children playing."

"We were only here for ten seconds and already Marshall met someone he knew that I didn't," Lily said triumphantly. "Do you think Alex knows who he is?"

"He knows. I'd bet everyone here knows by now. But word's out to play it cool. I think it'll be okay. I'd just watch those two," she said giving a nod to Louise and Colleen who were lounging on lawn chairs near Maddie. "Maddie's be cool, but neither of the other two has any filter. They both tend to say whatever's on their mind."

"I haven't seen the baby yet," Lily said. She felt the tug in her belly, she had to hold it—so young, so sweet—and was glad when Frankie said, "Let's go then." And led the way to the new mother.

As they approached, Maddie took the baby off her breast and, carefully holding his head, put him on her shoulder and gently patted his back.

Lily smiled down at them. "I haven't met the new guy yet. What's his name?"

"Liam. After Jake's grandfather."

Liam let out a burp that sounded too loud to come from his tiny body, and all the women laughed. "Good boy," Maddie crooned. "Just like his father."

"Can I hold him?" Lily asked.

"Of course. Why don't you sit here beside me?" When Lily was settled Maddie passed her the precious bundle. Warmth bloomed in her chest as Liam's head settled in the crook of her arm. She passed the other hand gently over the reddish fuzz on top of his head. Fed and burped, the baby looked up at her with a peaceful expression, his bright blue eyes looking into hers for a moment before the lids drifted shut and he fell into a blissful sleep.

"You have a knack," Maddie said. "I love holding him, I never thought I'd have another, but I'm glad to pass him off sometimes."

"I'll take him any time," Lily murmured. Tears pricked her eyes. She still wanted one. She looked up and blinked into the sun, her gaze falling on Marshall across the yard. Was it possible? Probably not. But you can't tell your heart who to love.

She seemed to have developed a radar where Marshall was concerned and followed him with her eyes. Alex had taken him under his wing and had introduced him to a bunch of men who were admiring a vintage GTO parked, hood up, in the driveway. It was in rough shape, must be someone's new project. She didn't know if Marshall knew anything about cars, but he seemed happy to sip a beer and hang with the guys. Probably safer than introducing him to Colleen and Louise.

A while later, Sean took center stage with a bull horn, and he and Jake herded all the children down to the lake for water sports and races. Lily followed them down, positioning herself near Marshall's children. Emily was pulling off her clothes, revealing the bikini underneath. Lily winced. She was the only five-year-old with a bikini.

"We have to do something about her wardrobe," Marshall said, his voice soft and breathy in her ear. She felt warmth coil in her belly again. *Enjoy it while you can.*

Most of the races were just fun, running through the water holding a blow-up toy or tossing balls back and forth with a partner in the water. Lily was glad to see both Emily and Boz joining in, but after a relay race through knee deep water, the older kids got down to serious business with Sean officiating swimming races from the dock.

Jake was cutting watermelon to keep the younger kids occupied, and although Boz was getting his fair share, Lily could see he was moping. She exchanged a look with Marshall.

He went over to Boz. "What's up, sport? Having fun?"

"Yeah," Boz said, his eyes on the racers. "But how come they all know how to swim, and I don't?"

"Well, most of them live here on the lake and they had to learn. To be safe."

"It kind of looks like fun," Boz said sulkily, throwing his watermelon rind into the trash bin. "Why can't we live on a lake?"

"Swimming is fun. You could learn too, while we're here."

Boz looked hopefully up at him and Marshall rumpled his straight black hair. "We'll get started first thing tomorrow."

"How's it been going for you?" Lily asked when Marshall returned to her side and took her hand so casually that she wanted to cheer.

"Fine. Really nice people. There are a few whispers, but it reminds me of family gatherings when I was a kid."

"Really?" Lily looked at him in surprise. "I've never been to anything like this in my life."

"Don't you have family?" he asked, his brows pulled together in concern.

"Not really. Well, I mean, you've met my dad." Marshall nodded. "And I do have a mother, although she moved away last year. But other than that..."

He put an arm around her shoulder, kissed her on the temple, and said, "Somebody give this girl a family."

She felt her cheeks redden. "I didn't mean I feel sorry for myself."

"No, I mean it." His gaze followed Emily as she went back for more watermelon. "You're great with kids. You deserve a big messy family. I didn't realize how much I've missed it."

"Aren't you in touch with your family? I mean, I know about your parents, but what about your brothers?"

He was quiet for a moment. "I left home, went on the road, and we drifted apart. I always thought I'd go back, take the kids to our old cottage when they got older. But time doesn't wait."

"I'm sorry."

He shrugged, but it held more pain than indifference "My own fault."

"Surely it's not too late to get together again?"

He looked at the ground. "I think it might be."

She shook her head vehemently. "It's never too late."

Marshall picked up a flat stone and skipped it over the water.

Boz ran over to where they were standing, slightly away from the crowd. "Wow, Dad. How do you do that?"

The moment of sharing confidences passed, but as she watched them skip stones over the water, she thought how unfair life could be. Marshall might think it was his fault, but family was family. Where were his brothers now that he needed them?

As potlucks often seem to be, dinner was an amazing spread. They ate at long trestle tables set under the maples. The wine flowed and after dinner, musical instruments started appearing.

When he saw the instruments come out, Marshall announced it was time to leave. With Emily draped tiredly around his neck, they said their goodbyes.

"If I wasn't feeling like a beached whale," Louise called from her lounge chair, "I would have snagged a dance with Marshall Mason. When will I get the chance again?"

Marshall was still for a moment, then said in a drawl Lily had never heard him use before, "You're lookin' lovely Darlin'. We'll make it next time."

"When you can get your arms around me," Louise said.

"You're beautiful just the way you are," he said, and bent down and gave her a kiss on the forehead, skillfully evading her arms.

As they headed for the door, Louise called to his retreating back, "I'll hold you to it." Laughter broke out behind them.

Marshall smiled as they walked to the car. "So, they knew."

Lily grinned back at him. "They knew. And what do you know? A riot didn't break out."

He shook his head, a smile quirking the side of his lips. "I love this place."

* * *

Alex came through with the motor boat the next day, a sixteen-foot turquoise outboard with the marina logo on the side and a pop up roof, a lot like the boat Marshall and his brothers had cruised in every summer, raising all kinds of hell. Those were good days, he thought wistfully, and part of what made them so good was the continuity of returning every summer to the same place, making friendships that lasted from year to year. He remembered the fun of arriving the first weekend in July and running from cottage to cottage to see who was up and who wasn't.

He'd like to give his children that experience. The security of belonging in a place like this. Knowing who lived in every house on the lake, knowing who your friends were. Like the kids he'd seen at the picnic. Might be something worth considering when the dust died down, getting a summer place.

The kids were thrilled with the boat. Alex had equipped it with six brand new life jackets and a full tank of gas. Marshall took the children to the General

Store to buy fishing rods and, of course, ice cream cones.

On the way out Boz stopped and read the sign in the window out loud. "Kids' Fishing Derby. What's a 'derby'?"

"A contest." He stopped to read the text. "It's in three weeks. At the resort. Want to enter? We should still be here then."

The excitement on Boz's face gave Marshall a thrill. *I missed this, all those years on the road.* He'd begun to feel like some good might come from all this upheaval after all.

As they walked back along the shoulder of the road, he felt a wash of pride to be walking with his kids, a fishing rod resting on their shoulder, an ice cream cone in their hand. When they arrived last week, he never would have guessed how quickly he would grow into his role as a father, because now he could see that although he'd loved them, he hadn't been much of a father before. He had to find a way to make this connection last when the summer was over and Mign wanted them back. A way to ensure equal access to his children.

That evening, an hour before sunset, they set out in the boat with the new fishing gear. Marshall cruised past the little island in the bay to the spot in the shadow of the mountain across the lake where they'd fished the week before with Sean and Amber. When their lines were in the water, Emily chattered non-stop about how much she loved swimming and how good she was getting, how much she loved her gymnastics class and how some of the girls in her class at school called her Shrimpy because she was so short.

Marshall listened with a smile on his face, staring at the house on the island, wondering if he could get a place like that himself. If an island was really a good thing, or if it would be too isolated for the kids. That would defeat the purpose of the feeling of community he wanted for them. And, he realized, that he wanted for himself.

Boz fished in concentrated silence, occasionally jigging the line up and down in a controlled manner, teasing the fish that lay in the darkness below. Half an hour in, keeping his voice low, he said, "Got one." Then he proceeded to reel it in, nice and slow. Marshall found a net in the bow cabin and let Emily help him net the fish. It was a nice trout, big enough to keep. Boz was so excited, he wanted to go home right away and cook it up, so they did.

Later, when the kids were in bed, Marshall sat alone on the porch, wishing Lily was coming by. But she wasn't. She hadn't brought Sweetie this morning, either, and tonight was her line dancing class so he wouldn't see her today at all. He'd become invested in their relationship. He counted on seeing her every day, less and less because he needed her to fix something for him—he was doing more for himself everyday—but because he wanted to see her, to talk over his day, and to steal a kiss in the dark on the porch when the children went to bed.

This was more than a casual summer affair. He knew where he wanted it to go and hoped like hell he could get there one day.

He dragged the sheet of paper on the coffee table closer and in the dim moonlight read the words he'd written last night. The words to the song he'd written last month. *Starting Over.* That was the title and thrust of the lyrics. He'd been a mess when he met her, and she'd helped him start over. When he had nothing to give, she was there. What else could he write about, but her?

His life was still a mess: Mign, the kids, the remnants of his career. But Lily had helped him find the strength to go on. Helped him see what was important; family, friends, and someone to share your life with. Maybe someday he'd have it together enough to share it with her.

Chapter 29

The childish fun that filled their days, reminded Marshall of the summers he'd spent with his brothers at the cottage. The response of his children was more than he'd hoped for, as they exchanged their urban trappings for shorts and flipflops and—most of the time—abandoned their phones and tablets for fishing rods and frisbees.

They played endless games of Go Fish, War and Yahtzee, and a horrible board game called Candyland that Lily had found somewhere, that Emily loved. There were play dates with Murphy kids along the shore, sometimes at their place and sometimes at the cottage, and for the first time Marshall really understood in his core what it meant to be a parent. And as he watched Boz on the dock, patiently untangling Emily's fishing line, he realized now that he'd felt it, he would never give his children up again.

A car pulled up behind the cottage, gravel crunching, but Marshall waited where he was, his eye on the kids, while Harry made his way to the shore. Although both children were coming along with their swimming lessons, after Emily's near miss, when they were near the water, Marshall never took his eyes off them again.

He scratched his bare chest and eyed Harry's city pallor as his old friend sauntered down to the dock. Although Marshall still wore his hat to protect the new skin on his cheek, he felt tanned and fit compared to his citified friend. Harry's pin-striped shorts looked ridiculously pressed, as, come to think about it, did his pale-yellow polo shirt.

Emily saw Harry and made a running dash down the dock to greet him. He scooped her up and tickled her until she shrieked in delight, before putting her down.

"Watch me swim, Harry," she said, racing into the water. She dog paddled out from shore and then turned around so that Harry could witness her fearlessly dipping her face in the water.

When she came up sputtering triumphantly, Harry applauded. "Bravo. Bravo."

"How's Boz doing?" he asked, watching his god son concentrate on the tangled fishing line.

"He's doing well. He's not as excited about swimming as Emily is, but I think he's having fun. Fishing's really his thing. We go out almost every day. Want a beer?"

"Twist my arm."

"Out of the water, Em," Marshall called and once she'd obeyed, the men made their way up to the porch. Marshall still kept his eye on the children, though, sending Harry in to raid the refrigerator.

When the men had settled on the porch, Marshall asked, "How are you coming with petitioning the court?"

Wondering what would happen when he got back to the city, was keeping him up nights. He was worried that Mign would want the children back full time and not let him see them as much as he wanted.

No, needed, he thought, his chest cramping at the thought of the control the court had given her over his family. How had he let that happen? Now that he was used to seeing them all day, every day, no other arrangement would work. And wasn't he the one who would be home all the time anyway, now that Mign had this job and his own career was in the toilet?

Harry nodded. "It's going well. I think we have a court date in early September."

Marshall's eyebrows shot up. "Just over a month away. That's fast."

Harry shrugged. "You get what you pay for and you did say, get the best. Well, Jenny Ling is the best divorce attorney there is."

Marshall snorted derisively. "Not like that crap lawyer we had the first time around. I must admit, though, I didn't really realize at the time what was at stake. It isn't about the money, it's about the time I get with them."

"And Mign was really sticking it to you at that point. I think she's calmed down a bit, and now that it looks like her career might be back on track, sticking it to you isn't as much of a priority as it was then."

Marshall raised his bottle to that. "Here's to Mign being too distracted to fight back."

The kids raced up from the dock. They raced everywhere now. Even Boz, whose slow, heel-dragging saunter had been his trademark.

"Hi, Harry," Boz said. "Did Dad tell you about the fishing derby?"

Harry flicked an amused gaze to Marshall. "No, he did not. What's it about?"

"It's a contest just for kids to see who can catch the biggest fish. You get a number, and everyone goes out in their boats at exactly the same time. Three o'clock. Then you fish until seven—that's the best time to fish, just before dark—and then you bring all the fish you catch to the resort dock to be counted and weighed by the judges."

Marshall grinned at Boz's enthusiasm. Harry shook his head in wonder and said under his breath to Marshall. "I've never heard him string this many words together at once."

"He's quite the fisherman," Marshall said, and Boz puffed out his chest with pride.

"I'm in it too," Emily said.

"You'll get the prize for most tangled lines," Boz scoffed.

"Will not."

"I won't have time to untangle your lines that day. I'll be too busy fishing."

Emily's mouth turned down at the corners.

"I'll do it," Marshall assured her.

"I'd better go practice," Boz said importantly, and ran down to the dock with his sister at his heels.

"Get your life jackets on if you're going to be down there alone," Marshall called after them.

Harry shook his head. "Such a difference. These are not the same kids I put on the plane in Los Angeles a month ago."

Marshall gave a satisfied nod. "It's done them a world of good to be out of the city. I almost hate to take them back."

"Do I detect a certain reticence about returning? Would it have anything to do with a certain woman?"

Marshall's mood took a nosedive. "I don't know what to do about that. I owe her so much. She really pulled me out of my slump."

"Yeah, too bad. But you know, summer romance."

Marshall focused his eyes on his kids on the dock and pressed his lips firmly together. "I can't help but think, if I could stay a while longer, it might turn into more."

"I think getting the kids back to L.A. and into school

is pretty important to the custody case. Mign is distracted, but not *that* distracted that she wouldn't notice if you dropped off the face of the earth with them."

"I don't know," Marshall muttered as he watched Boz cast his line into the water. "She's only called once to talk to them since they've been here."

After a few minutes of quiet contemplations, Harry said, "You're looking pretty good, too."

"I feel good." Marshall looked at his hand and flexed his fingers. They moved, but the skin still felt tight, the tendons beneath enclosed in a tight sheath. "I'd love to get this hand moving better, though. It makes it hard to cook for the kids, or to even hold a knife in that hand. I'll never be able to play chords on the guitar, but I've been messing around on the piano, doing a bit of writing. Maybe with more surgery I could play few chords ..."

"I could get you in," Harry said, trying to sound casual, but Marshall heard the underlying excitement in his voice. "In fact, I spoke to the surgeon last week and they're holding a spot open for you next month. I've got to let them know soon, though."

It was time to take a step. To see how far he could go. He owed it to his children to be the best he could be. "Hand and cheek? The hand is the big one. I don't really care about the cheek." Lily didn't care about his cheek.

"Hand and cheek," Harry said. "The cheek is just a bit of plastics to pretty you up. See what they can do with that scar. Just say the word and I'll book it."

Marshall had to go, to take the kids back and to work out the custody arrangement with Mign. And to see what he could salvage of his career. Satisfying as it was, he'd have to do more with his life than take care of his children. He'd failed his parents, not stood up for his brothers, at least he could be his best self for his kids.

And he was starting to feel like he *could* do more. The other night, when he'd put words to the song he'd written for Lily, a door inside him had opened and ideas were rushing out.

He wasn't sure what the future held for him, but he was ready to try.

"Book the surgery."

Chapter 30

Lily's job at the fishing derby was to count the fish caught by the under tens. Along with prizes for the biggest fish in the different age categories, there were prizes for the smallest fish, the most fish, the first fish and the biggest and smallest fish in the different species categories. The rules were that everyone had to fish on single barbless hooks, and that all fish had to be kept alive in a container of water and turned in for judging alive, then released immediately after being recorded by the judges.

Lily was happy to help, but she wished she could be out in the boat with Marshall and the kids. Not that they needed her—not anymore—something she had mixed feelings about. Seeing Marshall looking tall and strong, taking his place with his children in community events made her proud to have had a hand in his recovery—and thrilled by the man he had turned out to be. Neither the withdrawn and depressed Mr. Morris she'd first met nor the old Marshall Mason, either. Gone was the glitz and glamor of that life and really, she couldn't see him ever going back to it.

Although, this was Fortune Bay. She had no idea what his life would be like when he returned to L.A. He said it wasn't Hollywood, but his house was just a few miles from there and so many of the paparazzi shots were of him going in and out of this and that Hollywood club, with his wife or some other woman clinging to his arm.

And now that she'd held onto that strong arm herself, she could see the allure, because even though he might have lost some of the glitz, he'd lost none of the glamor. Not in her eyes. As Harry said, he had an intangible quality that drew people to him. He was *the man.*

There wasn't much action for the judges in the first hour, but her job was to be there on the resort dock with Johnny, ready for the first young fisher-folk to come in. She wore her green, Fortune Bay Resort tee-shirt and denim shorts and, to shield her from the sun, one of the straw cowboy hats with the Fortune Bay General Store emblem that Fiona was giving out. She'd been horrified to see, for the first time in years, the freckles that had plagued her as a young teen popping out across the bridge of her nose.

Just after four o'clock, the first young contestant came in with three tiny fish. Lily recorded the catch on her tally sheet and photographed the fish against the ruler with the contestant's name tag in the shot, in case of any dispute. Then the fish were returned to the water, which was almost as much fun for the kids as catching them in the first place.

The early trickle of returning entrants turned into a deluge as the afternoon wore on. Most contestants were in boats, but some fished from the shore and surrounding docks. She tried to keep her mind on her job, accuracy was very important to the contestants, but she kept one eye out for the turquoise fishing boat with the marina logo on the side.

A stranger with a camera around his neck who Sean said was a reporter from the local paper, approached her on the dock. "Mind if I take some pictures of the kids?"

"It's okay with me—if their parents agree."

He interviewed a brother and sister and took pictures of them as they released their catch under the watchful eye of their parents, then he hung around on the dock, zooming in on the boats as they drove by. After a while, he started to be in the way as the kids brought in their catch, so Lily suggested he move to a spot on the shore. A few minutes later she spotted him out on Frankie's father's dock at Cottage One.

Star came out to join her, her eyes focused on the reporter. "He was in the store asking questions," she said. "About Marshall."

Lily squinted into the lowering sun, glad to see the turquoise boat still across the lake. But then she noticed another turquoise boat slowly making its way towards the dock through the confusion of boats in the bay, and Marshall was at the wheel.

Her gaze shot to the reporter on the other dock who was scanning the bay with his zoom lens. He was continuously moving it though, so she didn't think he'd found Marshall yet.

She looked back at Marshall and when their eyes met, he gave her a nod.

Go back. Go back, she signaled frantically.

He waved and said something over his shoulder to the kids. They came to the side of the boat and waved at her. *Oh, no.* He thought she was waving. This was terrible. His first public appearance and it was going to be a disaster.

Sean came up to Lily on the dock—the smile on his face fading when he saw the panic on hers. "What's wrong?"

"The reporter's on Dock One and he's looking for Marshall."

Sean scanned the bay for the boat. "Where is he?"

"Right there, eleven o'clock," Lily said. "We've got

to distract the reporter. Marsh and the kids are coming in."

Sean pulled out his phone and turned his back to the noise of the boats in the bay.

"I have an idea," Star said, and raced off the dock.

Young contestants were lining up for Lily's attention, and soon Emily and Boz would be among them. She took the fish a little girl held out to her and out of the corner of her eye saw another turquoise boat pull up at Dock One, between Marshall and the reporter. *Alex.* He called out something to the reporter who went over to talk.

Then Marshall was right there, helping the children up onto the dock. Lily went over and took Emily's hand, unceremoniously hoisting her up. "Reporter on Dock One," she said.

Marshall's head shot around to see.

"Better go tie up at home." She made a sweeping motion with her hand indicating a circuitous route around the bay, and he nodded.

"What about the kids?" he called as he slowly pulled away into the crowd of waiting boats.

Stephanie stepped up. "I've got them." She put a hand on each of their shoulders.

Marshall gave Lily the *call me* sign and circled away from the dock, quickly losing himself in the mass of boats in the bay.

Lily breathed a sigh of relief and turned to Stephanie. "Thank you."

Stephanie nodded. "That's what family's for."

Lily heard a splash in the direction of Dock One, and Star's surprisingly loud cry, "*Sorry!* Let me help you out of the water."

A few moments later, as she was counting Boz's impressive catch, Lily saw Sean helping the dripping reporter into his car.

Stephanie gave Lily a wink as she herded the children off the dock. "I'll tell Marshall the coast is clear."

The shore was crowded with families waiting to hear the results and, at seven-fifteen, Lily and Johnny made their way to the stone steps of the dining room veranda to hand out the prizes. She had yet to see Marshall but when they announced the prize for *The Most Fish Caught by a Single Contestant*, Boz made his way to the front, and Lily pinned the ribbon to his proud chest.

When the last ribbon was given out, the crowd drifted away to the outdoor barbeque near the gazebo on the point. Lily looked around for Marshall and the children, but they seemed to have vanished. Probably just lying low. Lily's heart sank. It wasn't that she wanted him to be dependent on her—or maybe she did. Maybe she felt it was the only hold she had on him.

"Where's your friend?" Star asked.

"I don't know." Lily tried to keep her voice unconcerned but wasn't sure she succeeded. "I'm sure I'll run into them somewhere."

"Try the food tent," Marshall's familiar, deep husky voice said from behind her, and she turned to find him and the children, all eating cobs of corn, butter running down their chins.

Lily laughed, pushing down the feeling of concern over how relieved she was that he'd sought her out. Wiping the butter off his chin, she licked it off her finger. His eyes followed her finger into her mouth, and she saw the heat flare in his eyes.

"I've hired Amber to babysit for a few hours after

the dance," he said. "I hope you're free to take a ride in the boat."

Lust coiled delightfully in her belly at the thought of what they would do later tonight. She smiled. "Thanks for thinking of me. I was wishing I was out in the boat with you guys this afternoon."

"We'll make up for it tonight," he said softly, causing the heat to rise from her neck to her cheeks.

This was bad, on so many levels, but she pushed the underlying anxiety aside. She was a big girl and would take what she could from this relationship. While it lasted. It wasn't just who he was or where he came from that made her sure it was doomed. Sadly, she didn't have much hope for *any* relationship to be of lasting value. Look at her and Troy. And her parents. And Marshall himself, for that matter.

Life was hard. People change and move on, or at least that's how it seemed to her. If her life was going to be a string of meaningful encounters, she would count herself lucky for having known Marshall and his children for the time they'd had.

So she hooked her hand through his elbow and said, "Let's go. I'm starving. Show me where you got that corn."

There were hot dogs and Sergio's amazing burgers and salmon on a bun. Louise and Amber had baked salted pretzels, and Max had pulled out all the stops and brought in a candy floss machine. There was a beer garden up on the veranda and the band set up at one end, overlooking the dance floor set up under the trees.

Glittering lights had been hung from the branches, and with Boz firmly in charge of Emily, Marshall swept Lily onto the dance floor and into his arms. He held her tightly, as if he'd never let her go. Hot and possessive—and somehow a little desperate. She pushed that thought away, determined to enjoy whatever time they had together. Their bodies filled the dips and valleys of the other and she felt his breath warm on her temple.

"How long do we have to stay?" she asked.

"I told Amber she didn't have to come until nine. Tonight's a big night for the teenagers, too."

It was no hardship to sway in his arms on the dance floor, but after two songs they both knew it was time to check how Boz was doing as the man in charge. They found the children sitting together on the lawn chair, right where they'd left them. Emily was out cold, and Boz was not far behind.

"Good job, Boz," Marshall said softly, lifting Emily into his arms.

Lily took Boz by the hand and they followed Marshall to the cottage. By the time both kids were in bed, Amber knocked on the door.

"I'll be back by midnight," Marshall said. "It's a pretty wild night out there. I want you to lock the door and not let anyone in. That includes your friends."

"I know," Amber said. She rolled her eyes. "My dad's going to check on me to make sure I'm here alone. Don't worry. I'm cool. I didn't even tell anyone I was going to be here."

Lily gave Amber her cell number and, taking Marshall's hand, hurried to the boat.

* * *

Lily was ready tonight, Marshall thought as she took his hand and pulled him up the walk and to the cabin. They stepped up on the porch and she wrapped her arms around his neck. Snuggling close, her eager lips fueled the flame in his belly, but thoughts of what lay ahead doused the flame as quickly as a bucket of water. He couldn't do it. Couldn't satisfy his need without telling her exactly what lay ahead.

She must have felt his reluctance because she doubled her efforts, but a moment later her lips stilled. She pulled back a few inches and looked him in the eye. "You're leaving, aren't you?"

Marshall had trouble meeting her gaze, but blinked, and forced himself to look her in the eye. He owed her that much. Hell, he owed her everything.

"I knew it couldn't last," she said, pulling away. "Our lives are a million miles apart."

"Not that far. Not really." Who was he trying to convince? He couldn't drag her into his life. He had no idea what awaited him when he got back to L.A. Nothing pretty, that was for sure.

"Seriously? Think about it. You're going back with your kids to your life in Hollywood—"

"Not Hollywood. I'm up in the canyon—"

"Big difference," she said, a sarcastic edge that he'd never heard before creeping to her voice. She wrapped her arms around her ribs, a sure sign to keep his hands to himself. He wanted to feel her, to be with her tonight. For one last time. But it had to be up to her.

"And I'm here in Fortune Bay." She shook her head. "What future would we have?"

Sweetie had greeted them at the door, and now put her paws on Lily's leg. She scooped up the pup and closed her eyes. He could see her struggle to compose her features. When she opened her eyes, her expression was neutral. As neutral as a knife to the heart. "We knew this was coming. Are you going to have your surgeries?"

"Yes." Marshall straightened. He'd made that

decision and it was the right one. Having the surgeries on his face and hand was the first step to pulling the strands of his life back together. But why did telling Lily that feel so wrong?

"Good," she said from behind the soft shield of her dog. Sweetie licked her chin, sensing something was wrong and clearly choosing sides. "Time to see how much more they can do."

"I won't play again. Not like before."

"But you can still compose and produce. Isn't Harry setting something up with that young guy, what's his name?"

"Josh Bartholomew."

"Right." She looked at the floor, hiding her eyes. "Good. Good." One tear plopped onto the boards at her feet. "And the kids must be looking forward to getting back."

"Not really," he said, not taking his eyes from her face. "But their school year is starting in two weeks, so I have to get them back."

"Is your wife back?"

"Ex-wife. No. Not yet."

There was a long silence and he could feel the tension crackle, like ozone infused air before a lightning strike.

Lily rubbed her hand across her forehead. "Please. Just go."

His eyes stung at the sight of her pain, but he was unable to sooth her like she had him. "I never wanted to hurt you."

She looked at him with sparkling eyes. "You didn't hurt me. I went into this with my eyes wide open. If anything, you gave me a gift this summer. Renewed my faith in myself. Showed me there's more to life than Troy."

Marshall frowned, not really following the quick change of subject.

"*My* ex," she clarified pointedly.

His head jerked back, as if she'd struck him. Did she really think of him as her rebound guy? He pushed down the hurt. She meant a lot more than that to him, but, maybe it was for the best. Better than having her pining for him. Hell, he'd be doing enough pining for them both.

He couldn't help himself, he had to touch her one more time. He ran the back of his hand gently down her cheek. "You have so much to offer, Lily. I couldn't have made it this far without you."

She pulled away. "I was happy to help. And I was glad to help with the kids. So great to get to know them."

He looked at the floor, nodding to everything she was saying like his head was on a spring. "Maybe I'll bring them back next summer." He looked to her for encouragement, but her eyes said, *just go and don't look back. Let me get on with my life.*

That was only fair. He took her hand. Her eyes were unusually bright. He'd done that. *I never meant to hurt you.* "Goodbye Lily. And thank you."

She nodded, pulled her hand away and dropped her gaze to the floor. He couldn't stop himself. His lips grazed her forehead and as she leaned into the kiss, more tears joined the first spot on the floor, and he knew they weren't all hers.

When Marshall's boat tore away from the dock, Lily wiped her eyes and tried to convince herself that she was glad he hadn't really kissed her, because that would really have felt like goodbye.

Chapter 31

Marshall surveyed his ravaged face in the bathroom mirror. He'd vowed he'd face`./. the new scars head-on this time, not go down that road to self-delusion again, and now that the initial trauma was fading, he could see that the latest plastic surgery had smoothed out the initial scars quite a bit. It wasn't his old face—he'd never have his old face again—but it was a good face, a new face, to go with his new life.

He hadn't made it to Lola's wedding, counting himself lucky that it had been the same week as his facial surgery so he hadn't had to explain to her that he wasn't up to that kind of major Hollywood do just yet. The thrill had gone, and he'd be happy never to go to another gala. He thought back to Louise's wedding, what he'd see of it from the sidelines. Of Lily in that fitted dress and red cowboy boots, line dancing and laughing with friends on the stone veranda of the Lodge. If he ever got married again, he knew which kind of wedding he'd choose.

Before the facial work had healed, they had him back in the hospital for the hand reconstruction. Even now, three weeks later, the hand still hurt like a bear. He'd stopped the prescription painkillers after the first week. Another fork in the road he'd best avoid. Besides, he had to be sharp, for the kids.

He'd fired Christina, the former nanny, when they got back from Fortune Bay. The children didn't like her and neither did Marshall. Instead he'd hired a warm, motherly woman to cook and generally take care of them all. Janice. The kids loved her.

Harry had moved in to take care of the children while Marshall was in the hospital. That still tickled Marshall—the thought of Harry as nanny to his children. He'd kidded him about being a full-service manager but, good friend that he was, Harry had come and stayed, got the kids to school every day and visited Marshall in the hospital. Harry had also kept up with the contract they were signing to produce Bartholomew's new album. The kid had talent, and Harry had an ear for new talent. Together, he and Harry were beginning to sketch out a new direction for their business relationship. Producing. A new start. An exciting prospect. The question was, where to set up the recording studio. Harry was out scouting locations in the Valley right now.

Marshall absently rubbed the itch on his palm through the bandage as he walked out onto the back deck that overlooked the dry Hollywood Hills. Many artists had escaped to these canyons over the years, Crosby, Stills and Nash, Joni Mitchell and Mama Cass. Too many to name, going way back. But the canyon was changing. Every day dusty rock was being gouged away for new houses on the steep hillsides. He wasn't sure how long he'd stay. It was a long drive to the private school in the city where Mign had enrolled the kids last year when she'd moved to the condo in Hollywood during the divorce. But until he knew what direction their life would take, he thought it was better not to uproot them again.

He didn't know where he'd end up. He wasn't the same man he used to be. He'd always considered his guitar his fifth limb and without it, he didn't know where he fit in. For the first time in his life he was lonely.

The doorbell rang and a key scratched at the front door. It was too early for Harry, but Mign still had a key, even though she'd been gone for a year.

"Darling. You poor baby." She was talking as she swept into the room, dressed all in white, more stunning than ever. Marshall had never understood Hollywood's infatuation with starlets. In his mind, a woman in the full bloom of womanhood was immeasurably sexier than a skinny ingenue. It was a disinterested observation though. His interest in Mign was strictly as the mother of his children—and as the antagonist in their ongoing custody battle. So the question was, why was she here?

He held out his good hand, palm up. "I didn't realize you still had a key."

She closed her fist around the key. "I feel more comfortable having it when the children are here."

He thought for a moment. "Then you'll understand why I must have one to your house."

Her eyes narrowed a fraction, but the Botox didn't let them narrow too far. She dropped the key in his outstretched palm. "You're right. We have our separate lives, now."

He wondered for a brief second who was in her life now. Her constant need for adoration and sex had been the downfall of their marriage. If he wasn't around to provide it, she found someone who would. But he brushed that aside. He didn't care anymore.

"How's the show going?" he asked.

Mign's face brightened in a smile that he recognized. She wanted something. "Fabulous," she purred. "They are taking it on location to Europe until Christmas and after that we hope to keep filming abroad."

A cold lump fell into the pit of his stomach. She wanted to take the children. Well, he wouldn't let them go. Not without one hell of a fight.

"That's wonderful. When are you leaving?"

"Actually, we left last week. I just came back to get more things and to talk about the children. Thank you for taking care of them this month."

"They are my children. Of course I take care of them. In fact, I've had them for three months now."

"Yes, well, I'm supposed to have them back now—"

"You can't just say, *I've come to take them back*, like cd's you pick up at an old lover's apartment. They are not possessions to be bartered and traded, borrowed and lent. They are my children, and they need a stable home. I'm the one who can give that to them now. I want to keep them." *Forever.*

Her delicate eyebrows raised in amusement. "Now, after almost ten years, you suddenly want to be a father?"

Marshall took a deep breath. It was better to avoid falling into old patterns with Mign. When she was angry she hissed and clawed like a cat. So instead he said, keeping his voice level, "I've always been their father and provided for them. You did a wonderful job of taking care of them for all those years while I was on the road. Giving me a chance to work on my career. Now it's your turn."

He softened his voice. "It's wonderful about the show. Go, and give it your best shot. I hope it's a raging success. Don't worry about the children. I am happy to take over. Full time."

He held his breath. She could go either way. You never knew with Mignon.

She thought for a moment, then her face broke into a radiant smile. "Thank you, darling. I didn't know how they would take to Paris. And I'd have to find a new nanny..."

They were his. Relief washed over him. She wasn't going to fight him. But he had to be sure. "I'll have my attorney draw up the papers and hopefully you can sign them while you're here." He'd make sure she did, and make sure there was a clause to prevent her from taking the children out of the country without his permission.

"I'm only here for three days," she said, already turning to leave.

"We'll get it done. And Mign, I mean it, good luck on the project."

"Thank you, darling, I'm very optimistic. I must go. My driver is waiting." She gave him two air-kisses on his healthy cheek and swept out the door.

When the house was silent again, Janice poked her head through the kitchen door. "Is your wife staying for lunch?"

"Ex-wife," Marshall said absently. Then he smiled at his new ally. "And no, she's gone. I think we're getting the children. For good."

"That's wonderful," Janice said, her face beaming. "The house would be too quiet without them."

"It certainly would," Marshall said, pulling out his phone and punching in his lawyer's number. After talking over the terms of the new custody agreement, his attorney promised to courier the papers over that afternoon.

When the call ended, Marshall continued to sit in the leather club chair, gazing out through the floor-to-ceiling windows. He didn't see the dry hills before him, though. Instead, he saw images of his childhood cottage at the lake, the days with his brothers before everything went wrong. There'd been years when they hardly ever touched base. He'd missed both their weddings and hadn't invited them to his, either. He'd been too busy with his skyrocketing career, and then with Mign and the kids.

Then, last fall, a month after he'd filed for divorce, his parents had died in a three-car pileup on the Twin Cities expressway in a freak October snowstorm. In an instant, they were...gone. He'd spent a terrible few days with his brothers and their families at the funeral. Mign and the children hadn't come. She said she didn't know his parents and the kids didn't either, and at their age, they shouldn't have to go.

His nieces and nephews were there, though. Marshall hardly knew them, but they lived in the Twin Cities and had been close to his parents. He was sadly glad that his parents had known some of their grandchildren. They'd spent Sunday afternoons together and weeks at a new rented cottage every summer. Weeks when he'd been too busy to go. Too busy to take his own children while he'd had the chance.

His parents' death, and the distance between him and his brothers that week, had left him feeling rootless. Homeless—although that was crazy since he hadn't lived with his parents for twenty years. Without the comfort of either his parents or his children, he'd been alone at the funeral, and felt alone in the world. Watching his brothers with their wives and young families had only isolated him more.

Then, still reeling from his parents' death, he was thrown into the custody battle for the children. It was quick and brutal. Mign wanted the kids full time, said he was on the road so much they didn't even know him. The way Emmy cried in his arms should have convinced the judge otherwise, but the court awarded custody to Mign, along with heavy child support from Marshall and visiting rights at her discretion.

The night of the court decision, Marshall was fuming— judge had no right to give custody of his children to Mignon. He'd been faithful all those years on the road, but apparently she couldn't handle the loneliness. Instead of talking to him about it, she'd taken lovers—apparently more than one—and assumed he'd done the same.

But none of that mattered. What mattered was the children.

He'd gone down to the garage where he parked his motorcycle. He just wanted to ride, get out on the road and burn off some of the anger. He should have known he was too wound up to drive. Especially on a snowy night.

After the bike crashed into the guard rail, he'd awoken with his hand pinned to the burning muffler. He used his feet to push the bike away, but the muffler took most of the skin of his palm away with it.

He remembered the tires of a vehicle stopping close to his face, and the rest was a blur. He woke up in the hospital, aching all over, bandages swathing his hand and face.

The sun was slanting in through the patio doors when Marshall came back to the present, still sitting in the club chair in the house in the hills, with the phone in his hand. He looked at it blankly for a moment, then punched in his brother's number.

Chapter 32

Lily left the reception before Frankie and Sean cut the cake. She needed a break, and this was the time to take it. The cutting of the cake was always particularly poignant for her. The way the happy couple stood together, his hand over hers, making the first cut together—it always hit her hard. *This* was their first real moment in her mind. They'd pledged their troth, had the first dance, but this was the first action they did together.

She smudged a tear off her cheek and gave a wry laugh. Marriage was obviously not for her. Not now, not again, not ever.

Taking a seat in her office chair, she looked at the manila envelope in the center of her desk. The divorce papers had arrived today from Troy's lawyer, on the day of Frankie and Sean's wedding. If that wasn't a sign from the universe, then she didn't know what was. She pulled them out and started to sign on the lines indicated by a yellow X. It didn't hurt; she was over Troy now. Troy and Melissa and their happy little family. The baby had been born two weeks ago, a month early. She got a little jab of satisfaction at that, knowing how Troy wanted to be good and married before the baby was born. Well, you can't always get what you want. That was one lesson she'd learned and learned well.

When she finished signing, she straightened the stack of papers and slipped them into the envelope, glad to be finished that part of her life, happy to push it aside. She doubted it would cause her any sleepless nights.

The computer screen stood dark before her, the power button blinking. She willed herself not to turn it on, but one fickle finger shot out and flicked the space bar, waking it up.

It was a bad habit—a compulsion she couldn't fight—watching and listening to Marshall on the screen. When he'd first left, she'd waited for a phone call, an email, any message from him. As the weeks went by, she'd resigned herself to the fact that to him it really was just a summer romance. An affair of convenience. He'd been here and so had she.

But for her, it was much more than that. What started as a goodwill gesture had turned into a love that had burned a lasting imprint in her heart. She sniffed. She would never forget him. Heck, she couldn't stop thinking about him—how could she forget? He'd made her feel like she had something to offer. More than that, he'd made her feel desirable. Loveable. Although they'd never said the words, she thought he'd loved her. At least a bit.

When he left, the sparkle went out of her life. She'd gotten caught up in his life, working together as a team with the children and, for a while, she'd allowed herself to feel that they were a family.

When he'd taken the children away, he'd left another lasting brand on her heart.

She'd watched online for news of him and a few weeks later saw the shots of him entering a private hospital. He'd stood tall and straight, not shielding his face. She felt good about that, like at least she had helped him with that.

But she'd wondered what had happened to the

children while he'd been away. Had their mother taken them back? That would break Marshall's heart, and the thought made her own heart twist painfully in her chest. She'd looked up Mignon Noisette months ago. She was gorgeous. No other word for it. Lustrous black hair, tiny but curvy figure, luscious lips. And those cheekbones. Mign was in Paris now, working on a show. Had she taken the children with her?

Did they ever think of Lily and Fortune Bay? She shook her head. Why would they if they were in Paris now? Fortune Bay was probably a quaint stop on their journey, something to laugh about with the kids at school.

She scrolled down the screen to the pictures of Marshall coming out of the hospital in a wheelchair, puffy white bandages on his face and hand, not looking nearly so tall and strong as Harry helped him into the car. Lily sucked an anguished breath through her teeth—then reminded herself that was two months ago. He was undoubtable back on track by now. Unless he'd succumbed to depression again, which was entirely possible, especially if he'd lost his children.

Her hand reached for the phone. She wanted to call him. Had figured out his phone number from the resort records—although it could be Harry's, but even so.

She pulled her hand back, resigning herself to the truth. He knew where she was if her wanted to find her. Right here, where she'd been when he left.

But she missed him and the children, and weren't they still friends? He'd stayed friends with Lola—didn't she fit in that same category? Old lovers and friends.

How pathetic was that. She opened her browser bookmark to the trailer for the new song that kid, Josh Bartholomew had released. She'd heard it on the radio and a chill had gone through her—she recognized the melody but couldn't place it at first, then realized it was the song she'd played on the piano for Marshall. The song he'd written in the cottage in Fortune Bay. The song she liked to pretend, in her private moments, that he'd written for her.

But now there were words. Words he *could* have written for her. Particularly the chorus:

> *When I didn't have the strength to go on*
> *You helped me start over*
> *Now I want to start over with you.*

Lily sighed. *Dream on.*

There was a tap and the door opened. Lily clicked off the screen as Louise backed into the room and turned around, a baby in each arm. "Good. Nice and quiet. I've been trying to feed these two and Tabitha won't settle down long enough for me to feed Liza. Of course, I immediately thought of you—Aunt Lily with the golden touch."

Lily lifted her arms for the squalling infant, held her to her shoulder and patted her back. After a few snuffling squawks, Tabitha quieted down.

"You have the magic touch," Louise said as she settled into a chair and put Liza to her breast. "What are you doing in here, anyway?"

Lily smiled, determined not to let her sadness show. "Just taking a break. I think it's going well out there. Don't you?"

"Yeah. It was strange to see Frankie melt down like that this morning. She's always so *on*, so in charge. I guess the reality finally hit home that this time it was *her* wedding." Louise laughed affectionately, moving her daughter to the other breast.

"She looks lovely. That vintage ecru gown is stunning. That was genius. How old do you think it is?"

"From the forties, I think. It's a great store. I used to go to Seattle more and shopped there a lot." She grinned. "And didn't Sean look happy? So sweet he asked Amber to be his Best Person."

Lily smiled too. "It's been a long wait. I think they are all, including Amber, looking forward to finally living together." She sighed. "Lots of changes."

"How about you?" Louise asked carefully. "Any...news?"

"Nope," Lily said, putting a lilt in her voice. "That little episode is over. I think I'm here for good. I'll have to think about moving soon. The cabin's getting cold— heck, it's almost Thanksgiving. I don't want to be there when the cold weather really hits. But if I don't get looking, I might end up back with Dad." She gave a mock shudder.

Louise held the baby on her shoulder and patted her back. "I bet he moves in with Stephanie as soon as Sean and Amber move out. Then the farm will be empty."

"You think? I guess we'll see."

"Well, we better get back," Louise said, standing up and settling Liza into the crook of one arm. "They are getting so big, I can hardly hold the two of them at once anymore."

"I'll take Tabby," Lily said, and followed Louise out into the lobby.

Now that the meal was over, guests had spilled out into the lobby and The Cedars where they were serving drinks. Lily followed Louise into the dining room, dismayed to see she'd timed it wrong and Frankie and Sean were just walking toward the cake table.

Tucking Tabby into the twin stroller parked at

Louise's table, Lily walked over to the French doors out to the stone veranda. Her breath caught. It was snowing! Fat flakes drifted down under the parking lot lights. It must have been snowing for a while because the cars and the path to the lake were covered by a thin coat of powder.

Two children in bright parkas ran into the light, turning their faces up to the falling snow, trying to catch the flakes on their tongues. When their father ambled along behind them, Lily struggled for breath.

Marshall's hands were in his jacket pockets and his broad-brimmed hat shielded his face from the light, but she knew in a heartbeat it was him.

He said something to the children, and they moved up onto the path, but continued to chase the dancing snowflakes with their tongues. Then he turned to the veranda steps.

When he saw her at the door, he stopped. In the light from the veranda, she saw his lips widen in a slow smile. She pressed her palms flat against the windowpane.

He came toward her and when he reached the doors, he put his hands on hers through the glass. Her hands burned on the cold glass. He was back. Her heart spilled over with joy and she couldn't wait another minute to touch him.

He opened the door and she stepped outside, into his arms, laying her cheek on his chest. "I thought you weren't coming."

"I had a few things to work out."

She held herself a few inches away from him. "And did you?"

He smiled and rubbed his cold nose on hers. "I did. I'm here. For good, if you'll have me."

She pressed her eager lips to his in reply, snuggling

in closer to his warmth. He opened his jacket and drew her in. Wrapping her arms around his ribs, she pressed close to his fiery heat. This was home. The tears she'd been holding back for months rose to her eyes and spilled over. "I didn't know. You didn't call."

"*I* didn't know. What I was going back to, what my life would be like. My old life was gone. I was dropping into a void. I couldn't ask you to do that with me."

"We could have worked it out."

"I know and I'm sorry for leaving you hanging. I had to concentrate on keeping the children. They really missed you, by the way. They were so glad to come back."

Lily's cheeks ached with happy tears. She lay her head on his chest and listened to the slow strong beat of his heart. He spoke into her hair. "At first I was going through the motions. Move back into the house, get the kids back to school. Then there were the surgeries. They pretty well took up one whole month, going in and out of the hospital."

She looked up at his face. "Who took care of the children?"

Marshall grinned. "Harry." Lily threw back her head and laughed.

"He was great. Really. But I also hired a housekeeper. A motherly, Brady Bunch kind of woman who's been taking good care of us. But as I came out of the fog from the last surgery," he held up his still bandaged hand, "I kept thinking of you. Of us.

"Harry and I have been working on a plan to get into producing albums for other artists. But I really wanted to come back." The words were spilling out now as if he couldn't tell her fast enough. "Still, there were the children. One unfortunate fact of custody is that once you give up your rights, move out or give the children to the other spouse, it's hard to get them back, so I was determined not to give them back to Mign. Not without a substantial change in the agreement. The more time that went by—she was filming in Paris—the stronger my claim became. In the end, she wanted to go back to Paris, her contract had been extended, and was amenable to changing the custody arrangement."

Lily beamed. "You won."

"Yes, we won. For now."

The *we* made her pulse skip with hope. "So, you're back for good?"

"I am. We are."

Lily's brow wrinkled. "But what are you going to do? There's not much of a music scene around here."

"Produce. Harry and I have set up a company and I'm going to scout out a location for a studio. A home-studio."

Great as it sounded, Lily was afraid to believe. "This is not L.A. or Nashville."

"We think they'll come to me. I have quite a reputation, you know," he said matter-of-factly.

"I know," she said dryly.

"And I'll write."

There was a moment of silence while Lily let it all sink in. Then she said, "I heard the song on the radio." Her cheeks warmed as she thought of the million and one times she'd played it on YouTube.

His voice was low and gravelly. "I wrote it for you."

Now the tears did spill over. "I was hoping that was true."

"I love you Lily, and I want to start over, with you." He suddenly looked unsure. "If you'll have me."

"Oh, Marshall. You have no idea how long I've waited to hear you say that." Their kiss was fierce, but interrupted by the patter of feet on the stairs.

"Lily," Emily shrieked, and rushed to hold her around the waist.

"Is that a party?" Boz asked, pressing his face to the glass.

Lily disengaged herself from her warm cocoon and bent over to give Emily a hug. Then reached out and grabbed a mildly protesting Boz, but his stiffness didn't last for long.

Lily opened the door. "It *is* a party. And all your friends are inside." The children rushed in and disappeared into the throng.

Inside, people turned to see what the commotion was. Louise stood up and gave Lily a two-thumbs-up. Max held his hand up in greeting to Marshall from across the room and Marshall responded in kind.

"Good to see you, Marsh," Alex called out.

Then the music began to play. Marshall took her hand to his lips and kissed it gently on the knuckles. The love in her heart warmed her from the inside out.

"Can I have this dance?" he asked, holding his other hand out to her.

"Always."

* * * * * * *

Thank you for reading *Starting Over*.

Read on for a preview of
Star's Christmas Novella
Starlight and Tinsel

Get the e-novella of the series prequel
Lake of Dreams – FREE
By joining my mailing list
on my website at
www.JudithHudsonAuthor.com

or follow me on **Facebook at**
Judith Hudson – Author

Starlight and Tinsel

Chapter 1

Star packed the last heavy box into her old VW van and slid the side door shut. She and her mom had named it Eden because of the painting of Adam and Eve, in all their naked glory, on the side. Her mother had left Eden to her when she died, and in a strange way Star felt that through the beat-up old van, they were still connected. Like her mother was watching out for her from the other side, guiding her journey.

So, when Eden conked out a year ago to the day, right here in this workshop parking lot where there just happened to be a tiny apartment waiting for her, well, she felt it was meant to be.

A snowflake tingled on her nose. It had been snowing the night Eden had brought her to Fortune Bay, too. That dark blowy night, she'd thought Blue's workshop was still a gas station, as indeed it had been years ago when the mill was running and Fortune Bay was a thriving sawmill town. It was cold that night too, when her van had puffed its final breath.

Star knew serendipity when she saw it and had thought, for a while at least, that Blue might be the one. The reason she'd been led to Fortune Bay. But then Louise came back to town and in a flash, Star saw that he wasn't the one. Not her one, anyway. She still wasn't sure just why she'd landed here, but there must be a reason. She'd stay until she figured it out, then she and Eden would hit the road again.

She waited by the van, tugging her rainbow leg warmers up over her knees and pulling the fingers of her convertible mittens over her fingertips. Such a great idea, these knit mittens with the fingertip pouch that you could pull off, but that stayed attached to the gloves until you needed them. More trouble to knit, but definitely worth the effort. She was sure they'd be a hit at the Fortune Bay Christmas craft show later this month.

Stamping her feet to keep the blood circulating, she tucked her hands under her arms to hold in the warmth. She was kind of sorry to be leaving the old Station. Her friend and landlord Blue still worked in the attached garage bays that he'd converted into a woodworking shop and, although quiet, Blue was a nice guy and they had a relaxed relationship. He'd turned the old office and convenience store into a small—very small—apartment years ago, but the cabin she was moving to today was bigger and hopefully warmer. She was surprised by the excitement she felt to be moving there. She usually only felt this kind of rush when she was moving on to another town. Obviously, she wasn't finished with Fortune Bay yet.

A tow truck pulled into the lot. Star waved to the driver and Lorne lifted a hand in reply. He backed the truck up to the van, climbed out of the cab and loosened the big hook.

"I could fix this, you know. You could pay me a bit at a time." He cast a glance in her direction. "We could work something out."

Lorne was nice, but he was still a guy, and she had an idea what the terms of that deal might be. A regular at the café where she worked, she knew he was divorced and lonely. "Thanks, Lorne, but I think I'll wait. I'll have the money together soon."

"Okay then. Put 'er in neutral."

Star climbed into Eden, shifted into neutral, eased off the brake and hopped out of the van. The winch on the tow truck groaned and creaked as the Eden's front end lifted off the ground.

"Hop in," Lorne said as he climbed back into the cab of the truck.

Sure, hop in, she thought as she clambered up—way up—into the cab. These things weren't built for someone like her, someone who was five foot two. Okay, five foot one, but claiming that extra inch did wonders for her self-esteem.

The tow truck rumbled to life and started the slow drive through Fortune Bay: past the four streets of little crayon-colored houses that had been built by the mill long ago for its workers, past the park and the Hall, past the general store and the café where she worked, across the bridge and out of town. *Her town.* She'd been here for a year and it was beginning to feel like her town. Weird.

"How you going to get to work?" Lorne asked, eyes on the road.

"It's not that far. I'll figure out something."

He was right, though. The cabin was farther from the store and café than Blue's workshop had been, and the weather was getting steadily worse. But still, it was only about a mile. Except in the worst weather, she could probably hike it. The walk would do her good. Or hitch. In a town like Fortune Bay, odds were she'd know everyone who'd drive by. That was the upside of working at the café—even though she'd only lived here for a year, she knew everyone in town.

The downside was, well, working at the café. It was the longest she'd ever stuck to one job, and slinging breakfasts and burgers was not on her top ten list of dream jobs. But there wasn't a lot of choice in a town of less than a thousand souls—and even that was up from nine hundred since the resort opened last spring. New people were flooding into town, and that was kind of exciting to watch happen. Almost made her feel like a local.

The road followed the shore of Majestic Lake, and here and there she caught glimpses of the dark stormy water through the trees. The snow started coming down more insistently, wet flakes splatting against the windshield as they passed the old log farmhouse set back from the road. Then they turned down the dark, tree-shrouded lane to the cabin, Lorne easing the van carefully over the potholes in the dirt road. Big flakes the size of nickels hit the windscreen and created a lacy coating of snow on the fir branches that met overhead.

At the sight of the building, she felt excitement stir in the air. Star had always felt the cabin was a special place, had felt it when she'd visited her friend Lily there and, before that, Louise. She couldn't help noticing that, as if enchanted, everyone who lived in the cabin seemed to find their happily-ever-after. Not always exactly what they were expecting, but, in the end, just what they wanted.

The thought that it might be her turn both scared and excited her. She just hoped she didn't do something stupid to break the spell now that she was living here. And she could—she knew she could—without even trying. Her life never seemed to be entirely under her control, but she'd learned long ago to put a smile on her face and make the best of it. She was alive, healthy, and still young. Anything could happen.

"Just park it there, behind the shed," she said.

"Going to be pretty chilly inside," Lorne said, his eyes on the side mirror as he expertly backed the VW into the spot. "I could help you warm it up." He flicked a glance in her direction.

She laughed. "Good try. I managed in Blue's shop all last winter." It had been cold all right, but not as cold as spending the winter in the van. And she'd done that too. She could manage a woodstove as well as the next guy. Had been doing it off and on all her life.

Before Lorne had gotten Eden's front tires back on the ground, she'd climbed down out of the cab. "I see a bit of firewood stacked there against the house. I'll be fine."

When the winch was secured to the back of the truck, she counted out the agreed upon fee and handed it over.

"Well, you give me a call if you need anything. And remember what I said about those repairs. I didn't mean anything funny about that."

"I know you didn't, Lorne. And thanks. I'll remember." *Now please, just leave.* She couldn't wait to get inside, but didn't want Lorne to follow her in. She didn't have a lot of things in this life, but her privacy was one thing she valued.

Adam and Eve slid aside as she opened the side door of the van and hauled out the first of her boxes.

As he pulled away, Lorne called out the window, "I could help you carry your boxes in."

She kept on walking. "Got it. Thanks." Soon the tow truck chugged away down the driveway, and then—silence.

Stopping at the top of the porch steps, she took a moment to savor the solitude. Blue's was pretty quiet, but she'd still heard sounds of traffic going to and from the village. This was different. This was deep-in-the-woods-with-falling-snow quiet. She took a deep breath. The faintly metallic, musky smell was invigorating and, with a smile, she turned to go inside.

The front door flew open before she reached it and Lily appeared, a grin on her face and her arms spread wide. "Welcome."

Lily's twelve-year-old step-son Boz pushed past her and mimicked her gesture. "It's your new home. There's a ghost!"

"Take the box," Lily suggested, and he scooped the box out of Star's hands, almost bowling her over with his enthusiasm. Boz was a big kid, already bigger than Star, and rapidly outgrowing his baby-fat years. He disappeared inside with the box.

"Let's help Star with the rest of the boxes," Lily called over her shoulder as she started down the steps. They trooped out to the van and Star reached for the side-door handle, nestled between Eve's voluptuous breasts, which were barely covered by the proverbial fig leaf. When Boz's cheeks burst into flame, she shot Lily a grin.

"So, the cabin is haunted," she said, breaking Boz's rapt concentration on the couple on the door by putting a big box into his waiting arms. "Did anything happen when you lived here, Lily?"

"I did notice a few things," Lily said as they walked past the periwinkle shutters and silvered wood siding back to the porch. "I moved in last summer right when Dorothy was moving out. Dorothy was Augusta's sister—Augusta's the ghost, by the way—and they seemed to talk all the time. At first, I thought Dorothy was a bit batty, she is getting on, but then there were the other things..."

"Like what?" They piled the boxes on the living room rug and headed back out for another load.

"Well, Augusta seems to be sort of a matchmaker. Or at least she tries to nudge you along. Out of your relationship comfort zone."

Star gave her a skeptically amused glance as they loaded up again. "Really?"

"Really. She liked to pick out my clothes when I was going on a date and, well, she seemed to speak to me, inside my head..." She sent Star a sideways glance. "Sound crazy?"

Star shook her head. "No." This was nothing compared to the hocus pocus her mother believed permeated the world.

Lily laughed. "Well, at the time *I* often questioned my sanity." She walked into the cabin and over to a photograph on the wall by the back stairs. "This is Augusta. Maddie found the negative and developed this photograph when she lived here a couple of years ago."

Star walked over and studied the black and white photograph of a young woman, waving out the driver's window of a car with a split front windscreen, an exuberant smile on her face. Star grinned. "Well, hello Augusta."

Lily looked around the cabin. "I'll sort of miss her.

But onward and upward." They stepped back out onto the porch. "I'd better get back. We still have a lot of unpacking to do. It's been quite the week, seems like everyone in town has moved one door to the left. Harry—you remember Harry Brewster, you met him last summer—well, he and Marshall are making dinner. I'm not sure what to expect."

Marshall was Lily's new significant other and Harry was his former—maybe present, Star wasn't sure—agent. She pressed her lips together, then said, "Harry's visiting?"

"He's up from L.A. for a while. He and Marshall are looking for a place they can turn into a recording studio. Marsh is hoping Harry will stay and help him run it. Marshall's committed to staying in Fortune Bay, but I'm afraid Harry is still on the fence."

Star had met Harry a few times last summer but didn't know what to think about him. Not that she had to think anything, but he stuck out like a sore thumb in Fortune Bay with his pressed chinos and shiny city shoes.

"How long is he staying?"

"Harry?" Lily wiggled her eyebrows. "Why? You interested?"

Star laughed. "No. I mean, he's a good-looking guy—"

"And rich."

"I guess. That's never very important to me."

Lily grinned. "It is nice, though." Then she sobered. "But you're right, we can all see, after what happened to Marshall, that money doesn't always ensure happiness."

"You guys are happy now, though, aren't you?"

"Yes," Lily said emphatically. "But Marsh had a pretty rough time after the accident. I don't know what would have happened to him if it hadn't been for Harry. He did everything for Marsh and the kids."

"He looks..." Remembering his pressed shorts and polo shirts, Star searched for a word that wouldn't sound like a put-down. "Dependable."

"He's been devoted to Marshall since they were kids. Now, I think, he's kind of at loose ends. Harry always helped with the family before, but now Marsh has me. And Marshall's career has changed tracks, they are no longer touring with the band and the show, and that was something Harry always took care of. He doesn't really have a role here, and when he goes back to L.A. he doesn't really have a place in that scene anymore either."

"Can we go now?" Boz asked, jumping up on the porch.

"Sure," Lilly said, and Boz raced down the steps and up the lane.

A blast of wind blew in off the lake and Star shivered. "I should check the fire. Thanks for starting it."

"Boz wanted to learn, but it was just kindling so it probably needs some bigger pieces of wood by now. There are a few good chunks inside."

"Great. Want to come in for a coffee?"

"Tempting, but I'd better get back. Why don't you come for dinner?"

Star thought about the scant rations she had brought from the Station. "That would be great."

"Okay. Come at five. It's just the family."

When Lily disappeared around the corner of the cabin, Star turned once again to the door. The screen door stood open, but the wooden inside door was firmly closed. She turned the knob, but the door wouldn't budge. Locked. Seriously? They'd just been going in and out with her boxes. She put her hip to the panel and thumped, but it didn't budge. Standing back, she jiggled the handle—and the door silently drifted open. Her eyes dropped to the floor, and a voice in her head whispered the words printed on the mat just inside the door. *"Welcome home."*

She grinned. Haunted. This was going to be fun.

Chapter 2

T u v w x y z T

They had piled her boxes on the floor in the kitchen side of the big main room. The living room area occupied the right-hand side and was designated by a faded Persian rug. Placed around the carpet was a big old couch and chair set, the velvet arms worn thin from years of use. She pushed the furniture back until it hit the walls and with a feeling of deep relief, lay down on her back on the carpet.

She stretched as long as her five-foot-one-inches would stretch, then longer still with her arms reaching above her head. She swung them wide until she was as big as she could possibly be and thrilled that still she didn't touch the edges of the thick carpet. Paradise. How long had it been since she'd had a place to do yoga? There hadn't been room at Blue's apartment to do more than curl up in a child's pose. And in the van, it was out of the question.

She'd spent the summer before she arrived at Fortune Bay working in the canteen of a spa on the California coast where she'd made healthy smoothies and indulged in as many classes a day as her schedule would allow. She had racked up quite a few hours towards her instructor's certificate that summer but still needed twenty more and could use a few other courses before she'd feel truly qualified to teach. But this—she lifted her hips into a Bridge Pose, *Setu Bandha Sarvangasana*—this was pure bliss.

Exhaling a long breath, she sat up and faced the kitchen. Getting to her feet, she hurried over to check the cupboards and heaved a sigh of relief to find Lily had left the china dishes. Star hadn't thought to ask if the kitchen came fully equipped, but thank the Buddha it did, because she didn't have any kitchen equipment of her own except for her hexagonal, stovetop espresso maker. She'd spent half a year working at a Starbucks in Seattle and liked her coffee the way she'd learned to make it there. Strong.

Through the kitchen window Star could see the snow still coming down, big wet flakes piling up on the porch railing. The cabin was still cold, and a shiver wiggled her shoulders. In the stove, the fire had almost burned away so she put in a few more pieces of cedar on top, along with a larger split log. She'd have to source some dry wood soon if she planned to stay the winter and see about doing some winterizing.

If there was one thing she knew, it was how to tighten up leaky old buildings. The board ceiling suggested no insulation above, but a trap door at the top of the rough staircase at the back of the kitchen gave easy access to the attic. She could talk to Stephanie Murphy, her landlady, about throwing down some insulation up there. Maybe even pour some loose fill down the walls if they were open from above. She'd do the labor in return for rent if Stephanie bought the material. And she'd definitely get some insulating window film to cut the drafts. The fresh logs caught and soon the fire was blazing. It would be fine. Cozy. Paradise, in fact. A job and her own place to live? What more could she ask?

Swinging the door of the woodstove shut with a clang, she turned to her boxes. She traveled light but had learned long ago how to make a temporary accommodation feel like home.

First, she put her expresso maker on the kitchen counter beside the turquoise stove. An old beauty, Lily said most of the pushbutton burners still worked, but Star didn't think she'd be using it much because, although she enjoyed cooking, she did enough of it at the café.

The small box that held her mother's crystal collection was in the box of precious things, and she lined the colorful stones up on the windowsill over the kitchen table: Purple amethyst, yellow citrine, a chunk of turquoise they'd found together in the desert when Star was ten. A dozen in all. Her mother, Poppy, had ascribed magical and medicinal properties to each, but Star just liked the way they caught the light, and how they reminded her of her mom.

Next, she carefully unpacked the handmade glass vase she'd found in a thrift store in Utah. She knew a bit about glass from a short stint working with some glass blowers in Colorado, and this piece, with the blue and green swirls and punty marks on the bottom where the artisans had broken it off the blow pipe, was a real find. She liked to fill it with colorful flowers, wildflowers in summer and, her one extravagance, grocery store blooms in the winter months.

She set the vase on a small side table at the foot of the attic stairs. Above it, china ladies danced their way across a shelf and on the wall beside them, the black and white photograph of Augusta. Star took a moment to study it more carefully. Augusta's face at the car window had an exuberant smile, as if life was an open road ahead, there for the taking.

Star could relate to that feeling. After the shock of her mother's death had worn off, that was how she had felt when she decided to take Eden, her only real inheritance, and hit the road. Off on a grand adventure. What her mother would have wanted.

Now, three years later, that grand adventure was a wee bit tarnished. She wasn't sure what she'd thought she would find out there, and although she'd met many interesting people and done lots of, well, mostly boring jobs, something vital was missing in her life. She wasn't sure what. Job satisfaction? That was for sure. She was determined to spend the winter looking for something she could sink her teeth into. Something more fulfilling than slinging burgers.

A new life and someone to share it with?

Now where had *that* idea come from? She frowned at the photograph on the wall, remembering what Lily had said about Augusta being something of a matchmaker.

She shook her head and turned away from the photograph. No. Getting tied down with a man was the last thing she needed. Who knew when she might want to hit the road? Although it would be nice to go out on a date occasionally, she didn't need the complications that always ensued. From observing her mother's life, she knew you couldn't count on a man to stick around. Her father hadn't stayed, and none of the men her mother had tangled up with over the years had been with them for more than a few months. Then her mother, always the fragile Blanche Dubois, would be devastated, and they'd hit the road again. Until the next town and the next man.

And where were these men when you needed them? Where had they been when her mother got sick and it had been up to Star to keep a roof over their heads and care for her while she wasted away?

No, she'd decided long ago she was better off on her own, and she'd pretty well given up looking. But that didn't mean she didn't enjoy a bit of male companionship every once in a while. Sometimes it was lonely, living alone. If she was going to spend the winter in Fortune Bay, could be nice to have a warm body to cuddle with under the sheets.

"Okay, Augusta," she said aloud to the empty room. "Let's see what you've got."

* * *

You can find *Starlight and Tinsel* and the rest of the Fortune Bay series in e-book and paperback on Amazon.

Thank you for reading!

Judy Hudson

The Fortune Bay Series

Lake of Dreams
Colleen's back on Majestic Lake for the summer, living in the cabin, helping out at the marina and looking for romance with Mr. Right. A fun introduction to the series.

Summer of Fortune
Book One
Maddie wasn't looking for romance. Could a summer of freedom change her life forever?

The Good Neighbor
Book Two
Sean hates to see Frankie and her father estranged. He'd give anything to know where his own daughter is.

Home for Christmas
Book Three
Blue's carried a torch for Louise his whole life, but this time he's not sure he can wait around to pick up the pieces.

Family Matters
A Sequel Novella
Things are at a low ebb for Frankie and Sean. Be sure to read *The Good Neighbor* and *Home for Christmas* first!

Starting Over
Book Four
After a horrific motorcycle accident, Marshall's life seems to be over—until Lily knocks on his door.

Starlight and Tinsel
A Christmas Novella
Star finally gets her chance to shine in this Christmas novella.

Also by Judith Hudson

The Secret at Elk Horn Lodge

And writing as
J.M. Hudson
The Rocky and Bernadette Mystery Series

Temple of the Jaguar
A cozy travel mystery.

Murder in the Piazza
Coming in 2022

Starting Over is a work of fiction. Names, characters, places and incidents are entirely the product of the imagination of the author or are used fictitiously. Any resemblance to actual events, locales or persons, living or dead, is entirely coincidental.

Copyright